KR Paul

The Ballad of Ashes and Spring

A Hades and Persephone Retelling

Published in the United States of America by KRP Publishing

KRPPublishing.com

This book is a work of fiction. Except where noted, the characters, names, places, and any real people and places are fictitious or are used fictitiously. Any resemblance to people living or dead, or to places or activities is purely coincidental and the sole product of the author's imagination.

Copyright © 2025 by KR Paul

Cover copyright © 2025 by KRP Publishing LLC

Library of Congress Control number 2025948595

KRP Publishing eBook first edition – March 2026 ISBN-13 979-8-9898245-6-4

KRP Publishing first edition trade paperback – April 2026 ISBN-13 979-8-9898245-7-1

All rights reserved, including the right to reproduce this work or any portion thereof in any form whatsoever, now or in the future, without regard for form or method.

For more information on the use of material from this work (not including short excerpts for review purposes), please see KRPPublishing.com or address inquiries to via email to Admin@AuthorKRPaul.com.

Piracy is theft. For information about special discount bulk purchases of paper or ebooks, please contact

KRP Publishing Direct Sales via email at Admin@AuthorKRPaul.com

Manufactured in the United States of America

KRPPublishing.com

To my Hades, my lover, my partner, my King, and my muse

The Ballad of Ashes and Spring

A Hades and Persephone Retelling

Did Persephone descend or was she
taken?
Did Hades steal Demeter's bright ray
or did Persephone escape
to the peace of dark solitude
broken
only by her lover's touch?

Reference Guide:

The characters for *The Ballad of Ashes and Spring* are all based on their namesakes from Greek mythology. For those who are not super nerds like me and haven't been exposed to Greek mythology, this reference guide gives a basic understanding of each character's Greek myths and some of the symbolism woven into the story.

The Gods:

There were twelve primary gods associated with Greek mythology, each were associated with certain aspects of life (or death). These twelve were referred to as the Pantheon, the twelve Olympians who resides on Mt. Olympus ... except for Hades. The three strongest were the brothers: Zeus, Poseidon, and Hades. According to Greek mythology, the world was ruled by cruel Titans until they were overthrown by the brothers. After they emerged victorious, they divided the world into the Sky, the Sea, and the Underworld, or land of the dead.

Hades: The God of the Underworld, the God of the Dead. Implacable and stern, he ruled over the Underworld, supervising the dead when they descended to his realm. In Greek times, he was more like an administrator of the Underworld, rather than judging or applying punishments to the dead.

Persephone: Goddess of the Spring and Queen of the Underworld. She is known to have a dual nature: She is both Kore, "the Girl" and Persephone, the Queen of the Underworld. The Greeks associated her with grain, growth, and the cycle of the seasons. Many pieces of Greek art depict her holding a sheaf of grain.

Thanatos: The God of Death. Not the God of the Dead. Yes, it's confusing in our cultural context. Thanatos is the personification of death and brings the end of suffering and worry.

Eris: The Goddess of Strife. She personifies our modern phrase "the audacity of that bitch!" She likes to start things.

Hermes: The Messenger God and Herald of Spring. In the original myth, he is sent by Hades to help abduct Persephone.

Zeus: Considered the leader of the Olympians and the God of the Sky and weather. Also, a serial rapist and cheater. He's not a good guy. Seriously, this author high-key hates him. Brother to Poseidon and Hades.

Poseidon: God of the Sea, as well as earthquakes, and horses. Brother to Zeus and Hades.

Demeter: Goddess of Harvest. Mother of Persephone and goddess responsible for agriculture, harvest, and fertility.

The Nymphs:

Amalthia: A nymph known for the "horn of Amalthia" or our modern cornucopia, a magical horn that could produce an endless quantity of food and drink. If you watched "The Last Unicorn" you've heard the name before. Also, the author's preferred character name on many, many videogames.

Leuce: An ocean nymph brought to the Underworld by Hades. After she died in the Underground, Hades transformed her into a white poplar tree.

Minthe: A river nymph known to have been turned into a mint plant after it was discovered that she had a fling with Hades.

Stygia (Styx): Known as an ocean nymph or associated with the River Styx, the river in the Underworld that was the boundary between the living and the dead.

The Judges:

The Judges of the Underworld. They judged everyone who came to Hades' domain and determined their fate. Tartarus (tantamount to our modern hell) for those who were terrible in life and deserved eternal punishment. Asphodel (what we would think of as purgatory) for those whose souls were neither especially evil or especially good. Elysium (our heaven) for those whose souls we light with their good deeds in life. For those who choose to reincarnate, if the Judges sent you to Elysium three times, on the third time you could go to the Isle of Blessed, the most ideal of all afterlife locations.

- **Aeacus**: The record keeper
- **Rhadamanthys**: Valued wisdom and justice in the choice and presided over Elysium
- **Minos**: The Simon Cowell of the Judges. Mean. Temperamental. And often the deciding vote.

Charon: Ferryman of the Dead. Like modern Cajun ferrymen of the bayou, he uses a punting pole to propel the boat across the Styx to deliver new souls to Hades' realm.

The Myth of Hades and Persephone:

The original tales of Hades and Persephone were created to explain the cycle of the seasons. Depending on when the tale was told and where, Hades either kidnaps Persephone, daughter of Demeter, from the field where she was picking flowers or (debated) she went willingly. While in the Underworld, she eats six pomegranate seeds, unwittingly binding her to Hades and the Underworld. Above, Demeter wanders the world in grief for her daughter and refuses to allow plants to grow and bloom. Eventually Zeus must intervene, but because Persephone is now bound to Hades, they have to compromise: She will spend six months of every year above allowing plants to grow (spring and summer) and return to Hades for the next six months (autumn and winter).

Sources: Hazy memories of high school history and English classes combined with an amalgamation of Greek mythology in mainstream media (*Percy Jackson and the Olympians*, Disney's *Hercules*, *Battlestar Galactica 2004*, *Xena: Warrior Princess*, etc.). If you want something more formal than my fuzzy high school

memories, I can suggest the Greek Mythology article on Britannica.
https://www.britannica.com/topic/Greek-mythology

Act 1
The Descent

Chapter 1
Day 1

Persephone stared into the microscope, slowly swirling the knob until the slide came into focus. Pressed between the slide's two plates she could see the growth and death of her latest strain of wheat in one thin slice. Mold spores danced among the new growth, signaling that the plant's death was near. She was solely focused on her work to the exclusion of everything around her, which included two very large security guards and a holoscreen showing the never-ending coverage of a growing war. She sat perched on her stool, studying the results of her latest experimental crop. With one knee drawn tight to her chest, the other swung under her, kicking the stool's leg in a staccato rhythm.

She ignored a quiet cough behind her. Persephone sighed and pulled out the next plate, a slightly more mature slice of the same varietal. The cells showed robust growth and health. Persephone smiled as she hunched over the microscope, delighted at the mature plant's growth, but she was agitated. The yield was wrong once again. It was too high for her precise calculations, and she frowned because something was altering her outcomes.

Deep down, Persephone suspected she knew the source of the disturbance.

"Excuse me, Miss? I'm looking for Dr. Kore?" a man's voice called from her doorway.

Persephone sat up straight and spun the stool to face the man. She glanced at the clocks, set with times from around the world, each telling her she had gotten lost in her research and missed the start of an expected appointment. Tony, the head of her personal security detail, nodded to indicate the man had been vetted and was probably on her schedule. He clearly held back an amused smile as his chin lowered to his black uniform shirt. Beside him, his newest partner stood half a head taller than Tony and almost blank-faced. Only the barest twist to his mouth denied Tony's calm and a slight tightening of Henry's jaw indicated he was already annoyed with her visitor.

"Need something?" She rose and quickly wiped her hands on her dirt-caked, stained jeans. She nodded at the two men, giving Henry a little wink that she knew would make him roll his eyes, indicating the visitor could approach her. She wasn't the queen of the world but she was the queen of her lab and the two men ensured she only had the visitors she allowed.

The man stepped around Tony and Henry. "Yes? I'm supposed to come to work for Dr. Kore? Her new lab manager?" His voice rose as an annoying question with each statement. "They said I could find her here and that she was in desperate need of a lab manager." He finished the statement by licking his lips slightly.

"Lab manager?" Persephone asked, tucking her chocolate brown hair over her shoulder. She didn't need a lab manager. She suspected some high-level meddling, which set her on edge. If someone, probably her mother, was trying to play matchmaker again, she certainly wasn't taking this dweeb. He'd spent half his querying speech talking to the floor and the other staring at her admittedly minimal chest.

Henry shifted restlessly by her door. Persephone discreetly gestured for him to stay in place. He had only been on her security team for a few weeks, but it seemed he had already picked up much of the inner politics that made up International Bio-Chemical Corps, known as IBCC. His blue-gray eyes and close-cropped hair made the man look like a warrior made of marble. Beside him, Tony was a sharp contrast with sun-golden skin and a dark braid that went almost to his back. Despite the contrast in their appearances, they both had a look like if they had a broadsword pressed to their neck, they would laugh before destroying their foe. She had no doubt Tony would behave like a warrior if she was threatened.

"Look, girl," he scoffed. "I know Dr. Kore is the best bioengineer in the world, and with my credentials, I deserve to work for her. I don't need to get jerked around by some power-hungry intern. Go get her so I can interview with her and show her my papers." His earlier trepidation had clearly evaporated now that he'd assessed her to be nothing more than an intern, and the questioning tone was gone.

Persephone's eyes narrowed in her youthful face and her eyes darted to Henry. He gave her a quick nod. Her shoulders sagged in relief and the corners of his mouth twitched into a tiny smile before settling back into a neutral look.

"Yeah, I guess you'd hate to make the wrong impression." Persephone turned slightly as if heading to fetch 'Dr. Kore,' but paused. She smiled coquettishly over her shoulder at him. "What have you heard about Dr. Kore anyway that has you so impressed?"

"Her research into genetic and bioengineering is unparalleled!" he said with the warm smile of a professor about to embark on his pet topic. "She's unlocked ways to combine drought-resistant cultivars with less resilient species in unthought of ways. I've even read some of her more recent research into improving hydroponic systems to reduce evaporation and increase yield. Her research is extensive and some of the most cited in the world." He laughed and strode to where she sat, still perched on her stool. "The world of bioengineering, anyway." The man leaned in slightly.

Persephone leaned back, trying hard not to roll her eyes at his overt attempt to establish dominance, but didn't halt her security team from edging closer. She had no doubt that if she failed to keep him back, one of the two would have him on his knees with an arm yanked behind his back in a flash.

"Dr. Kore, huh?" she asked calmly. "Demeter Kore or Persephone Kore?"

"What?" The man jerked back a bit at her question.

With little space between them, now Persephone sat upright. "Dr. Demeter Kore is a biochemist, also well known for her research. But Dr. Persephone Kore is both a geneticist and bioengineer. Dual docs, ya know?"

"I'm looking for Dr. Persephone Kore, clearly," he sneered. "Who is Demeter Kore?"

"Dr. Persephone Kore's mother, clearly," she said in mocking reflection.

He sneered. "Oh, that's probably why I haven't heard of her. I only study cutting-edge technologies. If she's Dr. Persephone Kore's mother, she's probably well past her prime."

Persephone laughed, sharp and hard. He was a caricature of a boorish lecturer, smug and full of self-worth. Any doubt she'd harbored about not giving him a try had dissipated.

"I'll tell her you said that." She shot a look at her security team, now hovering mere feet behind him. Tony had his eyes locked on the man and was balanced on the balls of his feet, ready to lunge. Henry, on the other hand, stood tall and was still watching her, the slight bend in his knees only visible from the break in his pants the only indication he was prepared to strike. The way he looked at her as the domineering wannabe lab assistant loomed over her made her want to blush. It was hungry. Feral. Definitely not his usual cool composure. Her eyes shot back to the man before her.

He looked at her blankly before her words sank in.

His face fell by degrees as the truth hit him. "You ... you—," he stammered. "You can't be Dr. Kore."

"Oh, swing and a miss there, slugger. Look, *boy*," she gave him a saccharine smile. "I can and I am Dr. Kore. Dr. Persephone Kore, whose research is extensive and some of the most cited in the world. The world of bioengineering, anyway," she said, mimicking his rude tone. Her two guards inched closer.

His face fell from shock to anger. "Dr. Kore has been publishing for over a decade. You're like, twelve!"

Persephone's eyes narrowed and her mouth tightened. "You seem to suffer from hyperbole." She made an insolent face at him and cocked her head. "I'll have you know, I'm twenty-five. But you are right, I have been publishing for over a decade. I started publishing during my last year of my master's program and continued through my Ph.D., which, by the way, I finished well before I could drink. And I've been running this lab for almost nine years now."

The man looked poleaxed.

"You won't be joining me, by the way. I might need a lab manager, but a more open-minded one." She flicked her hands dismissively.

The man took a single step toward her, trying to tower over her small frame still perched easily on the stool, but before Persephone could blink, he was on his knees, one arm twisted tightly behind his back by Tony. Just as the two had been teaching her in their bi-weekly self-defense classes.

He looked at her questioningly as if he hoped to be rescued from her armed escort, but she shrugged. Her team was as restricted as she was.

Henry escorted the man out while Tony stood watch at her door, eyes sweeping the lab. Moments later, Henry returned, his uniform as unruffled as if he hadn't just thrown the man from the facility grounds. Persephone smiled at him, a silent *thank you*, and this time was rewarded with a full smile before he pulled it back into his professional mask. Something bright fluttered in her chest.

Sighing slightly, she uncoiled from her perch and stretched. She took in her messy lab, pots and soil scattered across worktables almost at odds with the high-end analyzers. "Okay, fellas, I'm gonna finish up for the day and head out for a hike." She paused because she already knew what was coming.

"Ma'am—" Tony started.

"Dr. Kore," Henry interrupted, "we'll have to check with the head of security first."

"*He's* the head of security," she said, pointing at Tony.

"I am the head of *your* security team, but I am not the head of *the* security team," Tony reminded her.

Persephone's eyes flicked to the unrelenting war coverage on a muted holoscreen above her workstation. She quirked one eyebrow. "Are you seriously worried about that?" she gestured to the muted screen. The news anchor's mouth moved silently as video of explosions showed in clips over his shoulder.

Neither answered, exchanging one silent look before Henry turned away to speak quietly into his radio. Persephone rolled her neck, occasionally twisting her head sharply in her hands to pop it.

"I'm sorry, Dr. Kore. You can only be approved for a short run and only on the compound tonight." Henry's face, usually expressionless, was regretful.

Persephone's eyebrows shot up. "By whose authority?" She'd been denied outings before, but this was an unprecedented level of restriction. She looked at Tony, who, as the head of her team, usually made the call on her restrictions, but he was looking at Henry.

"I'm sorry, ma'am, the head of our security team," Henry told her.

Her eyes narrowed over the odd phrasing. "Really?"

"Yes, ma'am," he said with his usual calm.

"How far?" she asked with deadly intensity.

"Ma'am, you may run as far as you like, but you must only run within the perimeter of the compound, and you need to be done before nightfall."

She gritted her teeth and held back the string of curses she wanted to let out. "Well then, I hope you enjoy running ten miles in three-mile loops through the corn, wheat, and soy," she told them. "I mean, I only assume you're on duty for a few more hours?"

They exchanged a look between them. Henry gave Tony a sharp nod.

She pushed back from the desk and stalked past the two men. A gentle hand on her upper arm halted her. She looked down, only then realizing that neither man had ever actually touched her before, as much as she might have welcomed that. She stared at the hand, pale on her sun-bronzed skin, feeling as if the world outside their compound had suddenly become all too real.

"Henry?" she asked quietly. She had gently flirted with and teased Henry since he had joined her team. He had a sweetness to him she liked. However, he had never reciprocated her flirting outright and had certainly never been so bold as to touch her.

Henry's mouth pressed into a thin line, and he didn't speak. Persephone stared up at him as fear built inside her. His eyes, a light blue rimmed in green, held her gaze with concern. If Henry was worried, she was scared.

"Ma'am, I'm sorry," Tony's voice cut their stare. "They've asked that you pack a small bag before you depart for your run. Just in case," Tony said with an anxious shrug.

"In case of what, Tony?" Persephone whispered and pulled against Henry's touch.

His hand stayed on her upper arm. Something unreadable flashed across his face.

"In case of what, Tony?" Persephone repeated, louder.

"In case this compound is overrun and we have to extract you quickly," he said calmly.

Persephone jerked her arm from Henry's grasp to face them both. "Are you serious?" She blinked hard to clear her contacts and narrowed her eyes at him. "Really?" she asked softly.

"Yes, Dr. Kore," Henry replied when Tony fell silent.

Chapter 2
Day 1

An hour later, she was running along the edges of the compound's many experimental fields, Henry and Tony jogging a respectful distance beyond to give her the illusion of solitude. Somewhere, far behind her, a small bag was packed with hastily assembled clothes, notes, and electronic drives.

Persephone held out a delicate hand as she ran, letting it slide along her various cultivars. Each was designed and mutated to counter a specific set of blights. She held eight patents for the crops she had produced over the last nine years, an unparalleled number among the staff of IBCC.

And yet, she winced slightly as her hand tapped each stalk, wondering if she was altering the outcomes of her current experiments. Farmers buying her genetically modified seeds expected a higher yield under static laboratory conditions. But she feared they would one day discover that her yields topped any other single scientist, no matter how the conditions were varied.

She gave a huffing breath as she ran, grateful that no one at IBCC had dug too deeply into her data to see the discrepancy. If it weren't for her mother's meddling, she would be at a real lab of her own choosing and could rely on the scientists around her to help double-check her results. At IBCC, she rarely, if ever, saw other researchers and most veered away from her when they spotted her during her leisure time, which was probably another trick of her mother's meddling.

So far, her closest companions were the ever-present security team her mother forced IBCC to employ on her behalf. She had been mutinous, resistant, and devious in giving them the slip until recently. When Tony had been promoted to the head of her team six months ago, she had settled down.

Tony was calm and unflappable. He'd broken the unspoken rule of never engaging with her directly to talk almost endlessly about his wife and life outside of work. Persephone, who had been devoid of real love for so long, had enjoyed their banter and stopped most of her shenanigans when he was on duty. On some level, knowing her mother's influence, Tony was likely as trapped in his duties as she was. Tony must have hired Henry because he had calmed her as much as Tony, if in a different way.

She glanced at Henry, keeping a steady pace just behind her left shoulder. She had been smitten the moment she saw him. He was tall and strong, his bulk filling out his uniform in an appealing way, like all her guards. But he was different, exuding a calm unlike any of her other guards. She basked in that peace. She half expected him to be like Tony, garrulous and open, but instead, she had spent the last few weeks slowly winding information out of him and flirting with him with all the subtly of a sledgehammer. Having been cloistered all her life, she had very little opportunity to practice. Yet, when he did speak, he exuded a gentle strength, sharp wit, and never made her feel like an awkward teenager trying to be subtle about a crush.

Well, she'd been subtle to start, which he ignored. Then she was open, which he gently turned aside while remaining friendly. When she asked if he was married, he had told her that he was single but didn't elaborate or hint that he had a significant other of some type. After that, she was blunt and still denied. Tony had dared to snicker at that. For the last week, it had been almost a game to see what was the silliest or most outrageous way she could flirt with him, knowing she'd still be denied.

"Enjoying the view?" she called over her shoulder to him and gave an extra swing to her hips for the next few strides.

Tony snickered, but Henry stayed silent.

"Henry, run up. Tony, fall back," she said.

They did as she asked, Henry running at her side and Tony, hopefully, out of earshot. For the sake of her ego.

"What do you know of what's going on out there?" she asked Henry.

"I can't say much more than what you've seen on the news."

"You're part of a security team. A security team at a secure facility, owned by a multi-billion credit corporation that sells to every nation on the planet. Well, almost all, some are sanctioned. I fail to believe you don't know more." She slowed down slightly, having realized she sped up as she spoke.

Henry paced her for a few strides before looking quickly over his shoulder at Tony. He glanced back at her. "I said I can't *say* much more, I didn't say I didn't *know*."

"Savvy."

"Since I can't *say* what I know, perhaps you could tell me what you know and I'd be happy to correct any misconceptions."

Persephone gave a light laugh then turned to look at Tony. He watched them but his face was blank and she hoped he hadn't heard Henry's offer.

"Zeus and Poseidon are at it again," she said quickly. "The two nations hate each other. They always have."

"Yes, the Sons of Zeus and Forces of Poseidon have been engaged in skirmishes for the last five months." They strode on a few more paces before he said, "And, yes, as far as I can tell, both sides fight like brothers over a rich man's inheritance."

"Poseidon's side is currently blockading key ports, keeping Zeus's people from receiving crucial shipments before what will likely be a harsh winter that far north."

"True. I feel that news has been negligent in mentioning acts of sabotage on several critical storage and processing facilities that would ensure those shipments are processed to feed, clothe, and house Zeus's people in the coming winter."

Persephone nodded. "And Poseidon's side feels justified because the accident on Rhodes spilled toxic, apocalyptic waste into their neighboring waters."

"Yes, the Forces of Poseidon are saying it was deliberate."

"And what would you say, Henry?"

"Could have been an accident. The Sons of Zeus aren't the most careful bunch. But it doesn't matter because the harm from it affected Poseidon far more than Hades."

"So much bad blood for so long," she said. "Does it ever end?"

"It ends when the struggle leaves both sides."

"How?"

"You know how," he said quietly.

They paced her for another mile before Henry finally spoke.

"We should cut it here, Dr. Kore."

"Call me Persephone—or Seph if you're really feeling close," she said with a smile.

"Dr. Kore, we need to get you back and positioned to move," he replied.

Persephone slowed to a walk and linked her arms in theirs. "You guys are sweet but absolutely no fun, you know that?"

"I'm incredibly fun," Tony responded. "Unlike him, I carry on a conversation well, or so my wife tells me."

"I'd like to meet this wonderful woman someday," she told him with a smile.

"Maybe you will," he said.

Henry shot him an unreadable look and Tony's face went blank.

"He's cranky because he's known me forever and is tired of hearing about my beloved wife while he stays single," Tony finally said with a sly grin.

"We'll get you back to your quarters, Dr. Kore," Henry told her, ignoring Tony's jab. "Based on our current intelligence, I suspect we may have to move you tonight. I'd recommend showering and eating as soon as possible so you're prepared."

"You really think we'll be attacked, Henry?" She shook her head. "That war isn't about us. I grow plants. I grow plants in a country that isn't an adversary to either side. What do the Forces of Poseidon or Sons of Zeus care about wheat and barley anyway?"

Henry gave her an odd look. "Dr. Kore, as you said earlier, you are world renowned. You can create what can save a civilization. Do not underestimate what people would do to control your knowledge and skills."

Chapter 3
Day 1

A ubiquitous holoscreen played silently near Persephone as she tidied her apartment. She ambled from room to room, hair still damp from her post-run shower and soaking the back of her shirt. It was easy to remain oblivious to the growing crisis on the news without her contacts or her glasses. Deliberately ignoring the screen as well as the conspicuous bag on the table, she purposefully moved piles of her belongings from one area to another while telling herself she was tidying up.

For weeks, Persephone had dodged each holoscreen displaying the rising tension between the world's two largest and most powerful nations. She and IBCC resided outside of both. Persephone knew enough history to know that if the big two erupted into open warfare, they might come through her tiny nation first. But from the little she'd allowed herself to see, it seemed unlikely.

A muffled boom broke her from the furious cleaning spree. From the window, the blurred, dimming light of a nearby blast faded. Persephone jerked upright, eyes darting to her bag. Reflexively, she sat at her console, which was transferring the contents of her desktop and her section of the IBCC servers to an external hard drive.

Persephone sighed and rose as the computer continued the long process of moving data. Her gaze falling on three stalks of wheat she plucked during her run, she didn't know why she'd snagged those cultivars, of all her current experiments. Somehow, they seemed vitally important now.

Another muffled boom was followed by a pounding at her door. Persephone's eyes darted to her well-worn t-shirt, faded tight joggers, and bare feet before coming back to the blurry entryway.

She hesitated. Somewhere in the back of her head, her mother Demeter's advice to *"never let them see you sweat or in sweats"* thundered through her consciousness.

The pounding sounded again. Disregarding her mother's careful advice on personal appearance management, she opened the door. Security personnel clad in black armor, different from their daily uniforms, flooded through. They flanked the walls of her entryway and hall, each rifle held down, but each trigger finger only a fraction of an inch away from a trigger. She was almost surprised to see there was not even a hint of feral lethality in their actions.

But clearly, every thought and every move carried purposeful intent.

"What—"

"Dr. Persephone Kore, grab your bag and follow me," a voice called out.

She reacted instinctively, only realizing it was Tony's voice ordering her around as she snatched the drive from her computer. She tucked the small drive into her bag as she followed him out swiftly. So swiftly that she left her contacts and glasses in the apartment as they fled. Nine years of memory drove her bare feet swiftly down two flights of stairs to a small concrete pad where a vehicle waited. Hands took her bag and lifted her into the vehicle. She settled, giving over to a false sense of calm that flooded her mind.

"CHARON 03, Hermes, the package is en route. Prep to launch and inform STYX 02 we'll be ready within the hour," the driver called into a radio at his shoulder.

"Copy, wilco Hermes," another voice crackled over the channel.

It was then Persephone realized that not only had she snagged her hard drive and bag, but the newest of her wheat cultivars were clutched in her hand.

Far beyond their vehicle, another boom echoed across IBCC's dark pastoral valley.

"Get down," Tony said calmly, but threw himself across her.

Persephone batted at Tony's muscular bulk ineffectually. "Get off, Tony!" she yelled, but he remained where he was, sprawled across her in the vehicle.

"Two minutes to the bird," someone yelled while they sped down the road.

Through Tony's bulk and more muffled booming, Persephone could hear the faint but growing *whump-whump-whump* sound of a helicopter. Her hands tightened on the stalks of wheat, seemingly the only thing she still had control over.

In a blur of motion, the vehicle stopped. She was extracted alongside her bag and loaded onto the running helicopter. Persephone would swear later that her feet never touched the ground during her abrupt abduction.

"CHARON 03, all souls aboard," she heard Tony shout into a headset as the helicopter lifted off.

"Tony, where's Henry?" she asked over the rush of wind through the open helicopter doors.

An unmuffled boom rocked the helicopter as it lifted off before anyone was buckled into a seat. Fire blossomed below and Persephone grabbed for anything she could get her free hand on as her occupied hand braced against anything else. They rose steadily from the ground, undamaged from the detonation only a few dozen feet away from their landing zone.

Persephone shivered from her place on the floor, hand still clutching the three precious stalks of wheat. She looked out at the destruction and shivered. Even in the growing dark, punctuated by explosive detonations, they were undoubtedly the only remaining stalks from several acres of experimental plants.

Chaos ruled the helicopter's movements. Persephone's shivers grew as they flew low across the terrain at speeds that whipped any warm air away from her body out the open doors. The helicopter yanked aggressively from left to right, skimming over the rolling terrain beyond the compound's valley. Persephone lost all sense of time as she flailed wildly for anything to grip. She grasped at the nylon webbing and straps that flapped around the helicopter as she fought for a more stable seat.

Whether it was seconds or minutes that passed, she managed to stay inside the maneuvering helicopter. Her eyes finally settled on Henry, whose presence she'd missed in their desperate evacuation. Relief flooded through her and Persephone would have smiled, but the damp shirt clinging to her back made her shiver in the ambient wind. Henry reached down, scooped her up with one arm, and draped her across his lap. He hunched over her, protecting her from the fierce winds whipping through the open cockpit.

In another time and place, Persephone would have smiled at

finally ending up in his embrace but not today.

Henry gently placed a set of headphones over her ears and she was immersed in the cockpit communication as they continued the flight away from IBCC.

"CHARON 03, reporting hostile fire outbound point Delta," a voice said in her ear.

"Copy all, STYX 02 is ready to receive you. Proceed on assigned vectors to RZ."

Persephone shivered in Henry's lap and he clutched her tighter. One arm wrapped around her thighs while the other pulled her torso tight against his chest. She tried to look up at him, to judge his expression, but the wind pulled her chocolate hair in a wild halo around her face, obscuring him.

"STYX 02, this is Hermes, sixty seconds from RZ," Persephone thought she heard the pilot say.

"Copy, engines burning."

"Hold tight, Persephone," Tony told her over the intercom.

Persephone nodded against Henry's chest, too cold to do much else. When the helicopter's skids touched down, Henry rose, still holding her in his arms. She was both dismayed she couldn't leave the helicopter on her own and thankful they didn't make her try, as personnel around her moved faster than her frozen body would allow.

"Keep holding on, girl," Henry told her as he settled into a seat of what she recognized as a plush business jet.

Persephone struggled to sit up on the padded leather bench seat.

"Here," Tony told her and offered an oxygen mask. He shot a quick look at Henry. "Flying at altitude can wind you."

She put the mask on her face gratefully and inhaled deeply.

"STYX 02, Hades Actual, package aboard," she heard over the hiss of the mask. "Authorized to depart."

"Copy, Hades Actual."

Persephone's eyes blinked hard. Her already blurry vision doubled. She realized no one else in the jet's cabin wore an oxygen mask. In a panic, she tried to push the gas mask away.

"It's okay, Seph," Tony told her and gently pushed the mask back to her face.

Henry put a gentle hand on her shoulder and she felt calmer.

"Tony? Henry?" she asked quietly through the mask. Her hand, still clutching the three precious stalks of wheat, folded gently across her waist. A strange lethargy spread through her body.

"You didn't accidentally," he hesitated, "you know?" Tony asked Henry as her consciousness faded.

"No man!" Henry replied harshly, then glanced down at her. "Get me the IV, it's a long flight to the Underground."

Persephone's eyelids drooped shut.

Chapter 4
Day 3

Persephone woke slowly, consciousness coming in fits and starts. With each waking, she could recall a fragmented memory. The dimmed lights of the business jet's cabin and an IV burning into the crook of her elbow. Bright runway lights on a pitch-black airstrip. Handcuffs and raised voices. Bright lights and a hallway that smelled like a basement: dusty, cold, and deep. The final time she woke, the only fragmented memory was of the soft whooshing of HVAC overhead.

Persephone opened her eyes.

She blinked.

She was surrounded by an unrelenting darkness that blinking failed to clear.

She rolled to her side and could feel a thin mattress or blanket under her. Every muscle in her body protested and she realized she had been unconscious for a long period. Persephone swallowed reflexively. Her mouth and throat were working to make enough saliva to swallow. A dim and fuzzy but narrow band of light was visible a few feet away, maybe the bottom of a door. Persephone sat up and slid back along the soft covering until her back hit a wall.

She sat with her knees drawn tight to her chest for an immeasurable time. The rough wall leeched heat from her back, as did the floor through the mattress's thin padding. Persephone shook as if the very walls were trying to pull life from her body.

Footsteps and a quietly rasping scrape beyond the narrow band of light caught her attention. There was a snicking clack before light flooded in. Persephone held one shaking hand up to shield her closed eyes.

"Doctor?" a deep, tentative voice called.

"Yes?" Persephone's voice creaked. She swallowed hard again, this time realizing how dry her mouth was.

"Dr. Persephone Kore?" the voice called again, muffled.

Persephone cracked her eyes open enough to see a figure move to block the door, then blurry feet approaching. She pressed up against the cold wall. "Yes."

A hand clasped her wrist and she made a croaking gasp of surprise. The strong hand yanked her to her feet. Staggering upright, Persephone winced at the blurry light coming through the door. She yelped in shock when pain lanced into her fingertip. Her finger was pinched and rolled until a bright crimson dot welled up.

"The machine needs more than that," a cold voice said in the darkness.

"She's dehydrated," a familiar voice chided. "You aren't going to get much more than that without a line." The hand holding her wrist ran a gentle thumb along the palm of her hand, as if trying to soothe her. "She shouldn't have been down here in the first place."

Persephone saw another hand swiftly collect the bright red drop of blood from her finger. She jerked her hand out of someone's grasp and brought it to her mouth to suck on the painful cut. While she inspected the finger, something near the bright fuzz of the doorway gave a soft cheeping.

The cold voice gave a sharp grunt. "Persephone Nestis Kore, daughter of Demeter Kore, and lead bio-genetic engineer at International Bio-Chemical Corps. Twenty-five years old, never married, and no children. Holds doctorates in biology and genetic engineering," the voice rattled off.

"I told you it was her," the familiar voice responded, annoyance making his voice tight. "I brought her in myself."

"This can't be right," the first voice argued. "You can't have two doctorates by the age of—what?—seventeen?"

"Sixteen," she corrected absently. Persephone wiped her finger on her t-shirt, wondering how long she had been wearing it, and squinted at the two vague shapes in front of her.

"Come on, Persephone," the familiar voice called.

"No, sir, she has to be judged." The second voice was testy, as if this were an argument had many times over.

"She was specifically requested."

"You know the rules. No dead weight," the voice said with cold humor.

"She was specifically requested by *him*," the familiar voice reiterated.

"He may be the Lord Commander and King, but even he has rules. Rules," the cold voice went on, "he has entrusted us to enforce, Thanatos."

A hand clamped onto her wrist again, presumably Thanatos, and gave a gentle but insistent tug. "This will be quick, then we'll get you settled."

Persephone had a moment's hesitation before stumbling along after them. It wasn't that she wanted to stay in a dark cell, but the idea of being "judged" held an ominous feel. She closed her eyes as she stepped from the cell into the brightly illuminated hallway. She had always welcomed the sun, reveled in its feel on her skin. This light was harsh, unnatural, and made her shiver.

The hand on her wrist released her. "This way," he said. "It'll be okay, Seph."

She blinked at him. She guessed he was no more than four feet away, but she was unable to see his face. Squinting after the men, or at least she assumed, men, all she could make out were darkly dressed, bulky figures. She stumbled after them, staggering down the hallway until a hand grabbed her elbow to steady her.

Persephone looked up to see the dark clad, armored guard, presumably looking down at her from a black, visored helmet. "Please, Persephone. No one intends to hurt you," he gave a little pause and Persephone guessed he was looking at the first person, a small, maybe slender man or a woman with a neutral voice.

"She must be judged," the voice said with a cool bluntness that conveyed an utter lack of care.

Listening more closely now, she realized the person was a slender woman in dark robes.

"Eris," growled the dark armored man with a familiar voice.

"She gets no more special treatment than anyone else," Eris replied calmly. "After all, we can't have anything stirring up the masses right now, can we?"

There was a moment of tense silence before the warmer of the two hands, the still helmeted Thanatos, tugged on her gently.

"Please, Persephone."

There was something in the way he said her name. A subtle reverence that unfroze her feet. She took a hesitant, stumbling step forward. A hand caught and cupped her elbow to keep her upright.

"Thank you," she mumbled.

"Are you alright?" he asked quietly, his voice muffled by the helmet.

"Tired, hungry, thirsty, and kind of pissed," she said. Her eyes swept from his helmet to the hallway, squinting, but still unable to see beyond the length of her arm.

There was silence as she tried to make sense of her surroundings.

"She's not wearing her glasses, Thanatos," another man said from her other side.

Thanatos' visored face turned to her. The hand at her wrist moved to cup her chin, turning her face up to his.

She glared up at his blank visor.

"I'll have to add it to the list," Thanatos said. His hand went to her arm and he guided her along gently by the elbow.

They led her, Thanatos by her elbow and the other two flanking them, down bright gray hallways. Their feet echoed sharply, in a way that made Persephone think the walls were stone or concrete, an idea reinforced by the dank chill in the air.

"Here," someone said, opening a door. "My duties as an escort end here. I will undoubtedly see you later, on the control floor." He stepped in closer and gave her a brief bow.

Persephone realized he had deliberately stepped inside of her field of vision to execute his respectful gesture.

"Thank you, Hermes," Thanatos told him and walked her through the open door. The blurry mass in front of her solidified into a pale dais with three forms seated atop it as they walked closer. Persephone squinted, able to see dark chairs and pale walls, but unable to make out anything more than vaguely human forms seated on the dais.

"I bring Persephone Kore before you for judgment," Thanatos told them, voice crisp and formal. "Not that it is strictly required," he said and Persephone got the impression he was looking at Eris from behind his dark visor.

"All who come here require judgment," a hissingly soft voice said from the dais.

"All," echoed two other voices.

"Send her data so she may be judged," the quiet voice hissed.

Eris tapped a key on her small machine and Persephone saw the figures hunch down, presumably reading. They stayed that way for several quiet and intense moments.

"Dr. Persephone Nestis Kore, you are here to be judged for a level of usefulness to us," the middle figure said.

"I didn't ask for this," she spat back.

"No, but the world as you know it will end. This facility will be one of only a few that survive. We wish for you to survive with us, but we must decide the circumstances of that survival. Those who are diligent workers or technically skilled can find themselves assigned to Asphodel, living a modest life until we can return to the world again. Those with useful skills or excellent minds could be assigned to Elysium, enjoying benefits equal to their contributions."

A spark of proud fire ignited in Persephone. She had never been considered anything less than an exceptional thinker.

"And those who refuse to obey the rules or carry their share of our burden find themselves assigned to Tartarus, fated to spend their time working difficult, dirty, or menial labors."

Persephone's mouth tightened. She knew she was arrogant and feared her smart mouth would get her smart mind shuttered away doing hard labor.

"Judges, you have reviewed the file," the hissingly quiet voice said, "state your cases."

"She holds two doctoral degrees in useful fields." There was a faint chuckle from the judge on the right. "One is quite literally *in* a field."

"She is too young," the quiet voice hissed from the left.

"Youth is a plus," the right judge quipped. "She isn't like the doddering old fools we have now who may not make it until we can open the doors."

"Headstrong. Impudent. Immature," the left judge countered.

"Young, yes, but she runs her own department. She has for years. Clearly, that makes for some level of maturity and leadership," the right judge argued.

"She holds multiple patents on genetically engineered plants. Her research has created food crops that are resistant to the most difficult and impactful blights. Something I believe we need," the center judge cut in.

"She will cause turmoil by her very presence," the left judge said. Persephone could see Eris nodding from the corner of her eye.

"Be that as it may, we need her," the center judge intoned.

"She is a risk. She will cause agitation with her very presence. She risks upheaval. She risks our existence."

"You have spent time in her presence. Would you speak for her, Thanatos?"

Persephone stiffened. His helmet-muffled voice was faintly familiar *and* he'd spent time in her presence? She squinted at his visor.

"She is headstrong, yes, but it is because she knows what is right and fights for it. She appears impudent if you don't see the care and humor that lies underneath," his familiar voice carried to the dais. Not loud, but inescapable. "One could call her youth 'immaturity,' but at their own peril. She burns with the fires and passions of those not yet worn down to callousness by great age. What you may point out as flaws, we see as features."

"We?"

"Yes, you know damn well, *we*. She is brilliant and innovative, both things we will need as our resources wane. And she was specifically requested," he paused, "by *him*." There was a strange emphasis to his statement.

Persephone looked back at the blurry shapes of the judges.

"Judges, your verdicts? Asphodel, Elysium, or Tartarus?"

There was a long pause and she could feel their eyes on her. Fear sank leaden into her belly.

"She has a fourth option," a deep voice called out behind them.

"She does not!" the querulous hissing voice on the left shouted.

"If she is the risk you say she is, then she has a fourth choice," the voice said heavily.

Another person stepped beside her, tall and bulky. The figure wore dark clothes and practically loomed over her. She peered at the figure, but they were just far enough away that it was a blur of darkness and a single flash of gold as they moved.

"Is this the choice you would have us make? You know what

it means, my Lord," the center voice asked. "You know you could make a place for her," he finished slyly.

"I will not trade lives like that. Given the dire need we have, but the security risk she presents, my recommendation is that she be judged Blessed."

"What is Blessed?" Persephone whispered to Thanatos in the silence that followed.

"Personally vouched for by him," his voice stressed oddly. "But if you breach faith, you'll be expelled."

Persephone blinked. "Okay, but what does that mean?"

"Accept it or be shoved out the blast doors into the middle of a war. Sorry, I can't explain more now."

She peered up at his mask, anger starting to overcome her fear. She opened her mouth, but his hand clamped over her mouth before she could curse him out.

"Do you take this obligation? Will she?" the center judge asked, unaware or ignoring her questions.

Persephone rolled her eyes toward the dark figure beside her. She wasn't sure if she could trust his words or not.

The horrifying memory of her compound burning beneath her as they barely escaped flooded her mind. A weight settled on her chest and her legs wobbled, thinking of the deep booms that had echoed across her pastoral valley. Something finally clicked into place in her mind and she realized that everyone she knew at IBCC was dead.

Persephone dropped her head as tears formed. She knew she couldn't break now, not with her future hanging in the balance. She swallowed down the fear, pain, and grief. She locked it away in a tiny box in her mind, to be opened, examined, and felt later. But not now.

Persephone nodded to the dark figure.

"Yes, we are both willing to accept the obligation," the deep voice beside her said with dignity.

"Judges, your verdicts?" the center judge asked. "Minos?"

"Blessed," Minos's querulous hissing voice said.

"Rhadamanthus?"

"Blessed," the right judge said calmly.

"And I, Aeacus, judge you Blessed."

There was a strange sense of finality to his statement and Persephone shivered. The shiver was accompanied by static, as if she stood beneath a clouded sky just before the first crack of thunder.

"Thanatos, I release her to the Lord's guardianship. And may you both have chosen wisely."

Thanatos' visor was still down and he nodded to the judges. Persephone saw his head swing toward her, but felt Eris shuffle back beside her. "Eris," he said coldly.

"Thanatos," Eris responded in an unruffled voice.

"Persephone, this way please," Thanatos said and took her elbow again, gently guiding her from the hall, the dark figure striding alongside them silently.

"Where are we going?" she asked and jerked her arm, but Thanatos' firm grasp remained.

"Just wait," he said.

"No, now!" she said heatedly.

They passed into the hallway and Thanatos shut the door firmly behind them as the dark, bulky figure continued. His helmeted head swung from side to side, likely peering down the corridors.

"You have been judged Blessed, Persephone. You represent too great a risk and are at too great a risk to be among the general Elysium population. I assume they would have judged Elysium had we not intervened."

"Why? Why am I dangerous?"

"Come on," he said and tugged at her elbow.

Persephone jerked her arm hard, freeing herself from his grasp. "No, now," she repeated.

"No, you have to formally meet one more person. I'll talk some as we walk. But quietly, so don't fuss at what I tell you."

Her eyes narrowed at his visor, but she held her elbow out. Thanatos set off at a brisk walk.

"This facility has been in place for a decade. It has had people living in it since it was declared operational."

"And what is this facility?" As they walked, she sensed the corridors widened. The sound of their footsteps became muted, they echoed less. The ambient noise around them increased but was more diffuse. A hundred voices murmured and were thrown back at her from raw, unpolished rock.

Thanatos huffed out a deep breath. "It is nothing more or less than a very well-built and stocked underground survival shelter."

"What?" Persephone squawked.

"Surely you aren't surprised?"

She considered for a moment. "No. With everything going on? No, I guess not." She shook her head.

Persephone could tell people were walking the narrowing halls. The sound had a similar diffuse quality of soundwaves hitting rough surfaces and scattering, but it was sharper, tighter. All around her, a cold seeped from every wall and the air had a strange flat smell to it. The people, whose faces she couldn't read at this distance, seemed to radiate a sense of hostility.

"Why me?"

"That's the dangerous part. We spent years bringing in the resources we needed to survive a full-scale war. Some of those resources are people. The last few years have brought an influx of the most intelligent scientists in the world. Brought in both to help us and to protect them. Since then, we've built a community from those minds and those who work under or for them. We've taken in no one new in almost nine months."

He sighed and they turned down another corridor. Unlike the corridors they had traveled the last few minutes, this was carpeted and had stately walls of dark wood and somber paint.

"I'm an unknown to a tight-knit group," Persephone said.

"You are. And while necessary, there will be some," he hesitated as if considering his word choice carefully, "*agitation* that there is now one more person in an already resource constrained population."

"Then why bring in someone new now?" she asked. "Why me?"

"You're the very best and we need someone who will keep food flowing from fields to kitchens."

They walked another moment.

"There's something else, isn't there?"

"Yes."

"I was 'requested'?"

"That too. We scout and vet everyone we bring in," Thanatos hedged.

"Kidnap," Persephone retorted hotly.

"Tactically acquire, might be more accurate. But most people come of their own volition."

"Who, Thanatos? Who requested me?"

Thanatos stopped in front of a dark wooden door. He was silent a moment before he opened the door and strode into the room, guiding Persephone in by the elbow. He walked her to a desk where a dark hulking figure stood.

The man towered over her and stood half a head above Thanatos as well. From where she stood, she couldn't make out his features other than to know this was a man with brown hair clipped or tied tightly against his head. She was close enough now that from across the desk, Persephone could make out an athletic form under a tailored suit. She took one step forward to see his face, then jumped a half a step back until Thanatos tugged her elbow.

"Dr. Persephone Kore, may I introduce you to Hades, Lord Commander and King of the Underground."

"Henry," she whispered.

Chapter 5
Day 4

Persephone's eyes narrowed as she studied the man in front of her. He was tall and broad with muscle, but she couldn't make out much more from across the desk. Before, seeing him lit a pleasant warmth in her belly, but now a feeling of betrayal started to burn there.

Raising her chin defiantly, she asked, "You're the reason I'm here?" She was pleased the words came out steadily.

At first, he didn't speak. She felt his intense stare, but she stood her ground, spine straight and worthless eyes fixed on his face. Whether he was mad, surprised, enraged, or merely bored, she didn't know. Not having her glasses was almost a bonus because she could face him without seeing his reaction to her hostility.

She raised her chin a fraction of an inch higher and waited. Beside her, Thanatos' hand eased on her elbow and he leaned back slightly.

The tension that had built since they entered broke suddenly.

"She is as strong willed as always, isn't she, Thanatos?" said his deep bass voice. "It's good to see that even now. We might just survive this yet."

Persephone stepped back as the hulking man came out from behind the large wooden desk. Thanatos put a hand at the small of her back, lightly holding her in place. She shot him a look, but his helmet blocked his expression and the armor he wore masked any other hints his body language might have given her.

A silence stretched briefly.

"It's considered rude not to shake someone's hand when it's offered," Hades' deep voice rumbled.

Persephone's blurry gaze dropped, finally seeing the hand he held out. She reached forward, bumping it once before he grasped her hand in his. His warm hand, thick and marked with calluses, engulfed hers.

Silence lingered between them as he held her hand, the air charged with something unspoken. When Hades released her hand, she thought the feeling had passed until he closed the gap between them, his hand rising to her cheek, guiding her gaze meet to his.

Like Henry, he was big. Not fat or extraordinarily tall for a man. He simply towered over her and held a bulk that spoke of muscle encased in suit cloth. Moreover, he carried a presence that radiated from him, making him seem to fill the room.

This close, she could finally make out his facial features. He looked like her Henry, but there were subtle and uncanny differences. Eyes that had blue-gray irises rimmed in green looked down at her from beneath dark lashes and thick eyebrows. Set against his pale skin, they were the only hint of emotional warmth on his face—flashing silver against marble flesh. Uncanny, but not unattractive. His silver eyes studied her intently, searching her face.

"Thanatos," he said, finally taking his eyes from Persephone to look at the man beside her, "our best notes didn't say she was blind."

Thanatos' helmet turned toward her sharply. "She's not—"

"I'm not blind. You kidnapped me and didn't bother taking my glasses," she cut in over Thanatos.

"*Tactically acquired*," Thanatos whispered.

Something behind Hades' eyes hardened. "You have not been," he frowned, "kidnapped."

Persephone arched a brown eyebrow at him. "Oh, yes, I suppose I came here willingly, knowingly, and having given my consent to travel? How many weeks did you guard me and you didn't catch on to how dependent I am on glasses and contacts?" Persephone spat, disgust dripping from her voice.

"It would be trite to say, 'this is for your own good,' so I won't. But there are forces at play here that you don't understand yet."

"Then tell me," she said. "I'm not a damn child who needs coddling. I have a fully functioning brain and don't enjoy high-handed assholes doing things *for my own good*," she said in a mocking echo of his words. "I have a life. A job. I have experiments that will need my attention soon."

Even as she said it, she knew it was a lie. Somewhere in the back of her mind there was a tiny box full of horrors witnessed over the last few days. She had locked it away, but now it threatened to explode.

She watched his eyes flick to Thanatos and back. "That is gone. I'm sorry to be blunt, but that life is gone. Everything you knew is gone or will be in a matter of days to hours."

"No. I'm not staying here. You can't hold me and I need to go home."

"You are and I can. I am sorry, Persephone," he said with genuine sorrow in his deep voice. He held up a hand to halt her outburst. "I will have better proof than a patronizing 'because I said so,' in a day, maybe less. Until then, we need to get you settled."

Persephone bit back an angry retort. Raising her chin to meet his eyes, "Fine. Tell me what 'Blessed' means."

Hades rocked back slightly and Thanatos leaned away from her once more. "You didn't tell her?"

"I didn't have time," Thanatos said.

If Persephone could have seen his face, she would have assumed his jaw was clenched. Hard.

"The Judges explained the three levels, yes?" Hades asked, voice brisk.

"Yes. Labor, scientists, and uh, criminals, I guess."

"Not quite, but close enough for now," Hades shrugged a shoulder, his muscles rippling the material of his suit. "There's more nuance than that, but for now, it will do. Did Thanatos explain what he or I do here?"

"No."

Hades' eyes narrowed at Thanatos again but he addressed Persephone. "I am the Commander of this facility. Thanatos is the head of Defense."

"He called you a king," Persephone told him. "Others refer to you as a lord."

"That too," Hades agreed.

Persephone's head whipped toward Thanatos, realization growing in her mind, and she stared at him intently, trying to see the man beneath the armor. Slowly, she turned back to Hades. "And what is this facility? Thanatos said it's a survival shelter."

"It is. A survival shelter. A lifeboat. A chance to live." Hades' deep voice held a hint of something unfathomable. "Know that we are fully stocked to live in the facility for up to five years, self-sustained, provided our population remains stable, both in size and attitude. If they revolt or riot, Thanatos and I would be able to quell it, but the method by which we subdued a riot would harm the population size."

"You'd kill everyone?" Persephone said, shock creeping into her voice.

"I would avoid that as much as possible, but I cannot allow a cancer to grow."

Persephone turned to Thanatos. "I'm a late addition. They're unhappy you would alter the population by even one person?"

"In a way, yes. It's not just that I've added a person. It's that I've added someone, so close to the end game, and I haven't brought in the others' extended family members or granted requests for couples to start families."

"Wait, they—" Persephone started, but Hades cut her off.

"Yes, I manage populations down to how many of our personnel are allowed to have children."

Persephone stared at him in shock.

"My resources are limited."

Persephone closed her eyes and organized her thoughts. "For the third time, what does 'Blessed' mean?"

"Because you are being added in a way that many would perceive as against the rules or as a show of extreme preferential treatment, we are designating you as under protection. As far as they are concerned, I have taken you as my," he paused, clearly seeking the appropriate word, "ward."

Beside her, Thanatos shuffled slightly.

Her eyes narrowed and she stared at him. "They consider me his ward? And how will I perceive this?"

"You will be under his care and protection at all times," Thanatos said.

"Prisoner?"

"You will be with him or one of his personal guards at all times for your protection, not a prisoner," Thanatos told her.

"We anticipate the outbreak of full-scale war within the next day. I will begin locking down the facility in the next few hours. I don't anticipate that to be an event without significant emotional turmoil. Your presence, in addition to that, will cause more turmoil and I want you to be safe," Hades told her. He caught her hand again. "Please know, I left you in the world as long as I dared. I," his eyes darted to Thanatos, "wanted you to have your freedom as long as you could. But we always planned to bring you here for your safety. I couldn't stand the idea of letting you die on the surface."

Persephone took a deep breath, ready to start howling her thoughts on the matter, but she was halted by a blaring alarm.

"My Lord?" Thanatos asked over the alarm.

"Yes, it is time," Hades said simply. "Take her down to the fields. Show her what parts of her research we've already replicated. I'll initiate the lockdown."

"You stole my research?" The words burst out of her, equal parts accusation and outrage. Her chin lifted, defiance blazing in her eyes.

"You don't want me commanding security?" Thanatos asked over her outburst.

Hades shook his head. "No, they are loyal to us. They know their orders. I'll call if I need you." He turned to her, one hand raised placatingly. "It's not so much stolen as prepared for your arrival," he said then turned back to Thanatos. "Keep her safe."

"What's going on?" Persephone asked. Fear and anger laced her voice. Fear that she already knew the answer and anger that, as of right now, there was nothing she could do about it.

Hades slapped a panel and the blaring alarm cut out. "I measure various parameters all over the world. All current signs indicate that full-scale war will begin in the next twenty-four hours. I'm locking us down. For the final time." He leaned over his desk and punched a large button with one thick finger. "Control? Execute the lockdown."

Hades raised his face to her once again. "Welcome to the Underground, Persephone."

Chapter 6
Day 4

If the residents of the Underground were shocked or at all perturbed to see Thanatos hauling a screeching, fighting woman over his shoulder as he strode through their halls, they didn't indicate it in any way Persephone could see. Of course, her line of sight was limited to Thanatos' backside and a few floor tiles as he carried her out of Hades' office.

She had started howling in fury as soon as Hades had turned away to execute his lockdown and didn't stop until a warm, soil-scented breeze wafted across her face. Thanatos set her down gently and for the first time in days, she felt the softness of soil underfoot.

Persephone immediately crouched to examine the soil. She raked her hands through the loose dirt, rubbing it between her fingers to feel the density, sand, and moisture content. It was good, dark soil that left a darkened line under her nails.

She stood and turned her face up to the overhead light. Unable to see the source, she let her eyes close and felt its warmth on her face.

"It's not real, is it?" she asked. Persephone had regained a measure of calm. The feel of soil underfoot and in her nails was so normal that she felt her muscles loosening.

"What?"

"The sun? The light source? It's not our sun. It's a lamp, right?"

"Yes, but you already knew that," Thanatos answered, surprise coloring his muffled voice. "It's as close as they can get, I've been told. But, no, it's not the real sun."

She squinted, unable to see anything in the brightness, but she assumed that if she could, there would be a matrix of lights with varying outputs. The vital mix of light across a spectrum of electromagnetic energy, perfectly tailored to growing plants.

Persephone nodded, her eyes still closed, as she basked under the lamps. A slight breeze ruffled her hair, strands flowing across her neck and face.

"Will I get sunburned here?"

"No, ma'am."

"Then they aren't strong enough. And the breeze?" she asked, fingers tucking the errant strands over her shoulder.

"It's a good HVAC system," Thanatos told her. His voice held a gentleness at odds with his dark mask and armor.

Persephone considered him. While his voice held a haunting familiarity, his armor and mask, combined with her inability to see clearly beyond the length of her arm, made it impossible to guess who he was. "Take off your helmet."

"Excuse me?" Thanatos didn't sound mad so much as surprised.

"I want to know who you are," she told him.

"You haven't guessed?" he asked quietly.

Her eyes narrowed again. She thought a moment before shaking her head. "While your voice is familiar, it's muffled," she said, surprising herself that she wasn't verbally eviscerating him, "and your mask and armor obscure any other detail that might give it away." Persephone was almost proud of how well she held her calm.

"I can't—"

"You say you are here for my protection, but how can I trust you when I don't know who you are?"

His mask turned to her. Whether he tensed with anger or relaxed knowing he was beaten, she couldn't tell under layers of fabric and armor. She could see his head tilt slightly, but everything else was lost to her blurry vision and his armor.

Persephone waited. She was good at waiting. No specimen achieves its full growth overnight. A blossom doesn't bloom because you force it. Plants grow in their own time and way. She waited, watching him under slightly furrowed brows and an expressionless face.

Slowly, hesitantly, his hand went to the mask, releasing one clasp. The plastic covering dropped to one side. Under her blurred gaze, his fingers toggled open the helmet's chin strap and visor. He ducked his head quickly as he stripped away the helmet and mask. Underneath was a familiar face, framed by a neatly trimmed beard and a long, braided stripe of hair down the center of his head, with the sides trimmed close.

Persephone let out a single breath. "Tony."

Anger and betrayal flooded through her. Twice. She had been duped by both men she trusted the most. Henry was one thing. She had pursued him with only a hint of response. The barest of smiles had given her hope that one day he might be receptive to her inexperienced flirting. One day he might reciprocate the little flutter in her stomach she had each time she saw him.

Tony was different. Tony had been the head of her security for months. He was so open about his hobbies, his favorite books, and his wife. She had been duped by someone she liked and trusted.

His soft expression held wariness; He knew her well enough to expect an outburst. She swallowed it down.

She inhaled slowly and exhaled. "Thanatos."

He nodded.

"Why were you my bodyguard at IBCC? More to the point, how did you and Henry—Hades," she grimaced, "manage to secure positions on my personal security detail?"

He seemed as shocked as she was that her voice was calm and steady. His eyes were wide but beneath them, his mouth twitched into a quick smile.

"Hades and I believed your protection and safe passage here was the most important thing in the world as we prepared for the end of it. I couldn't trust anyone else to retrieve—" he faltered.

"What, Thanatos? What am I?" Persephone raised a single eyebrow. "What am I to you?"

Fake sunlight and a manufactured breeze wafted over them as silence stretched.

"*Salvation*," he whispered so low she almost missed it.

The world above raged and raced to a civilization-ending war but for her time skittered to a halt. The silence between them pulled as taut as a trellis line stretched to guide life to the sun or the golden cord of the Fates trembling before the snip. Life and death hung for a moment before her.

"You're far more important than you realize," he said quickly and louder. "We need you. We need what you can offer."

It was half an answer; even she could read that on his newly exposed face. Too tired to fight him, she simply said, "Okay."

"Would you like to see the rest of the fields?" he asked with barely disguised relief.

"Why not?" Persephone answered wryly.

Thanatos slipped his helmet back on. He left the visor up but the clasp of the lower half of the mask made a slight click as it slid into place. She gave him a look but said nothing. With the mask on like that and only his eyes visible, she lost any idea what he was thinking while he could read her face and body language with ease. She wanted to be mad but couldn't summon the energy.

Wordlessly, he offered his arm. She took it, wrapping her hand over the hard, dark material of his uniform.

Persephone was surprised, holding his arm as they walked. She had expected the armor to be thick, giving him the impression of great bulk, but it was a thin, firm material like plastic. Underneath was solid muscle. She hadn't paid much attention to the appearance of her security team other than Henry; her annoyance at being forced to even have a security detail made her deliberately blank them from her mind while working.

She gave him a sidelong look as they passed through neat rows of wheat, her free hand trailing against the growing stalks. She idly noted the head of the wheat was just emerging from its sheath by the feel of the stalk under her fingertips. They were still weeks from harvest. Beyond them stretched an almost endless sea of gold, waving slightly in the fake sunlight. Open spaces where other plants grew capped many of the rows, but nothing she could distinguish without glasses.

Persephone focused on Thanatos for a moment as they walked. Maybe it was her poor eyesight, but he seemed subtly different. Had his beard always been that thick? Had his hair been that long? Surely it was only a little long on top? And had he been this muscular?

"Why do you look different?" she blurted out as the field of wheat ended.

Thanatos stopped and she stopped with him. Beyond him, the next field was a blur of green.

"There are a few things here that are," he paused as if weighing his words, "different," he said finally. "Some people have said that reality itself seems different here. It could be a trick of the mind, protecting itself from knowing the person is stuck in the Underground for the next few years of their life. Adjusting to what life is now and trying to forget what was before."

"You don't seem certain."

His masked head turned to look at her. "Do you believe that reality could be different here?" he asked in a neutral voice.

Persephone frowned. "No."

A silence stretched and she realized he wasn't looking at her but beyond her and she turned to the wheat behind them. Along the edge of the neat rows, the last stalk in each row stood higher than its neighbors. She rushed forward to grasp the closest stalk. It was tall and robust, its grain perfectly ripe.

"I—" she started, but he cut her off.

"You knew, or suspected at least, that you were the source of your high yields."

"But—" she stopped, gaping at the plants.

"Maybe you didn't know you could do it. But we saw the consistently higher yields your patents produced during testing. Our researchers have been analyzing your work for years. It only took two days of being in your lab to see that you suspected it too, even if only subconsciously." His voice held a reverence, as if he had enjoyed watching her work. "By the third day, I knew Hades had made the right choice. Here, it will be more powerful."

Persephone swallowed hard. "How did you even know to suspect something like this?"

Thanatos shrugged. "Do you want to walk more?"

She nodded silently and he offered his arm once more. They walked slowly through the next field.

"You planted corn, beans, and squash together?" she asked once she was able to get close enough to identify the plants.

"Yes. I mean, not me, but yes, clearly."

"It's companion planting. The three work well together. Each providing something the others need." She reached out a tentative hand to caress the corn. Releasing her grip on his arm, she leaned in closer to touch the beans climbing the stalk and bent down to run a finger over the rough squash leaf before gently touching the ripened squash underneath.

From where she knelt in the dirt, she looked up to see Thanatos watching her silently. He looked so out of place—a silent, dark-armored sentinel among the verdant colors of the growing field. She frowned. The feral lethality that had been absent when they took her from IBCC lurked on the edges of her vision now. Where earlier, he and his team had been all precise movements and calm tactical execution, he stood with a strange, rigid grace that said he was ready for violence at a moment's notice. She couldn't see his eyes, but she had the impression they were constantly scanning, seeking death for the next threat.

It was so at odds with the growing life around her that she rocked back on her heels.

"Thanatos?" she asked hesitantly. "Tony?" she said quietly when he didn't answer.

"Yes?"

"What are you looking for?"

He was silent for a long moment. "Threats," he said finally.

Something in that single word sent a shiver down her spine. Part of her trembled at the calm way he said it; his cool detachment meant death to anyone who approached with violence. Another, deeper part of her felt relief that she had someone she knew here. Well, sort of knew. She inhaled sharply and let it out slowly.

"Tell me more about the plants," he told her.

"The corn is the structure," she told him, straightening. "It gives the beans something to climb. The squash protects the soil for both, spreading to kill off any weeds. And the beans climb the corn, strengthening the stalk as well as feeding nitrogen back into the soil, making it fertile."

She wiped her hands on her clothes, trying to ignore how dirty they were after what was probably several days' wear, even if she had been asleep for most of it. Thanatos offered his arm once again and they walked on toward a grove on the far side of the corn.

"Are there other plants we should be growing together?" he asked as they walked.

"Of course," she replied absently. Half her mind was on how she could get clean clothes and glasses. "It just depends on what you want from them. I assume shade isn't a problem and possibly you've sanitized the soil from insects like aphids." *Will I need to steal clothes? That was probably a one-way ticket to the Tartarus group.* "Beets and garlic grown together will improve the flavor of the beets. Chives will similarly improve the flavor of carrots when grown together. Of course, basil, tomatoes, and onions are a classic combination that work together as well and make for great food."

She saw him nod as she talked. Persephone wondered if he would give her clean clothes if she asked.

"But, I also assume you've," her mouth twisted slightly, "acquired other scientists who've already told you this."

"Several," he said without a trace of apology. "They all helped design and build the vast fields that feed our population."

"But?"

"But," he said as he stopped at the grove, "my understanding is they don't have your intelligence and acumen for research. There are other talents you have that they don't possess."

Persephone dropped his arm and looked at him. She wanted to grind her teeth in frustration. With his helmet on she couldn't read his face. His body language was masked by his armor. The subtle nuance with which he infused his words was lost to the muffling of his mask. Fatigue washed over her. She didn't have the energy to pick apart the nuance she couldn't read. Instead, she turned her attention to the cultivars surrounding them.

She stepped away from Thanatos and toward the tall, broad plant. Its thin trunk held leafy branches aloft at her height. Persephone smiled when another step closer showed her the large red fruit hanging hidden among the small leaves.

"The pomegranate is a real bastard, you know?" she asked, her mouth quirked into a smile. She reached out to brush her hand along the underside of a branch. As if obedient to her unspoken wish, the leaves expanded, the few orange blooms opened, and the pale pink fruit hanging midway down the branch blushed to a deep red. With no glasses, Persephone was only able to see the bright red of the fruit.

Persephone turned to smile at Thanatos. The Tony she knew had a mouth that held a hint of laughter as his eyes danced with mirth. But Thanatos had his mouth covered by the lower half of his helmet showing only the pale blue eyes. Once friendly and familiar, now they were unreadable.

She turned back to the tree, unwilling to decipher the enigma behind her. "They're not really trees," she said quietly. "They aren't really shrubs either. They're too small for one and too tall for another," her voice was a whisper, yet somehow she knew he heard every word.

Persephone's hand stretched up to the dark red fruit and a large pale hand caught her wrist. She stumbled back, unsure how a man so large and wearing so much armor could move so silently, but he held her gently upright. His other hand stretched out to pluck the fruit, dwarfing it in his hands.

Persephone only knew Thanatos had set the fruit gently in her hand when she felt the weight of it in her palm; her eyes were locked on his. The cool look that had made her turn was broken by the crinkle of skin around his eyes and the warmth in his pale blue eyes, betraying the smile she couldn't see.

"You have a gift," he told her. "A gift that may just keep us alive. I promise that I will do everything in my power to ensure your safety because I think losing you would mean we never emerge again."

She was confused by his statement. It was so simple, reassuring, but she left like they were having two separate conversations. Persephone let her eyes close, allowing the rest of her senses take in the growing fields.

She was aware of her pulse thrumming under her skin, the warmth of the lights on her cheeks, and the slight breeze that blew soil-scented air across her face.

She felt his hand closing hers over the fruit. Her pulse surged and she felt a spark of hope. At his sharp intake of breath, she opened her eyes. Behind him, the whole tree had suddenly bloomed. Every branch was weighed down with ripe, bright red fruit. Persephone's mouth opened and she stared at Thanatos, her eyes wide with fear and confusion.

The squeal of a radio and quiet chirping broke the strange sensation.

"We need to go back," Thanatos told her. His eyes were flat and emotionless.

Persephone closed her eyes and sighed once before taking his proffered arm. Nothing made sense to her. She wrapped one hand around his armored forearm and used the other to hold the pomegranate to her chest.

Thanatos walked her briskly through the fields and she kept her hands and arms close to her body, frightened of what would happen if she skimmed her hands along the crops. She kept her questions to herself as well. They left the fields, returning to the rough stone hallways she remembered from only a few hours before, when they had brought her out of a cell to face the mysterious judges. Rough stone walls that looked like they had been hewn from a mountain turned to smoother stone, then concrete, before becoming drywall. Her bare feet felt the change from concrete to tile. Clearly, the area around the farms was utilitarian and needed no polish. As they walked further, the little she could make out indicated more social or personal use from the domed lights to the tile or carpeted walkways.

People gradually filled the halls as well. At first, Persephone ignored them, trying to blank them out of her mind along with the slew of questions that threatened to spill out of her mouth. But her eyes caught a harsh glare from one passerby and she started taking in the people who passed them. Her feet drew her closer to Thanatos as they walked.

He sensed her unease and the arm under her hand pulled her tighter to him. Something in his posture and stride altered and the feral lethality she'd seen in the fields returned. His helmeted head was held high and his shoulders, already broad with muscle and armor, were thrust back. His stride, firm and certain, propelled them along the corridors with a predator's grace.

She knew that anyone who approached them with violence in mind was already dead—their body was simply unaware of it yet. It should have scared her, being pressed against the side of walking death, but in a way, she found comfort.

They stopped in a well-appointed hallway at a dark wooden door flanked by two guards. Thanatos released her hand and removed his mask.

"Where are we?" she was unable to stop herself from asking.

"The safest place I can leave you," he told her, but wouldn't make eye contact as he knocked on the door.

"As you're the head of security, wouldn't that be with you?" She regretted the words as they left her mouth. They sounded flirtatious, even delivered in a mild tone.

Thanatos' head whipped to look at her. She held her hands up placatingly.

"Sorry, that came out so wrong."

"That's good because you already know I am happily married, Persephone," he said lightly.

She flushed a bright red and wanted to sink into the wall but gave a light laugh. "So that part of Tony was real? I need to start making a list of how Tony and Thanatos are the same," she said. Persephone shuffled back a half-step just as the door opened.

"My Lord," Thanatos said while giving him a quick nod. "Persephone was just showing me her incredible way with words."

Persephone's mouth dropped open and she realized he was grinning at her. He may be Thanatos, but he was still the same Tony who enjoyed teasing the rest of the security team. Her embarrassment started to fade.

Unlike Thanatos, Hades and Henry remained an enigma.

Hades stood in the doorway, his muscular frame still swathed in an elegantly cut suit. If a man could be called beautiful, he was. The betrayal that had burned in her before was taken over slightly by the attraction she had felt for Henry.

Damn it, she thought. *This would be easier if he didn't look so damn much like Henry.*

"The lockdown is initiated and proceeding smoothly, Thanatos. I'll take her while you make the last security arrangements."

Thanatos opened his mouth, then snapped it shut on whatever he had intended to say. He gave Hades a slight bow and said, "My Lord." Turning to Persephone, he gave her a deeper bow, one hand going over his heart as his head dipped, "My Lady."

Persephone was surprised by his words but more surprised by the dark look in Hades' silver-blue eyes. Thanatos' lips slipped into an impish grin and he winked at her before turning away, suddenly looking like Tony once more.

"Persephone," Hades called as she stared after him in shock.

Persephone blinked, shaking her head, and looked at Hades.

He stared down at her from sharp silver-blue eyes. His straight patrician nose, high cheekbones, and strong jawline spoke of royalty not many generations back and gave him a fearsome stare so unlike Henry's gentle calm. She inhaled once and stood straighter, not wanting to appear to be withering under the baleful glare, even if inside she wanted to shrink back away from him.

"Come in," he told her.

Steeling herself, Persephone walked into Hades' lair.

Chapter 7
Day 4

Persephone didn't know what she expected as she followed Hades through the door. Perhaps another elegantly appointed office. But as the door clicked shut behind her, she realized how very wrong she was. Even without her glasses, she immediately knew she was in his personal space. Just beyond him lay a large, dark room. Not dimly lit, but dark gray walls and dark marble accented with a lighter color, which Persephone thought might be gold if she got close enough to see. In a way, it mirrored the same understated elegance of his suit.

"Persephone?" Hades asked. His voice was cool and calm, the complete opposite of the anxiety coursing through Persephone.

Her eyes darted up to the man in front of her. Even several feet back, he loomed above her, almost filling the entryway. He raised one hand, palm up, for her to take. Her eyes flicked back to his face, and she was relieved to see his glare was gone, melted into an open, if not quite friendly, demeanor. Somewhere in that look, the Henry she knew peered out. Hesitantly, she closed the gap between them and took his hand, which was warm and surprisingly soft.

"Thanatos," his voice tightened slightly on the name, "said your glasses were left above?"

"It all happened so fast," she said in a rush, "and I didn't have them on. I got my bag, my notes, and my computer, but glasses were in another room and—" she stopped, voice cut off by a sudden rush of emotion. Yesterday, maybe two days ago, she had been safe and comfortable in her home, surrounded by her notes and plants. It may not have been a stretch to say her stay was involuntary—she had few freedoms, but she was safe. Now all she knew was that she was both in danger and dangerous.

Hades' strong hand squeezed hers. "We have your medical records on file. I've already contacted our optometrists for a rush order on a pair of glasses."

"You have optometrists here?" she spluttered. The emotional whiplash between her escape and his hand wrapped warmly around hers was staggering.

He frowned before laughing. It was rich, deep and throaty, more open than any laugh she'd elicited from Henry, and it bounced off his dark walls. "Yes, we have almost everything we need to be self-sustaining." He caught her confused expression. "I'm sorry, I thought Thanatos had told you more."

"No, he's been remarkably tight-lipped."

"In the many, many years I've known Thanatos, tight-lipped isn't the phase I would assign to him. But that's good," Hades said firmly. "No, I'm sorry. I'm glad he hasn't said everything yet. Some things require you to have a greater understanding of the foundations first."

Persephone looked at him quizzically. Her head hurt trying to follow these men and their half-answers. It was like seeing only half the cards and when the next one was turned over, you were playing an entirely different game. Throw in Thanatos, balancing deception with humor and Hades projecting calm while being physically imposing, she had felt on edge since being pulled from her darkened cell.

Hades held up a placating hand. "I will tell you everything as the days go on. For now, I want you to have time to adjust."

"And that's why I'm here? To adjust?" She looked pointedly beyond him to where she could see the back of a plush couch.

"Yes and no," Hades told her. He tugged lightly on her hand, drawing her along with him deeper into the room. "This is my home," he said gently. "For the time being, you will reside here."

"What? You're so tight for space that I can't have my own? No wonder people would be so mad you brought me in at the last minute."

"No, you misunderstand," he told her with a shake of his head. "There are a very small number of rooms available still in Elysium and Tartarus, but they are not safe for you there. Alone."

The angry, petulant eyes of the people they passed in the hallways and Thanatos' sudden shift in body language, visible even under his armor, flashed through her memories. She closed her eyes, weighed down by worries of what the next few years of her life would be like.

Hades' hand tipped her chin up. "Look at me," he said gently.

When Persephone opened her eyes, his silver-blue gaze was waiting for her. He had stepped closer and she could read the concern clearly on his handsome face. Something warm fluttered inside her.

"You won't be harmed. I won't allow it. But to keep you safe, you're going to have to stay by my side. Trust me. And do as I ask." His thick brows furrowed with earnest concern. "Please, can you do that?"

She'd heard this line before. *"I've sacrificed a lot to keep you safe, Persephone, don't throw that away," "The world out there is dangerous, that's why you need to stay at the IBCC compound, trust me,"* and *"Staying here means I can guide you away from your mistakes."* It was like hearing Demeter's words in Henry's voice. Pain, betrayal, and anger washed over her. She may be caged again, but she'd find a way out this time and guard her heart from someone using her emotions for control.

Persephone's eyes closed again, unable to face him, but she nodded. The hand on her chin skimmed down the side of her neck to land lightly on her shoulder. Her eyes flew open again. Something deep, something she'd hidden for the last few weeks lurked. She may have teased Henry, but like a schoolgirl teasing to cover her crush. The warmth she felt turned to heat that coiled low in her belly.

Her body was a damn traitor.

"Thank you," he said simply.

Persephone took a step back, out of arm's reach. "Tell me what I have to do."

"For now? For tonight? Just stay in my apartment. We'll work out a more permanent solution with Amalthia and Thanatos in the morning."

"Who?"

"Amalthia is my head of Administration and Logistics. She is on an equal level with Thanatos and the Judges."

"The assholes who wanted to throw me to Tartarus?"

Hades' eyes narrowed briefly, but his tone was calm. "Yes. They comprise my head of Law and Order. They are," he hummed as he thought, "quite strict with policy enforcement. And they should be. If I allow any laxity, any wasted resources, I will lose the Underground." His face was grim. "Persephone, you must understand, the moment I ordered the lockdown, this place became a completely enclosed society. Nothing gets in or out."

"Like a terrarium," she said.

"Yes. The balance must be held in perfect harmony, or the system dies. That," he squeezed her hand, "is what I control. The balance. Life and death."

She nodded and waited silently.

"For now, may I offer you a place to shower and change into fresh clothes? Then we can have dinner and talk more." At her nod, he led her even deeper into the apartment.

Persephone passed a charcoal gray sofa, suede from the feel of it under her trailing fingers. The U-shaped couch took up most of the room and surrounded a low brown table. Here and there, small colored pillows stood out against the dark palette of the room. Despite how dark it appeared, everything her fingers skimmed over was soft, smooth, or suede, giving the room a feeling of cozy comfort despite its formal elegance.

The next doorway led to a darkened room, but as she entered, discreet recessed lighting illuminated a space done in soft tan tones, accented by browns and reds. Two steps in and she realized the large object dominating the middle of the room was his massive bed. She hesitated.

"The main ensuite is through here," he said, catching her unease. "It's the nicest of my bathrooms."

When he neither tugged insistently at her hand nor pressed the issue, she started forward again. He led her wordlessly into a bathroom as enormous as he was. A beige and gold marble countertop with two sinks dominated one long wall. Across from the sinks, a large tub was framed by dark red glass tile.

"A shower and a steam room are beyond that door. Feel free to use anything in there you need. I'll leave your clothes out here," Hades told her at the entrance to the second set of doors. "There's a light switch just inside." He released her hand and started back toward his bedroom.

"Thank you," she said to his retreating back.

At the door, he nodded and closed it behind him.

Persephone felt immeasurably relieved that he wasn't going to stay and lurk as she showered.

She entered the room he'd indicated and turned on the light. It bathed the room in a soft glow that reflected off creamy tile with gold accents. The room was so large, she could barely make out the fuzzy outline of what must have been an entire bank of shower heads.

Persephone sighed with anticipated pleasure at washing several days' worth of grime away. She stripped out of her pajama pants and t-shirt, kicking them toward the door before stalking to the shower in her underwear. She had almost no opportunities to spend the night in someone else's home, but she knew enough to figure out how the shower worked before stripping down completely.

Upon closer inspection, the shower featured multiple shower heads. They protruded from the pale glass tile at knee, hip, and head height. Persephone had never seen anything so ridiculous and luxurious. So, of course, she turned on every tap and squawked in surprise when the water that came out from each head was hot. She had nice quarters in IBCC, but even she had to wait a few minutes before hot water reached her shower head.

Having assumed the handle would only turn on the shower heads at her knees, Persephone was instantly soaked from head to toe, including the undergarments she had left on for her inspection. She wiggled out of the sodden underwear and left the water running as she walked to the room's door. Wrapping herself in a towel, she cracked the door open. The bathroom beyond the shower was empty, so she darted out to drop her clothes on the counter.

Persephone scurried back into the shower room and dropped her towel in a messy heap. She didn't sprint to stand under the warm spray, but she moved faster than was safe. The feel of the water washing away days of grime was like heaven. She felt reborn. Persephone dipped her head under the closest shower head and let the water cascade down her body.

Small niches evenly spaced in the tile wall held a variety of soaps and hair products, some of which were familiar. She washed, scrubbing vigorously until even her light brown skin was pink. Persephone would have stayed in there for hours, but the rumbling of her stomach finally drew her out.

Persephone snagged a fresh towel from its golden peg as she stepped from the opulent shower. Once back in the main bathroom, she scowled as she searched the countertops. Her grimy clothes and sodden panties were nowhere to be seen. Instead, a tiny scrap of silk lay neatly folded on the countertop.

Persephone huffed once and stormed through the bathroom door.

"Hades! What. Is. This?" she ranted as she fumbled into his living room, one hand clutching the offending scrap of fabric, the other holding the towel tight to her chest.

"A nightgown," he said, completely unperturbed by a tiny, irate woman waving a silken garment under his nose.

"Why?" She infused enough anger into a single word that he should have taken psychic damage.

Hades' eyes narrowed as he considered her. "Your clothes were two days overdue for a wash. I assumed you would have preferred clean and dry clothes."

"These aren't clothes! This is a nightgown!" she screeched. "And what made you think I wanted you intruding on me in the shower?"

Hades looked at her in stony silence. His penetrating gaze, while not directed at her naked form under the towel, seemed to take in every aspect of the room. Persephone shrank back involuntarily and shivered. It wasn't a cold shiver; it was a trembling she felt to her core.

"I'm sorry to have made you uncomfortable by my presence in an adjacent room. But I'm the commander of this facility and I am unused to doors being closed against me. I will do better in the future."

Persephone's eyes narrowed as she regarded him. "Am I getting different clothes?" she finally asked.

"No."

"Not even to eat dinner?"

"No. Your bags have not finished passing quarantine and nothing I own would fit you."

Persephone nodded once, frowned, and stalked back to the bathroom. The dress, nightgown really, barely came to the top of her knees. Its golden-bronze silk crept to her mid-thigh any time she raised her arms above her shoulders.

She grimaced at the reflection in the mirror. Somewhere in this underground terrarium was a bag packed with soft, thick pajama pants, a comfy sports bra, and a battered shirt from her university. Until then, she was stuck half-blind with a man who took up an entire room.

As a scientist, she calculated that there was a non-zero chance of bumping into and off him and she was both scared and delighted by the prospect.

Chapter 8
Day 4

"Will you join me?" Hades asked, hand extended palm up.

Persephone looked at his hand, only barely on the edges of her clear vision, and realized he was asking about more than dinner.

"Join you?" she asked, hoping to clarify his meaning.

He stepped in closer. Perhaps he wanted to be close enough for her to see him clearly, but he loomed over her. His hand reached slowly for hers, carefully telegraphing his movement. He drew her to him with a thumb brushing gently on the backs of her knuckles. To Persephone's horror, she could feel her body react in ways she could neither control nor hide. Her cheeks flamed as he raised her hand, the movement shifting silk over her nipples, now standing out against the fabric.

"For dinner? And preparing it, of course," he said. His eyes never wavered from hers; he wasn't ogling her, but something changed in his voice.

It was deeper. Darker. Feral.

Persephone ruthlessly pushed down thoughts of how her body reacted to his stare. She cleared her throat and gave him the smile she gave at lectures: bland, professional, and devoid of her real emotions. "You don't just order in? You make things yourself? Don't you have a whole army of cooks at your beck and call?"

He gave a little laugh. "I suppose that's a fair question, but the answer is," he paused, "nuanced."

Her eyes narrowed. This was better. It was calmer, rational, and the heat that had flared across her was cooling. "Nuanced? Do tell."

He gave a quick nod. "Very well but walk with me. It's easier if I'm explaining while I cook." Hades turned, slipping his arm under hers in a courtly gesture, gently leading her out of his room.

"You? Cooking for me?" she asked him. His skin was surprisingly warm on hers as he deftly guided her across his living spaces.

"Why not? Here, we all play many roles. No one is too good to take out their own garbage and everyone carries their own weight."

"Except me," Persephone countered.

"Even without the wild politics and policies of my realm, you know that's not true. How many patents do you hold?" When she shrugged, he continued. "Every one of them is for a new, hardy crop. You are a genius at developing crops that survive."

He stopped them at the threshold of what was probably a brightly lit kitchen. She squinted again, trying to focus on the room. The hand wrapped around her wrist tightened briefly and she looked up. His gaze was intense, piercing straight into her soul.

"We must endure, Persephone. Whatever unfolds above, we must survive, and you are essential to that. To our survival. To *my* survival. I may lead this entire facility. I may hold the power of life and death here," his mouth twitched with something unsaid, "but my hold is delicate … fragile. It is give and take. I must appear strong and in control and provide the tight discipline that keeps a closed system running. But I also must give people what they need. They need food, water, and shelter. If you can ensure they have food, crops that grow and thrive in the artificial light of a world away from real sunlight, you are helping me save my people."

"But I am still the extra. I am 'Blessed of Hades,' not my own person. I can't exist in this world without your protection, your name. My vision may be bad, but I could still see the faces of people we passed as Thanatos walked me to your office. More to the point, I could feel them. They *hate* me."

"They will calm down," he said bluntly.

"Or what?" she asked. "What happens if they stay hostile to me? I've lived cloistered in one compound with little freedom of movement, but at least I was well regarded. Now I'm entirely trapped in a place where I'm nothing more than a brain and a drain on resources. And what am I to you? Some accessory?"

Hades' face darkened and his presence seemed to grow, filling the whole kitchen. "You aren't a slave, if that's your worry."

"I'm certainly not free to leave and you want me to work for you. What's my pay? My compensation?"

"Food, water, shelter. Entertainment, if you desire it. As you work, your reputation will rise. And, for the next few hours or days at least, you have the choice to leave."

Persephone blinked and a glimmer of hope stirred in her chest. Demeter had never even hinted that leaving was a possibility.

"Leave? You'd let me leave?"

A flash of her escape from the IBCC compound hit her. Her home, her life, and her work were gone. Her heart beat faster and she felt a strange out-of-body, shivery sensation. Even if he would let her leave, she had nowhere to go.

Hades watched, expression intense, as the thoughts flashed across her face and his hand tightened on hers briefly. "Yes, as much as it would pain me, I would let you leave. When someone from Tartarus is still unable to positively contribute to our society, we have no choice but to release them above. They are equipped with a backpack, a knife, a filled two-liter water bottle, rope, and a pack of matches. I could do the same for you. Arguably, a resourceful person could survive quite a while with that. But," he gave a little shrug, "once war kicks off, I cannot make guarantees."

Persephone let her hand drop from his arm. He was right, there was always a choice, but with no glasses and a full-scale war coming, she didn't like her odds. Her shoulders sagged and she let out a long sigh.

"I'll stay."

Hades gave her a slow nod that was almost a bow. "Then please join me in making dinner."

Persephone's brow furrowed. "You aren't kidding, you really do make your own meals."

"I take pleasure in creation," he said with a smile. "I do indeed take many meals from our various cafeterias, because I am a busy man. But I enjoy creating. I enjoy taking something from raw material and transforming it into something that nourishes the mind, body, and soul."

She turned away from him as he spoke. It was as if he was in her head. She skimmed one hand along the arm he had held, thinking of the feeling of sheaves of wheat under her fingers.

She took in one sharp breath, centering herself after the whiplash of their short conversation. "What's for dinner then?"

He gave a soft chuckle. "Do you want to have a say in it, or do you want me to make the choice?"

"I haven't had a say in almost anything for the last, what, two days?"

Hades tilted his head slightly. "Three."

"Three days. And I feel like my oh-so-famous brain is scrambled. You seem to have something planned, so let's go with that. I don't feel like playing the dinner time twenty questions game."

Hades smiled, a real smile that seemed to light his face and more of Henry shone through. Persephone reminded herself he had her kidnapped and this was all part of some plan to control her research. Her body, however, reacted strongly to his smile.

"Seared steaks, haricots verts blanched and topped with butter, and whipped potatoes."

"To drink?"

"Wine?"

"I'm asking you!" she laughed, relaxing over what was a very normal conversation, finally veering away from their earlier charged conversation.

"I can pour us red wines, white wines, I have sparkling wines, and I have a full bar. I'll be honest, I had a meal planned, but no idea what you drink."

"I guess 'Tony' didn't get invited into my home to see me eat supper, so you don't have spies to rely on for that." She looked at him slyly. "And 'Henry' seemed to make himself unavailable."

Hades' face darkened at the mention of Thanatos' role as her bodyguard. "No, he was primarily there for your protection, not as a spy."

"And yet, you seem to know quite a bit about me," she spat back. "I'll have red wine, Cabernet Sauvignon if you have it."

He moved into the kitchen, leaving her at the edge of the well-lit space. "There's very little I needed to have anyone observe and report, you know," he said as he reached under the counter before setting a bottle on it. "You are world-famous. You have articles written about you, your upbringing, and your school career before you started at IBCC."

She frowned as he pulled the cork from the bottle. "But you still needed a look at my personal life. You sent Thanatos to spy on me, even though you just denied that."

He slid a full glass to her. "Yes. A bit."

"You aren't even ashamed, are you?" she asked.

"No," he said simply. "A toast?"

Persephone scoffed. "A toast? To what, my capture?"

He gave her a smile, tinged with sadness, and tilted his glass toward her, his voice barely above a whisper. "To the illusion of control," he said. "And to the beautiful, terrifying moment we let it go."

Persephone's jaw dropped. He had managed to summarize her entire adulthood in a single line: the illusory control she had over her lab, Demeter's invisible strings pulling and tugging, and her growing surrender to him. She sipped the wine to cover her shock. It was the ideal balance of dry, bold, with a hint a spice. It was perfect. She frowned.

"You aren't the only one whose life is only a thin veneer of control," he took his own sip. Even at the edge of her vision, she could see his obvious enjoyment. Perhaps he had the red stocked for her, but perhaps he enjoyed it as well. "You were going to be the last person to join us," he continued. "You would have the least amount of time to assimilate, adjust, and decide this was a fit for you."

"I'd say kidnapping me really kills that," she said with a voice as dry as the wine she sipped.

"Indeed. But I needed you to stay. To want to stay with me. With us," he corrected. "So, I knew I needed to create an environment that you would enjoy and appreciate. Something palatable from the start. Which, yes, required gathering more information than is readily available from your multiple interviews."

"Not really going like you planned, is it?" She set her glass down.

He shrugged and took another sip. "I assumed you would be resistant. It's a horrible situation you've been placed in. But I also assume the more you learn and understand, the less resistant you will feel. I hope that, eventually, this feels like home to you."

Persephone gave a noncommittal "Hmm."

What was home, anyway? It wasn't the compound where her mother had kept her as a child. The labs were sterile, smelling like bleach and control, devoid of warmth or personality. Only the expansive gardens, full of modified cultivars, felt like life and belonging. Her early interest in those plants had Demeter push her into advanced schooling, eventually revealing she was a protégé. But even brilliance hadn't bought her freedom. Her overprotective mother had seen something that drove her to shelter Persephone at the compound, insulated from the outside, and caged by the illusion of protection. Even during her advanced schooling years, she had lived a sheltered life, returning to her mother's compound each day, as if Demeter feared what would happen if Persephone were unleashed on the world. Finally at IBCC, her quarters had been bare. A room but not a refuge or home. She had only ever truly felt a sense of home among her plants, with her fingers deep in soil or curled around a growing leaf and the simple promise of growing life.

"Let me have unfettered access to the fields and maybe I can," she told him simply.

Hades set his glass down and studied her. "That's all? No demands?"

"What would I even ask for? I've been confined almost my entire life. I suppose this is no different." She thought for a minute. "Okay, no. This is very different. I still have no idea what being 'Blessed' means or how I am going to convince an entire population that I'm useful, but I suppose splicing genes by myself in one lab is no different from any other lab."

"How terribly lonely," Hades said quietly.

His words were like a slap in the face. Not vicious or malicious, more the sudden realization of how long she had been alone, locked away from the world and genuine human connection. No wonder she had latched onto Tony and Henry so eagerly. They were the first people in her life who had felt real and genuine when they were around her. And they betrayed her.

Why did he have to be so damn attractive?

"Yes." She reached for her glass and took a huge gulp.

"Perhaps that is something we can remedy here."

Chapter 9
Day 4

Hades broke the heaviness in the air with a simple, "Shall we start?" He gestured to the sleek kitchen.

Persephone gave a choked laugh. "I guess so. What do you want me to do?"

He took her arm again, his hand warm on her elbow, gently steering her to a thick chopping block. He pulled a knife from its block and put a bowl of potatoes next to her. "You can chop the potatoes before we boil them."

Persephone took the knife and turned to him. "You really trust me with a knife? You kidnap me and then put a knife in my hand?" An eyebrow arched over her bemused expression.

"You couldn't hurt me, Persephone," he told her, silver-blue eyes staring intently at her.

The way his deep voice practically growled her name made her shiver. It was the voice of a predator. A predator that was absolutely certain of its place at the apex and she was trapped with it. She gasped quietly as fear thrummed through her.

Every protective reaction she had keyed up, months of self-defense classes playing across her mind, interspersed with her recent abduction. Classes that had been taught by Tony and later by Henry.

She nodded and turned back to the potatoes.

Persephone worked quietly, chopping on a thick wooden slab as Hades moved around his kitchen, pulling out pots, pans, meat, and green beans. At one point, he moved her wine glass closer to her workspace. She jumped and whirled around when the glass touched the counter, not having realized he had been behind her. Instinctively, the knife came up before she hastily dropped it.

Hades retrieved it from the floor, gave it a light rinse and returned it to her silently.

"Sorry," she mumbled and returned to the potatoes.

"Instinct is a powerful thing, Persephone. Embrace it," his deep voice rumbled behind her.

She nodded but focused on her task. Tension pulled taught through the quiet kitchen.

Hades continued moving around the kitchen behind her. Persephone's focus was torn from the potatoes whenever he walked by. He never came close enough to touch her, but she could swear she felt the body heat radiating off him. She flinched with each passing.

The tension hit a high when he brushed past her to grab something from his utensil drawer. With lightning reflexes, she dropped the knife and turned toward him. Her body went into automatic. Her right foot hooked his left ankle and yanked, pulling him off balance. Her left palm flashed forward, giving his shoulder the push it needed to knock him to the floor.

Persephone stood in shock for a fraction of a second, taking in Hades sprawled across his kitchen floor, surprised by her own actions and their effectiveness. Then she met his eyes and saw the apex predator she heard in his voice staring at her from behind them.

Like prey, she bolted.

Years of running around the IBCC compound, dodging trucks and large farm equipment, had made her agile. Her feet flew down the hallway and she tempered her speed only to keep from running blindly into his furniture. There were no real thoughts, only adrenaline and the lingering look of Hades' predator eyes staring up at her from the floor.

Had she studied fauna more than flora, she would have known that fleeing a predator only entices them to chase.

She reached his front door and her hand was on the knob when he caught her. One hand covered hers and prevented her from wrenching the door open. The other snagged her right hand, dragging it above her head. His body, which had seemed large before, now felt massive. He pressed against her, creating a cage to hold her in place. He may have looked like cold, chiseled marble, but he radiated warmth. The heat reached her as a current that set her pulse stuttering.

"Don't," he commanded.

Persephone writhed, fearful of what he would do. Raising a

knife against him was bad enough. Now she had knocked him to the floor and ran. She pushed against him with her shoulders and hips, trying to twist out from under him.

"Don't," he repeated, growling.

Persephone realized he didn't mean escaping. She froze against him.

He let go of the knob and turned her back to face him, her right hand trapped beneath his, her wrist pressed to the door as his breath brushed her cheek.

Her free hand came up to push against his firm shoulder, but he didn't budge. She gave a gasping breath and looked up at him. He opened his mouth to speak but stopped, staring down at her. She got one glance at those silver-blue predator's eyes and looked away.

Hades seized her chin with his free hand and tilted her head up. She closed her eyes and pushed at him again, trying to writhe away from his grip once again as his body held her in place. His legs pinned her, one between her knees and his hip on hers.

"Look at me," he commanded.

Her eyes flashed open and she stared defiantly at him. He responded by pressing his body closer, the knee between her legs making the bronze nightdress's hem slide higher.

"I told you to stop," he said as she felt him against her, his hardening length pressing against her hip through the silk nightgown.

She pushed away, pressing her back to the door, a familiar friction between her legs where his thigh loomed. She stilled.

"Good girl," he said and ran his thumb over her bottom lip.

She shivered and sucked in a breath. A flash of heat sank deep into her belly. The look he gave her now said he'd replace that thumb with his lips or cock if she gave him the chance.

They stared at each other for a moment that walked the knife's edge. Predator and his prey, each waiting for the other to move before acting.

He gave a pleased hum and ran his thumb across her lips once more. "As much as I'd like to see where this goes, we still need to eat dinner." He dropped her hands and took a step back.

Persephone rubbed her wrists to give herself a reason not to look into those eyes again. Her wrists didn't hurt, but the ghost of his hands, warm on hers, lingered. She wanted to be mad. Or scared. But somehow it was one of the most erotic moments of her life.

"I'm not mad," he told her. "You don't know me and I scared you. I apologize for that and your reaction was appropriate. But you understand why I couldn't let you out that door, right?"

"No," she said quietly.

He held out his arm and she took it with only a moment's hesitation. "It's about balance. I hold this society together with the support of my three branches. They maintain the order of our people through their administration, but I lead at the head of it all. I must display control, empathy and acumen, but always control. Of myself, of my surroundings, and of my people."

He led her gently to the kitchen's breakfast bar.

"I'll take it from here," he said. He returned to cooking as if she hadn't just tried to stab him, flipped him to the ground, and nearly escaped. "You are in the precarious position of being directly under my protection and to a certain extent, control."

"I don't like how that sounds," she told him bluntly. The feel of his thigh pressing between her legs was all too fresh but not entirely unwanted.

He held up a mollifying hand. "Don't worry, Persephone. If you find yourself under me in my bed, I promise it will be because you were willing. And you would come, a lot. You would beg me for it." He gave her a smirk and her cheeks flamed. "But I would want you to want it, to need me."

He juggled dishes as she absorbed his statement, her mouth hanging open.

"The control that I mean is that you follow our rules and aren't openly defying me. If you had made it out that door, first, you would have been caught by one of my guards."

"Guards?" There hadn't been any as they entered earlier.

"Yes, two of my most loyal group of guards stand watch over my door at any time I am inside my quarters."

"For someone who seemed unperturbed by me raising a knife against you, you seem awfully preoccupied with defense."

"Indeed. I have some," he paused, his head tilting to the side slightly, "personal defenses that are very effective, but I don't want to be caught unawares."

Persephone had no idea what he was talking about, so she stayed silent.

"The other thing that would have happened is word would get out that not only were you able to escape, but I allowed an environment that my Blessed fled from me."

"For the last time, what does that really mean?" she cried.

Hades slid two laden plates across the countertop. "More wine? I'll explain as we eat."

Persephone nodded silently and followed him to the table, carrying their wine glasses.

Chapter 10
Day 4

"Blessed. What does it mean?" Persephone said bluntly as she set the wine glasses down. The table was a dark, natural-looking wood set with rich red placemats and black napkins.

"I feel a bit of context is necessary to get there." When she looked mutinous, he continued quickly, "I will tell you, but the society here is different than above and the context is important."

"Hmph. Fine." Persephone took a sip of wine and looked at him pointedly. Three days in a chemically induced sleep made the wine hit her with each sip. A warmth that was entirely different from what Hades induced in her spread across her body.

"I have been working to build and grow this facility for over a decade."

"You knew a decade ago this would happen?" she asked as she pushed food around her plate. Her belly gnawed with hunger, but even after watching him prepare the meal, she didn't trust the food until she saw him eat first.

As if picking up her thoughts, he cut a large slice of his steak and popped it into his mouth. She followed his lead, taking a small bite at first.

"This is delicious," she mumbled around the bite as she frantically sliced more. He had said she was out for three days and she could feel three days' worth of hunger clawing at her belly.

"I can make more if you want it."

"No. No. Tell me about this place. The people." Perhaps unwisely, she took a heavier sip of wine to wash down the steak before shoveling a forkful of whipped potatoes into her mouth.

"To answer your question, no, I didn't know that this specifically would happen or the exact timing, but I watched for signs. I studied the nations above and a war between the Sons of Zeus and the Forces of Poseidon was inevitable. There is too much bad blood between the two to ever bring lasting peace. So, I hedged my bets: I started with a small facility and staffed it with only a skeleton crew as a test. When that went well and signs indicated full-scale war was more likely in the next decade, I pressed on to the next stage."

"You've been building this and collecting people since then?"

"Yes, but it takes time. I set up the leadership functions first to ensure an orderly influx and they primarily occupy the original spaces. The rest of the people joined us above until the spaces were ready below."

"Why three classes of people? Why not just let people be people?"

"This isn't your lab, Persephone. We aren't all scientists collaborating in harmony."

"Harmony?" Persephone laughed and sipped her wine again. "Clearly, you've never been to a quarterly budget meeting when programs are getting axed."

Hades nodded his agreement. "True, but—and I don't in any way want to belittle your research, as it does save lives by preventing hunger—my world is a matter of life and death. This facility and I are all that potentially stand between life and extinction."

"If one of IBCC's programs goes unfunded, hundreds, if not thousands, die of starvation," Persephone said hotly.

"If my control fails, this entire facility will fall into death and chaos, bringing the end of the human race. The chances that anyone above survives the next week are slim." He took a quiet sip of his drink.

Persephone absorbed his words. He truly believed this was the end of the world above. She wasn't even sure she could deny it. She nodded once.

"Why three? You still haven't answered that." She inhaled another mouthful of potatoes.

"It's cleaner, neater this way. We were able to group housing types into three categories. Three tiers. Same thing for luxuries and food. Your tier is directly related to what you can provide or produce. We don't value things here like they do above. In a close society, with finite resources, if you don't produce or if you take more than you provide, you are of little value to us."

"And is there mobility?"

"Mobility?"

"Can you move up or down? In the tiers, I mean."

"Down, certainly."

"Well, yes, I figured. You mentioned kicking people out. But up?"

"To a limited degree, yes. But only if a position opens above." He looked down as he sipped his wine.

"Someone must fall for another to rise?"

"Or die. Or otherwise leave us permanently."

"That's dark."

"That's our life, Persephone."

"And if someone in Tartarus goes rogue? Decides to simply stop working?"

Hades cut another bite of his steak and ate it quietly without meeting her eyes.

"Hades. You don't have a jail, do you?" she asked quietly.

Hades shook his head, still avoiding her stare. "Our confinement cells are extremely temporary. You are given three days' grace to decide if you will change, then it's exile."

"But once the door closes? Now?"

Hades finally lifted his gaze to meet hers, cold and aching with regret. "Death."

The word hung in the air between them.

"Perform or die," she said simply. "As a scientist, that gives 'publish or perish' a new layer of horror."

"You follow the rules and you survive a world-ending war. If you don't, your chances are the same as if you had not joined us."

Persephone considered his statement and shrugged. "I've been a prisoner all my life, one way or another. This is just a little more extreme." She finished the last bite on her plate and washed it down with the last sip of her wine while Hades stared at her.

"Surely you haven't been a prisoner your entire life?"

"I grew up under the green thumb of Dr. Demeter Kore. World-renowned bio-scientist, fourth rate mother," she said dryly. "Is there any more wine?"

"Yes, one moment, I'll get it." He flashed her a concerned look as he rose.

"What? Don't give me that," she said, leaning back in her

chair. "You said yourself you had to send Thanatos to find out what wasn't in the scientific journals. And my mother's extreme control over her only daughter, and a science prodigy at that, is certainly not published."

"Your childhood?" he asked as he pulled another bottle from its shelf.

"Ha," she spat mirthlessly. "Spent behind the walls of an IBCC compound in the south while she spliced genes for tropical fruits. Ignored until I misbehaved, then I never knew which version of her I would get: the cold calculated scientist measuring the effectiveness of a punishment or the virago tempest howling at me across the compound. But never sent away or allowed out. All punishments were meant to bind me closer."

"Surely during your advanced schooling? You had to have some freedom then." He gave her another hefty pour of the dark red wine.

Persephone raised the glass, considering. "Thank you," she murmured. "I suppose you could say I had some freedom then. I was allowed out of the compound. I was allowed to attend classes and spend free time on campus. But she required me to live on the IBCC compound. I was a teenager, so I didn't have much of a say."

"You didn't fight it?"

"How? I had no money and I was a minor. Besides, if you have all your basic needs met, you certainly don't need to leave the compound," she said in a mocking tone. She took a deep sip of wine and let its effects calm her.

"Hmm, somehow I hear the elder Dr. Kore's voice coming from your mouth. She controlled your environment." It was a statement, not a question.

"She controlled everything. Even at my IBCC compound, I had guards. You weren't there for my safety, you were there for her control," Persephone stated and sipped the wine. "She didn't want a daughter; she wanted a protégé."

"I'm sorry," Hades said plainly.

"You're sorry, but you aren't able to alter the fact that I am a prisoner in a gilded cage again." She took one more sip. "At least the wine here is better."

Hades looked away. She stared at him, wondering what he

was thinking.

"What do you want?" He asked after a long moment had passed.

"Freedom. The ability to control my own destiny. Real respect. Real friendship, not sycophants who are trying to earn my mother's approval through me."

"I can't give you the freedom you think you want," he said. Before she could protest, he went on, "But I can provide you an opportunity to earn the respect you crave. And I can give it to you within a society completely disassociated from your mother. I know I can guarantee you will never meet one of her sycophants here."

Persephone's mouth opened to argue but snapped shut when the full implication hit her.

Her entire world was gone.

Destroyed.

More likely than not, her mother was dead or would be shortly.

She set down her glass of wine and began sobbing.

Chapter 11
Day 4

It took Hades nearly an hour to get Persephone calm enough to sleep. He had placed her gently on the long side of his huge couch, then scooted to his kitchen to put the last of the food away, before escorting her to his bathroom to clean up.

She was so tired and distraught that she didn't comment on his earlier presumptions regarding her in his bathroom.

"You are welcome to sleep in my bed," he told her gently. "I know the quarantine bunkers are not as comfortable as I would like. Your sleep must be wrecked."

"No," she said, shaking her head vigorously.

"I'll sleep on the couch; you may have the bed to yourself," he told her.

"No. It's too …" she searched for how to phrase her thoughts, "intimate. Even without you there."

Hades gave her another deep bow of his head. "The other option is my couch."

"That's fine. I've slept on the couch in my lab more than once while data was processing or compiling."

"Very well." He spread a blanket over her as she lay down on the plush couch. "I'll close my door, but if you need anything, feel free to open it."

Persephone mumbled something unintelligible before her lips parted in a light snore. If either of them had assumed it would be a calm night, they were both mistaken.

The sound of an explosion rocked her from her sleep. Drowsy and disoriented, she staggered from the couch.

"Hades? Hades!" she cried into the darkness. Around her, flames began to engulf his luxurious apartment.

Another explosion rocked his spaces, the concussive shock vibrating her body and pushing air from her lungs. Persephone could see helicopter skids lifting away from the flames below.

"Hades!" Her scream cut through the roar of fire below her.

"Persephone!" Hands grasped her shoulders and lifted her up.

She drew back, confused. Up? She was already up. She was standing in Hades' burning living room with bombs exploding around her.

"It's a dream, love. It's just a dream," his voice called to her.

Love? Persephone frowned and her eyes opened. The room was dark, the only illumination coming from a dim light in his kitchen. A dark form moved toward her and she put her arms up. Warm arms encircled her as Hades' scent washed over her.

"The bombs. The bombs, Hades," she mumbled, pressing her head into the soft skin of his bare chest.

"It was a nightmare, Seph. Just a nightmare," he said, holding her gently.

Persephone let herself sink into the feeling of his chest, still in the miasma of sleep. His skin was soft over firm muscle with only a light dusting of hair. She inhaled the scent of sandalwood, charged ozone, and burnt cinnamon. She felt peace and calm as she rested against him.

"Seph, wake up," he urged and gave her a gentle shake.

The room was now washed in a dim glow from a table lamp and she was seated across his lap. She must have dozed off as he held her, exhausted. Persephone's eyes locked onto his. The silver gray of his eyes was clouded with concern and the wild predator behind them was safely locked away.

Her hand clutched his thick arm. "IBCC was on fire. It was a dream, just a horrible dream."

"You're safe. You're here with me."

Persephone scrubbed her face and wiggled out of his grasp. "Thank you. For reassuring me," she said quietly.

"Whatever you need, Persephone," Hades said as he stood. His pajama pants were untied and threatened to slip off his hips.

"Sleep. Please, just let me sleep," she said and fell back against the couch cushions.

Her eyes closed before she could see the look that crossed his face: fierce, brutal, and tender. It said he would tear down the world to keep her safe and destroy anyone who dared to hurt her.

Persephone dozed fitfully. A combination of wine and stress kept her body on edge, keyed up, and ready for the next fight.

An hour later, she woke up again, screaming. In less than a minute, he was at her side, cradling her against his chest.

"It's a dream, Seph," he told her quietly.

"Dr. Kore, to you," she countered.

Hades gave a long inhale, his breath going deep into his chest. "Dr. Persephone Kore, you are having nightmares. I need you to relax so that you can sleep and be brilliant tomorrow."

"I'm always brilliant," she mumbled against his chest. She snuggled in as if they had been intimate for years.

"Yes, you are, love," he whispered.

"Mmm, not your love," she said sleepily.

"Ok, Seph," he replied. He scooped her into his arms and walked her to his bed chamber.

"I should sleep on the couch," she muttered.

"You tried that. Three times, in fact. One time, you were cradled in my arms and fell asleep before I could put you down. Two times it failed. If a crop fails twice, what do you do next, doctor?"

"Attempt a new introduction or revert to the species that worked," she muttered.

Hades lay her gently on the side of the bed and pulled his covers over her. Her only reaction was to yank the comforter to her chin and sigh with contentment.

"Goodnight, Persephone," he whispered as she dropped into deep sleep.

Chapter 12
Day 5

Persephone woke slowly. Her mind felt like it was climbing out of some dark morass. The nightmares slowly evaporated as she woke. She inhaled deeply, eyes still closed, and stretched. Her back arched and her head shifted across the pillow.

The feel of a hard chest pressing against her back and an arm wrapped around her waist stopped her cold. Before she could speak or react, the hand tightened. She drew in a sharp inhale but otherwise stayed silent and motionless. The hand relaxed and she could hear Hades' breathing drop back into the rhythm of sleep.

He had carried her to his bedroom after her nightmares disturbed both their sleep. She must have been so exhausted that she hadn't fought him on it. She had let this man sweep her up in his arms like a heroine of old and carried her off to his bedroom.

There was something dark, erotic, and primal about it.

She wasn't ready to examine that thought too deeply yet.

With Hades asleep, Persephone took the quiet moment to appreciate the delicious feeling of his warmth at her back. His bare chest was warm and solid against her. The scent of him was subtle on the pillow. She wiggled appreciatively into the soft mattress.

The feel of something hard pressing against her ass told her he was more awake than she thought, perhaps waiting. Without warning, she could feel the soft caress of his hand at her hip, skimming across her waist where the silk nightgown had bunched up in her sleep and stopped just short of her breast. She gasped and her heart caught in her throat.

The hand stilled as they both waited silently for the other to move. Tension and static crackled between them.

Persephone's breath came faster now and she could feel the hand on her ribs lightly brush the bottoms of her breasts as her chest moved. Something darkly feral possessed her and she pushed her chest up to meet his hand, her hips arching back to grind into his lap.

Persephone could hear the faintest inhale behind her. If Hades was shocked, he didn't let it hold him for long because he pinched her nipple, rolling it through the silk. She gave a little cry as her heart rate rose. The hand on her breast skimmed down her belly, leaving a trail of heat in its wake. His knee nudged between her legs.

Hades skimmed the flat of his hand over her, gently cupping her, and pushed a single finger against her lips. They parted easily and Persephone was surprised to find she was already dripping wet for him. She gave a quiet moan and the arm under her head wrapped around her, pulling her close to his chest.

Persephone could feel the rise and fall of his chest against her as his breath whispered across her neck, hot and primal.

"Don't," she whispered, "stop."

The hand on her slit stilled. "I'm sorry," he mumbled and moved back.

Persephone grabbed his hand, pulling it back to her. "Don't stop."

Hades growled. A fierce growl, deep in his chest, that rumbled against her back and made her remember every erotic through she'd ever had.

He pressed a single finger into her, curling it inside as he rubbed her clit with the heel of his hand. Persephone whimpered and clutched at the arm across her chest, greedy for more.

"Don't stop," she whispered. To hell with rules or propriety. To hell with the circumstances that brought her here. In the moment, she let go of everything and surrendered to his hands.

Hades pushed a second finger into her, keeping the gentle pace that left her aching for more. She rocked her hips, at once pushing into his hand and brushing her ass along his cock.

With another growl, he dropped his head, kissing the hammering pulse. His pace was slow but deliberate and she could feel the slowly building tension rising. Persephone could feel the dampness from his pre-cum soaking where the nightgown covered her ass. She moaned, knowing she couldn't hold out much longer. His pace quickened and she could feel her orgasm coming. Clutching the arm across her chest, she rode the wave of pleasure as her walls fluttered around Hades' fingers.

Hades' hands moved away from her as she lay panting in

his arms and she could feel him reach to position the head of his cock against her. She bit her lip in nervous anticipation but didn't stop him. He pushed gently, just penetrating, her lips barely parted. Persephone gasped again and arched into him.

The sound of a sharp beeping shattered the moment. Hades groaned in frustration but rolled away, slapping a button Persephone couldn't see. The intrusion was like a knife to her ribs.

"Yes?" his voice was sharp and spelled doom for whoever interrupted them.

"My Lord, it's started," Thanatos' voice was clear across the room.

"Now?"

"Yes, Lord Hades."

"I'll be up shortly," Hades said and slapped the button again. "I am so sorry," he told her, "but it appears we are being interrupted by the end of the world."

Act 2
The Aftermath

Chapter 13
Day 5

Persephone never dreamed she would attend the end of the world in pajamas. Certainly not in oversized, borrowed pajamas.

She had refused to follow Hades to his command center in the thin silk nightgown she was wearing when his comm link buzzed. He refused to let her stay in his quarters alone. After one frazzled squabble, they had compromised with her wearing a pair of his pajama pants, rolled at the waist and hem, and the smallest shirt he had, still several sizes too large for Persephone.

Hades, on the other hand, was resplendent and every inch the King and Commander in dark trousers, a crisp black button-up shirt, well-worn boots polished to an onyx shine, and similar armor to what Thanatos wore the day before.

"If you were hoping I would make a good first impression with your people, this was not the way to do it," she whispered harshly as they crossed the threshold from the communications center to Hades' command suite.

"If the timing had been better, your own clothing would have arrived at my quarters and you would have been clad in something more professional," he whispered back and his hand, warm even through an armored glove, grasped her wrist. "If the timing had been better, right now you would be writhing beneath me begging for more."

Persephone's cheeks flamed red and she looked away from the fuzzy flicker of the command center's screen to stare at the floor.

"I'm sorry I couldn't schedule the end of the world more conveniently," his whispered words brushed across her ear and Persephone felt her whole body respond. Heat flooded her and she pressed her thighs together to stop the feeling. Hades straightened and walked to join Thanatos at the screens as if he didn't just light her entire body on fire.

Persephone stayed back. She wanted space from Hades as

she processed the last few hours. She had enjoyed it, more than she was willing to admit aloud, but the memory of how easily he'd unraveled her left her cheeks burning. Each glance in his direction sparked something in her she didn't fully understand and heated her cheeks once again, but she was conflicted about the level of control he held over her. Besides, she had no useful input in this situation. This was war. This was death. This was the realm of Hades and Thanatos. She was a woman of life and growth. She knew how to coax life from the most dire pastoral situation, but she couldn't defy death. Could she?

Persephone was used to leading. She was used to running a lab that designed and grew thousands, even millions, of credits' worth of food. She was almost always the smartest person in the room. She knew how to direct her supply and logistics teams. She knew how to teach and lead the assistant researchers who flowed in and out of her lab seeking a moment's reflected glory working for the world-renowned Dr. Persephone Kore. She had some tough luck with stubborn security teams who followed her mother's orders and not hers. But overall, she knew how to lead and manage her environment. To be almost completely devoid of knowledge or control was a disturbing new feeling.

She needed to find a way to regain some semblance of control. First step: know more.

Persephone walked toward the sound of Hades' voice, deep in conversation with Thanatos.

"No signs of either the Sons of Zeus or Forces of Poseidon bringing out their big guns yet, my Lord," Thanatos reported. "They're still pounding the hell out of each other. We're losing sensors at an alarming rate."

"Keep the surviving ones scanning. The ones that will detect anything truly world-ending are hardened."

"Yes, sir," Thanatos replied. "The early reports show that Athens was leveled by multiple large rockets fired from the Sons of Zeus."

"Hmm, certainly sends a message to Poseidon if you take out their main seaport."

"Not just the port, the entire city is rubble," Thanatos said, his voice heavy.

Persephone blinked and peered at the screens. From her spot beside Hades in the commander's suite, everything was a blur of blinking, shifting lights down on the floor.

She left the command suite and descended a short open staircase to the communication center's main floor.

"Persephone?" Hades called to her.

"Let her go, she'll need to come to grips with it on her terms." Thanatos' voice drifted after her.

The sound of their tactical discussion faded as she approached the massive wall of screens. The screens were so tall, they nearly disappeared into a darkened ceiling. Twenty or more screens comprised a massive wall in front of the command center's personnel. Two rows of desks arced in front of the wall: each station manned by someone staring intently at their personal screens as well as the massive wall. Occasionally, one would toggle a switch, speak rapidly into their headset, then return to watching the horror unfolding in front of them.

Persephone stood abreast the front row, their desk lamps glowing dimly, and she was able to see the closest screens with clarity now. Some showed only fuzzy green lines, indicating levels of something, but what that something was, she didn't know. Others showed a mixture of video feeds that looked like they were taken from security cameras at street level or just above the street.

Most showed varying levels of destruction: burnt out cars and structures, toppled buildings surrounded by rubble, or vast smoking ruins with no signs of life. One screen showed nothing but static in one corner, the fuzzy green lines beside it a riot of action.

"That was Thebes," the woman at the console next to her said quietly. She had a small gray flower embroidered on her sleeve. Persephone guessed the technician was of the Asphodel class and she was certainly earning her place today.

"What?"

"The static," she said. "We lost the camera a few moments before you arrived. But those green lines? It's an overlay that shows communication waves. Thebes lost everything above ground but must have a bunker with a hardened communications system; they're still broadcasting to the Sons of Zeus."

Persephone nodded as if she knew more than the facts that

some people were dead, some people still lived, and the war raged on while she was in a gilded cage, unable to help.

She turned away from the screens and rejoined Hades in his suite. A woman had joined him and for a moment, Persephone felt a flash of jealousy. As she got closer, she could see that the woman was tall and beautiful, with a willowy grace in her charcoal gray suit. Persephone felt positively frumpy standing barely at the woman's shoulder in baggy, borrowed pajamas with unbrushed hair, morning breath, and undoubtedly smelling like the morning's passion.

"Maintenance and Logistics both report our facilities are holding," the woman said in a calm, even voice. She gave a single assessing glance before dismissing Persephone from her mind and stepping a half-pace closer to Hades.

Persephone bristled with unexpected malice.

"They should be," Thanatos countered, "none of the sensors report detonations near our facility."

"Good," Hades said simply.

Persephone cleared the last step and Hades held his hand to her. She could barely read his expression, but something on his face told her his gesture was more of a formality than to offer assistance.

"Persephone, this is Amalthia, the head of Administration and Logistics. Amalthia, this is Dr. Persephone Kore, Blessed of Hades."

Amalthia's beautiful face cracked for a fraction of a second, something ugly peeking through her serene mask. The mask was back in place as she greeted Persephone, "Our late guest. A pleasure."

Thanatos and Hades looked at her but said nothing.

"Lovely to meet you," she said blandly as if their meeting wasn't the product of kidnapping and world-ending war. Persephone knew Amalthia's greeting had been some kind of snub from the men's reactions, but she was unwilling to respond in kind when she had no allies aside from Thanatos and Hades.

"Thanatos, would you show my Blessed to a chair so we can continue the discussion?" Hades asked. At his words, Amalthia seemed to flinch again but said nothing.

Thanatos extended his elbow to her and Persephone accepted it gratefully. She had no desire to be near that woman and it seemed the feeling was mutual.

"What's her problem?" Persephone asked quietly when they were finally out of earshot, tucked in a small alcove.

Thanatos gave a small sigh. "The closer we got to now, Hades started changing. Pulling away emotionally from everyone. We," he gestured to himself, Hades, and Amalthia, "always knew you would be the last person pulled in. We also knew that if the Judges didn't grant you Elysium, being declared Blessed was the only way to save you from Tartarus, or worse, expelled."

Persephone nodded. She realized she'd asked Hades multiple times what Blessed really meant last night but had been sidetracked every time.

"Hades, he ..." she started, but Thanatos cut her off.

"He took a calculated risk. He knew what he stood to lose. You may not see it, but he is a man of passion and follows his heart more than his brain sometimes. It's why he has a council to guide him."

Persephone blushed at the mention of Hades' passion.

"What I was going to say," she said, "was that Hades still hasn't told me what that all means."

Thanatos straightened, eyebrows raised in shock. "Still?"

"We kept getting sidetracked last night."

Thanatos gave her a wicked grin but didn't say anything.

"I know you said it meant he was personally responsible for me and my actions, and Hades reiterated as much last night. But everyone seems to be tiptoeing around telling me anything more."

"You understand why we have the designation?"

"Uh, other than protection for an extra person, no."

"When we pulled people in, we knew everyone had to have an occupation, something that kept our society going. Many of our top brains, scientists like you, had families with small children. We knew they would never abandon their families to die above, so we designated them Blessed. But it comes with restrictions."

"Hades is responsible for my behavior," she said.

"Yes, that's one. The spouse is required to find an occupation and the couple is not to have additional children. If the spouse dies, they are not allowed to remarry. If any of the Blessed misbehave, they will be expelled. And because no one in their right mind would let their family die like that, we assume the brains would go with them."

"Grim."

"But necessary," he told her.

"Wait. Does that mean Hades can't ever marry?" The thought hit her like a punch. "Oh gods, that's why Amalthia hates me already. She was hoping to—" Persephone stopped and glanced up at Hades' platform. Amalthia was watching them from the corner of her eyes, mouth pursed into a thin line.

Thanatos placed a gentle hand on hers and she tore her gaze from the platform. Thanatos' face was serious.

"Persephone, he *is* married."

"What?" Shock, embarrassment, and shame flooded into her. She closed her eyes, trying hard not to think of how she started her morning.

He was married.

"Oh no, Thanatos. I—," she stuttered in horror, "I'm a terrible person."

She opened her eyes to see Thanatos studying her closely. He squeezed her hand.

"He's married to you."

Chapter 14
Day 5

Persephone took a deep breath, then another. Her already horrible vision fading at the edges.

"Hold your breath, Seph, you're about to hyperventilate."

Something about how Thanatos, her Tony, called her "Seph" knocked her back into reality.

"I'm married? To Hades?"

"Mostly," Thanatos told her.

"How can you be only mostly married? It seems pretty binary."

"Not here," he told her. "Here, things, *reality*, work differently."

"You can't be serious right now," she choked out.

"There is something here that binds us, something inherent in Hades. It's what really keeps the facility protected from the war above." He held up a hand for her to stay quiet. "It's why we know this facility can survive. It's why a Blessed marriage is different."

Persephone shook her head, unable to understand.

"When the Judges decreed you Blessed, did you feel anything?"

"Yeah, I shivered. I was cold and scared."

"Anything else?"

Persephone thought. "Yes, there was a sensation, like static when I shivered."

"That was Hades' binding. But," he looked at her, slightly embarrassed, "it's not complete. It's why I said you were only mostly married. The Blessing isn't finalized. Close, but not complete."

"What?" Persephone's brow furrowed. "What completes the—" she stopped. "No."

"Yes," he said, his pale blue eyes unable to meet hers.

"You're joking with me. This is a joke. You cannot possibly be serious?"

Thanatos shook his head, still avoiding her eyes. "It's not a joke."

"And you can tell?" Persephone blushed a crimson that extended down her neck to the collar of Hades' too large shirt.

"There's an aura," Thanatos said. "Yours should be the same as Hades and it seems to have taken on some of his aspects, but the shift isn't complete." He gave her a sly grin. "It must have been an interesting night last night."

Persephone dropped her face into her hands and mumbled, "I'm not answering that since you seem to already know."

"That's all the confirmation I need."

"Who else can see this aura?"

"Only a few of us," he assured her.

"Amalthia?"

He nodded silently.

"Fuck."

"Well, yes, that would be what's needed here," he said dryly.

Persephone opened her mouth in outrage but fell into a fit of giggles. She laughed while the screens around her showed the end of the world.

Here she was, worried about some level of propriety and the world was literally going to hell. It was too much; she laughed until her sides ached and she was gasping for breath.

When she calmed down enough to finally look up, Hades loomed over her beside Thanatos with a grim expression on his face. She shot to her feet.

"Hades," she yelped, stumbling back against the chair.

"Are you alright?" he asked and held out his hand.

Shooting Thanatos a quick look, she took his hand. The odd feeling of static washed over her with his touch.

"You told her?" he asked Thanatos.

"Yes, my Lord." Thanatos looked pointedly at Hades. "You didn't."

Hades gave his second-in-command a long look before returning his attention to Persephone. His gaze was dark and his brows furrowed.

"Finding out we were married sent you into a fit of laughter so loud the entire command center could hear it?"

"I'm sorry, it was a shock," she said.

Hades gave her another of his subtle bows. "Thanatos, take over for a little while. Events will stay at this level of war for at least a few more hours. I'm taking my Blessed to walk her fields and let her find her balance again." He looked at her with a cold expression, "I suspect you'll have some questions for me that I can no longer delay answering."

"Yes, my Lord," Thanatos said with the deepest bow she'd seen yet.

"Come with me," Hades said and shifted her hand to his forearm.

They walked in uncomfortable silence for several minutes. Persephone took in what she could with her limited vision. Walls ranged from clean drywall to bare limestone. The floor under her feet was a mixture of stone, concrete, fabricated plastics, and carpet. The air smelled flat, slightly metallic, and stale.

"You need more plants in your common spaces," she told him, finally breaking their silence.

"We don't do a lot of decorations here, Persephone. It's a waste of resources."

"It's not a decoration. Or at least, not *only* for decoration. Several species of ferns help to pull pollutants from the air, things left by manufacturing or," she looked up at him, "closed systems. It might reduce the load on your filters."

"If you can grow it and put it out with what's on hand, you are welcome to do so." Hades' voice was stiff and formal.

"You're mad Thanatos told me," she said. "Don't blame him, I pushed him."

"I'm not mad at Thanatos, Persephone. I'm mad at myself. I've had multiple opportunities to tell you and I've squandered them. Now things have progressed in a way that I feel you will think I broke your trust."

Persephone straightened as she walked. The information was all so fresh that she didn't even consider that if they had continued this morning, their bond would be complete without her ever knowing what they had done.

"I commend you for identifying and telling me the problem I had not yet seen." She was as stiff and formal as he was. The information settled on her uncomfortably, like a wool blanket with no warmth.

She looked up at him to gauge his thoughts. His pale face was blank except for a slight frown at the corners of his mouth.

"If you had been trying to trick me into completing the bond, I assume you wouldn't have told me that just now."

Hades was silent.

They continued their walk to the gardens in silence.

Persephone's mind rolled. If he was so concerned about finalizing the bond, did that mean it was revocable before it was sealed?

"What happens if the bond is never sealed?" she finally asked as they walked through the fields' airlock.

"It can't be broken, if that's what you're wondering."

"Hmm, I was," she admitted. "But then what is the advantage of completing it?"

They stepped out onto the dark soil of the fields and Persephone gave a sigh. She wiggled her toes, sinking them into the soil. She dropped Hades' arm to scoop a handful of the dirt, then dusted them off on her borrowed pants. Persephone took a step toward the corn growing in neat rows before them, but Hades caught her hand.

"The advantage," he said quietly, "is that you will have a somewhat enhanced protection that comes from me. It solidifies your place here so that you can never be expelled."

"Unless I do something horrible," she told him. "Thanatos told me about that too. You said you took personal accountability for me. I didn't realize it was that deep. You said I was your ward, but really I'm—"

"My wife," he said gently.

Persephone stole a glance at him, but his face was still unreadable.

She looked down. "And what if I never want to do wifely things? The kind of things that would seal the bond? You won't," she swallowed hard, "you won't force me, right?"

His hand came to her chin and very gently raised her head. She was scared to look up. Scared to see what the answer would be.

"Look at me," he said. "Please."

Persephone opened her eyes and saw him, how close he

stood to her. His face wore an unexpected and almost timid smile. Fear and hope warred in his silver-blue eyes as he looked down at her. For a moment, he reminded her of Henry.

"I have no desire to ever force that. As I told you last night, if you chose to grace me with that beautiful gift, I want you to be excited, ready, and filled with passion." His thumb ran along her lower lip again, sending a spark of heat through her. "Because when I take you, it will be more than sex. I will worship you. I will draw every moan from you like a symphony. And when you come for me I will give you only one breath before I start again, because you deserve to be worshipped like a goddess and fucked like one too. Believe me, you are a goddess to me."

Persephone could only stare at him with her mouth slightly parted in shock. She had no idea how he could sound so dirty, so possessive, and make it sound so deliciously hot.

"Even if you never complete the bond, like now, it protects you," he continued like he didn't just turn her world upside down. "It protects you from harmful acts, even from me. It would be stronger if complete, but there is still a level of protection there."

"How?"

"Magic."

"Ha ha. Very funny."

"I told you last night, I wasn't scared of you wielding a knife against me. Perhaps a practical demonstration will help." He pulled a knife from his boot and offered it to her, hilt first.

"No," she said, knowing what he would ask.

"I promise I am perfectly safe."

Persephone frowned. "Okay, but I'm aiming for your thigh where there are no vital organs."

She eyed his leg and bit her lip. The sudden memory of that thigh pressed between her legs as he pinned her to the door stoked the embers inside her.

She lunged, arm flashing out to jab his thigh.

He didn't move, but the blade slid harmlessly over his thigh and her momentum sent her tumbling forward. Hades caught her before she fell and drew her to him.

"Your protection is not that strong," he said as he pulled the knife from her fingers. "But it would turn a mortal blow into mere grievous bodily harm. And I beg you, please don't ever come to that level of harm."

"Magic is real," she breathed and blinked up at him.

"Yes. Here, it is. It's real for certain people above too," he said and looked down at her.

Persephone stepped back as she took in what had happened. "The aura Thanatos mentioned, that's how you knew, wasn't it?"

"Yes."

"You didn't have to look at my data on yield inconsistencies, you already knew."

"Not quite," he said slowly, as if thinking or remembering. "We had a list of potential bioengineers to vet and possibly recruit. As my scientists dug into your data they noticed the anomaly. That's when I directed Thanatos to join your security team. He wasn't there an hour before he reported back about your aura."

"I had one? Even then? I thought we had to …" she trailed off as heat flushed across her again.

"Yes. You've always had your own aura, like me. Like Thanatos. Like the others. But when, *if*, the bond is completed, your aura would take on an aspect of mine."

"I need a moment to think," she told him. Her mind whirled through the implications of what he said.

Hades nodded and took her hand, leading her along the rows of corn.

Persephone let her mind empty as they walked. She allowed her body to feel the lights above them, simulating sunlight, the breeze that was perfectly directed from an impressive HVAC system. She could even smell the moisture in the dirt as they walked.

These fields. This place. They were so complex it boggled the mind. Thousands of people living in a closed system. The science of it all was so advanced that it was practically magic.

"Okay," she told him.

"Okay?"

"I accept it."

"That was fast."

"I'm a fast learner," she told him with a smile.

They had stopped at the pomegranates she had seen the day prior. Bright red fruit dotted the plant, swaying in the artificial breeze.

"Do I—" She stopped herself. It was stupid to ask.

"Do you have magic?" he finished for her.

"Yes."

"Dr. Persephone Kore, whose yields always exceeded what they should, even in controlled environments. You could never make the math work because it was you. If you hadn't run along your plants so often, I think your yields would have been normal."

She looked up. "I did this yesterday, didn't I?"

"Yes. Or so Thanatos tells me," he answered.

"Growing plants. You have to admit, for a magical power, it's not exactly exciting," she said dryly.

"No," he said and pulled her close, "but it may be what saves us all."

Persephone looked up at him. His smile was warm and genuine. The feral predator lurked in his eyes again and she smiled back. Very slowly he leaned in to kiss her, as if afraid of rejection. At the last inch, she stood up on her toes to reach him.

Their lips met in a way that sent the static feeling along her body, practically crackling with energy. Fire filled her, deep in her belly, and she clenched her thighs together. His arms wrapped around her, pulling her sharply against his chest and he deepened the kiss.

They broke apart slightly, with Persephone gasping for breath. Hades' lips went a scant millimeter from hers, a deep growl coming from him, and the feral predator that lurked behind his eyes seemed to rise to the surface.

"You don't know," Hades said slowly, "how long I've yearned for that." He cupped the side of her face and ran his thumb over her lip. "I know I said I would never require it of you, but if you allowed me, I would taste every inch of you. I would burn the world down to make you happy." His hand tightened on her back and pulled her close. Eyes closed, he rested his forehead against hers.

Persephone allowed herself one moment to bask in that desire before she writhed away from Hades' grasp to gather herself. As with this morning, she allowed herself to be drawn to him without thinking. Hades stood his ground, eyes closed as he breathed hard.

Persephone looked away, unable to follow the shift of emotions across his face. She looked at the pomegranate plant surrounding them. The limbs that had been heavy with fruit now bowed under the weight of hundreds of heavy red orbs.

"Hades, look," she said.

His eyes flew open and he took in the plant. "Your magic," he said.

She reached for a fruit, but a hand on her arm stopped her.

"Wait. You have to understand there is more to my magic," he said. "I am like you, but the opposite. Where you create and grow life, I bring death."

Hades reached for the nearest pomegranate and touched it. The bright red fruit shrank to a withered gray husk at his touch. He caressed the branch, weighed down almost to snapping with the weight of its own fruit. It dropped every fruit at once before turning a dull brown. Then it sprang back, dead and desiccated.

"No!" Persephone cried. Fearful of him, what he could do, and fearful that the death of the fruit plant could negatively impact her new world.

"I'm sorry, Persephone. If I so choose, I bring death with a touch," he told her.

"But this is life, this is what feeds your people," she cried. His insistence that they were a closed system played in her mind; she feared even one branch could tip the balance.

Persephone lifted her hands to the branches. Her mind opened, reaching out to the plants, seeking to undo what he had done. Her hands found the dead branch and caressed its length, bringing life back to it. As her hands moved along the branch, leaves and blooms sprang back to life. She gasped, glad to see it returning to life. She took a step, then another, hands sliding along the branch, filling it with life.

When she reached the trunk, she set her hands to it, pushing more life into it, feeling the strain of her efforts. The bark fairly pulsed under her seeking hands.

"Persephone, no. Slow down," Hades cautioned.

She ignored him, pumping more life force into the plant. Her life force, she realized, when the beat of her heart slowed to match the pulse of the magic. The plant stretched its branches toward the fake sky and she gasped. Her vision swam with gray and a buzzing sounded in her ears. She tried to pull her hands back, but she seemed locked into the plant.

"Hades," she tried to cry, but her voice was barely a whisper. "Help me."

His arms wrapped around her and pulled her back, breaking the deadly life bond as she slipped into a reeling darkness.

Chapter 15
Day 5

Persephone woke slowly. Her vision had gone fuzzier than usual before a strange gray haze crept from outside in. Dreams, strange and disjointed, hit her like reality fractured by a hammer.

Persephone opened her eyes, one, then the other. Nothing made sense and they closed again. A noxious smell pressed against her nose and her head lolled right to left as she tried to escape the smell.

"Seph," a voice called, familiar and warm.

She turned to the sound of the voice, ignoring the beeps and cheeps of the room.

"Good girl," the voice said.

"Hades?" Persephone's eyes fought to open. The first thing she saw was Hades, seated close to her. He looked at her with concern, his fear evident in the tightness at the corners of his eyes. Beyond him, Thanatos stood with arms crossed over his black body armor.

"Who's running the end of the world?" she asked and tried to smile.

"Amalthia," Thanatos said briskly. "And now that I know you're alive, I'll return to take over once more." Thanatos bowed to her, gave Hades a nod, and strode out.

"What happened?" she asked Hades.

Hades took her hand silently. It was warm and callused and he rubbed his thumb gently along the back of her hand, mindful of the IV Persephone had missed.

"Hades?"

"I demonstrated my control over death," he told her. He turned her hand over to caress her palm. "And in showing I could control death, I nearly lost you to it."

The gentle touch on her palm made little tingles. She let him stroke her hand a moment longer while she thought.

"I went too far," she said. It wasn't a question.

"Yes," Hades said and kissed the palm of her hand. "Don't ever do that again."

"I'm not sure I can control it, Hades."

His hand tightened on hers. "You have to learn control. I can't lose you."

"I know, Hades. The Underground apparently needs what I can do, even if I can't control it."

"No," he said harshly. The hand on hers gripped tighter and he brought the back of her hand up and caressed it with his cheek. "*I* can't lose you. Me. Hades."

There was silence broken only by the hum of machinery as she processed what he said.

She shook her head. "I've never done this before. I didn't know I could. I mean, I suspected, maybe, but it seemed so unrealistic. I'm a woman of science; everything must be proven to be true."

Hades kissed her fingers before putting her hand to his cheek and leaning into it. "But doesn't the scientific method call for updating a hypothesis and testing again if you are given new data? New information?"

Persephone nodded. She rubbed her thumb on his cheek. "Yes. I don't even know where to start."

"Start small, aim for control," he told her. He covered the hand resting on his cheek, tracing its path down her arm to her elbow, igniting a flutter low in her belly as the monitor betrayed the quickening rhythm of her heart.

Persephone sighed. "I can do that."

"Once you learn control, increase it, but slowly. Today showed that you are like a baby serpent. A young serpent is more dangerous than an adult. An adult knows how much venom to release in a bite. A baby serpent has not learned that control and injects everything it has into its victim, even at the risk of harming itself." He turned his head to kiss her palm, then set her hand back into her lap.

"I need time to recover first," she told him.

"Fortunately, we have a lot of time on our hands for the foreseeable future."

There was something decidedly wicked in the smile he gave

her. Persephone opened her mouth to respond when a woman barged in. She wore medical scrubs with a golden sheaf of wheat embroidered on the sleeve.

"My Lord," she said briskly.

"Yes?" Hades rose to face the woman.

"I need you," she said quickly.

"Nurse, you know I no longer offer that," he said shortly.

"I'm sorry, my Lord, not that. My patient." Despite her denial, her face was flushed and she looked entirely too hungry when she looked up at Hades.

Persephone was surprised to feel another flare of jealousy. *Did he and this woman have a past? How many of his former lovers lingered in this place?* Persephone worried she would spend the next few years of her life tied to a man surrounded by his exes; Amalthia's glare had been bad enough.

Hades glanced at her before addressing the nurse. "Is it urgent?"

The nurse cocked her head to the side and scrunched her face. "Every second I delay is more pain. He's at the end and I want to ease his passing painlessly."

"He agrees?" Hades asked quietly.

"He requested it."

"Unhook her," he said, pointing at Persephone. "I want her to see this."

The nurse's lips pinched into a line, but she did as he asked. In a moment, Persephone was free of the IV, a bandage neatly placed over her hand. They followed her down a well-lit corridor. Persephone had very little reason to visit a hospital or medical facility in her life, but she recognized it when she saw it. The hallway was lined with rooms, but most stood empty. They turned into the first occupied room.

A man lay on a hospital bed. His face said middle-aged age, but his frail body looked older. Clear IV lines rested against his skin, no longer intrusions but companions, their steady pulse a lullaby for a body ready to rest.

"Thomas," Hades greeted him warmly.

Thomas's head lifted from its pillow slightly and a thin smile spread across his thin, hollow cheeks. "My Lord."

"She tells me it's time, my friend."

"Please, my Lord. They've told me it's spread even further. Lymph nodes, belly, lungs, they found a tiny one in my brain today. I want to stop fighting it. I want to be free of this pain, the aches, and the burn of the medicines."

Hades looked up at the IV bags that hung over Thomas's head and nodded. "You've been with me since the beginning, Thomas. You were the second man I hired for the job, do you remember?"

Thomas' thin smile spread further. "Yes, my Lord. I was proud to do it too. Ten years, my Lord, it has been my honor."

Hades placed his hand on Thomas' thin hand. "No, Thomas, it has been *my* honor."

From where she stood, Persephone could see the pain in Hades' eyes. He genuinely loved and respected this man. He must have been terribly important to the expansion of the Underground.

"Thank you, my King," Thomas whispered.

He dipped his chin in a tiny bow. On any other man, it would have been a slight against his king, but this nod, given with the very last drop of his energy, conveyed gratitude and respect beyond measure.

"Rest friend, your work is done. We have it from here," Hades told him and leaned over to kiss the man gently on the forehead.

At his words, Thomas gave one last sigh and sank into his pillows. If not for Hades' gentle hand on his and the blaring of his monitors, Persephone would have assumed he was merely sleeping.

Hades stepped back and gave the man a slight bow before striding from the room. Persephone trailed behind him, only catching up as they crossed the threshold to her room.

"Who was he?" Persephone asked. "Who was he to you?"

Hades helped her to settle onto the bed again. "He was my first waste management specialist." A proud smile lingered on Hades' lips and a hint of unshed tears in his eyes.

"Janitor?" Persephone asked.

The smile vanished, replaced with a tight-lipped frown. "I suppose it could be accurate to label his position as such. But the connotation betrays how vital he was to us."

"You told me you valued production, creating more than you take. But a janitor only cleans; they don't make anything."

"While I still don't like the tone in which you refer to Thomas, I understand your confusion. In a closed system, with limited resources, disease would bring the waste of lives, of precious medicine, and productivity. Thomas was vital to ensuring we were as shielded from disease as possible. He defeated what could end us all by the sweat of his own brow and a dedication to our community. He was also loyal and honest, two qualities I value highly."

Persephone took his hand and gave it a small squeeze. "Thank you for explaining. I'm sorry you lost him."

Hades was quiet a long moment as they held hands, very obviously processing the death.

"You took his life," Persephone finally said quietly. "It wasn't a coincidence that he died while we were in the room; you did something."

"Yes," he said bluntly. "Thomas has been sick for many months. He fought hard but was ultimately switched to palliative care within the last week. What he asked for was the chance to end his suffering and go with dignity, something I can grant."

"Like with the pomegranates?"

"Yes. But for him, it was painless."

Silence lingered between them.

"The way you say that implies you can make it painful as well."

Hades remained silent, staring at the pale beige wall behind her.

"Have you?" Persephone whispered and tugged gently on his hand.

Hades pulled his hand back from hers. "Yes."

"Why?"

Hades frowned. "Are you sure you want to know?"

"Yes."

"Once was in self-defense. I was attacked by a man intent on killing me. He clearly didn't know of my personal defenses. As he thrust the knife, I grabbed his wrist and made him regret every decision that led his life to that point. He died screaming."

Persephone let a silent moment pass before asking, "And the other? It sounds like there was another."

Hades looked away from her. "There were people with me

when I was attacked. It was before we started work on the Underground and they saw what happened. It frightened them, but it also solidified in their minds that I would be able to lead and control this daunting project. The only other time I've used my power that way was several years into construction. A man tried to betray us. He was caught attempting to sell diagrams of the facility to the Sons of Zeus. I executed him publicly, at an assembly of every member of the Underground at the time. He also died screaming and I did not make it quick."

Persephone leaned back. Part of her was aghast at how easily he admitted to torturously killing a man. It was cold, precise, and calculated. Intended to keep people in line.

Another part of her was slowly coming to understand why. Everything Hades had explained about showing control over a change of this magnitude and keeping the machine running seemed to click into place. If this was the first betrayal, the first crime of that magnitude, he needed to demonstrate that once the doors were closed, if you refused to follow the rules, there was only one outcome possible.

"I must return to the communications center," Hades said briskly. "You need more rest and your bloodwork is not complete yet. If we find that you have not harmed yourself, I will ask that you be returned to my rooms." He avoided eye contact.

"I would like to go back to the command center," she told him. "If it goes as bad as we expect, I want to witness it myself."

Hades bowed his head. "Very well, Persephone."

Chapter 16
Day 5

A nurse came in later as Persephone lay considering what Hades told her.

"I won't need to hook you back up to the IVs," she said and gave Persephone a smile. "Your bloodwork all shows good signs."

"Thank you," Persephone said.

The nurse hit a button and started raising the head of the bed. "He didn't do that to you?" she asked quietly.

"No," Persephone said ruefully, "I did it to myself."

"Hmph. Magic hands, that one."

"So, he told me." Persephone swung her feet over the side of the bed.

"Slowly, please. Don't want you passing out again." The nurse gave her a sly smile. "Has he shown you yet?"

Persephone shuddered. "Yes, he killed my pomegranate tree. *A* pomegranate tree," she corrected herself. "Bringing it back to life was what got me here."

"No, dear," the nurse said and laid a hand on her arm, "the other death. The little death." Her smile was wicked now and her eyes danced with laughter.

Persephone's eyebrows shot up. "What?"

"The man has control of death in many ways; I'm surprised he didn't tell his beloved about his control over the little death. I'd certainly want my husband to share that with me," the nurse muttered.

"I am not his beloved. I'm Blessed, which I guess makes me his wife." Persephone stopped before saying "in name only" and pressed her mouth in a firm line. Hades' insistence on giving the appearance that she was under his control probably extended to not exposing the fact that their bond was not complete while she denied their *de facto* marriage.

The nurse gave a little snorting laugh. "I wouldn't be so sure

103

about that."

When Persephone looked at her pointedly, she smiled.

"When we first came Underground, he was known to occasionally use the little death as a reward. Oh, it's not sexual, not really. If he was pleased with your work, he'd put a hand on your wrist and … let's just say the rest of your day was brightened."

Persephone's mouth hung open, but no words came out.

"But over the last few years, he's stopped. We wondered if he was displeased with us but later found out it was because he had found you." Her smile softened. "I think he's been saving himself for you since then."

"Thank you for letting me know. It's certainly going to be a topic of discussion at dinner tonight."

Persephone had no doubts that it would be the topic of many discussions in the near future. The nurse looked like a cat who'd just found freshly dried catnip and would no doubt spread the hot gossip as soon as Persephone was out of earshot.

By the time she was dressed in Hades' pajamas, a woman arrived in the dark, armored uniform Persephone associated with Hades' personal guards. She thanked the nurse and followed the silent guard through the corridors.

Chapter 17
Day 5

Persephone found Hades in his command suite. Her guard, a golden bident of Hades' personal guard flashing on her chest, gave her a deep bow and departed, her short blonde bob making a pale curtain over her face. She took a moment to observe the trio standing in the command suite before entering.

Thanatos, unmasked but dressed in his armor, followed the remaining camera feeds, occasionally turning to speak to Hades. Amalthia's willowy body swayed through the room, as clearly checking their supplies as she was attempting to attract Hades' attention. Hades was seated in a chair that was part throne and part individual command suite. The black leather was elegantly stitched and layered over a base that held its own keyboard. Arching up from the chair's back on an articulated arm was a set of three monitors, no doubt broadcasting the most useful screens from the floor below.

Hades was sprawled in the chair, one foot propped up on a footrest, knee cocked into the plush leather of the chair's side. He slouched, the only hint that he was more than lounging was his eyes locked intently on the trio of screens.

Persephone watched him. He listened intently to Thanatos' comments and mostly ignored Amalthia despite what were no doubt her best attempts to get his attention. The third time Amalthia touched his arm, Persephone decided she'd had enough and pushed the suite door open.

Alarms immediately started blaring across the whole communications center. Persephone froze, wishing to shrink into the floor as every eye in the center turned to her.

"Stand down," Hades said as his personal guard pounded up the steps from their positions around the room. "Persephone, welcome back. Next time, have the guard let you in."

Persephone blushed bright red and tried to ignore Amalthia's smug smile. "Of course," she said as blandly as she could.

Hades pushed the trio of screens up on their articulated arm and launched himself from the chair. The languid façade he held together on his digital throne evaporated as he crossed the space to her. He took her hand, raising it to kiss in an elegantly outdated gesture.

"My Blessed," he said, lips lingering over her knuckles.

His breath across her fingers sparked something in her again.

"Hades," she said and nodded.

His mouth firmed into a hard line, but he said nothing. Over his shoulder, she could see Thanatos wince.

"*My Lord*," Thanatos mouthed silently.

Persephone's face scrunched in annoyance before she put her polite social mask back in place.

"While you've been napping," Amalthia's sharp voice snapped, "the war continues. We may be nearing the end, though."

Persephone gave Amalthia her most practiced bland social smile, as if nothing Amalthia said could possibly matter. "Indeed? I'm so glad you've settled an entire war by yourself, Amalthia. Well done."

Persephone's tone was so mild that no one eavesdropping could have accused her of an insult but combined with her utterly uncaring face, it was a stiletto to Amalthia's pride.

"She won't love you for that," Hades said quietly in her ear.

"As if she was ever going to love me anyway," Persephone responded, equally quiet. "You, on the other hand," she said and let her voice trail off.

A quick squeeze of her hand was his sole response.

"My *Blessed*," Hades said, stressing the second word, "our intelligence network predicts the war will end in the next handful of days."

"So quickly?" Persephone had lived through only a few wars but knew they almost always dragged on like two bloodied fighters duking it out until the bell.

"Both sides were swift and brutal. They went for each other's throats and not much of either remains above." He said it coldly, factually, as if the end of the world weren't happening.

Persephone let her gaze wander to the massive screens on the command floor. By squinting, she could just make out that many of the screens were now a haze of static. The people working the floor were nearly still as well. They no longer buzzed with action, passing information from one station to another. Most seemed to be sitting, shocked and staring at the few screens that still bore data.

"May I go look closer?" she asked Hades as she blinked to clear her eyes.

"Please, sit here," he gestured to his digital throne. "You should be able to pull up any feed you wish."

Persephone could feel Thanatos' and Amalthia's eyes on her as she settled into the chair. She couldn't read either face from where she sat, but she had the distinct impression from the tension in the room that she was the first person to be invited to sit on Hades' throne. She tugged gently on the screens, bringing them close enough to her face to see them clearly.

"What am I looking at, Hades?" The three screens were split into multiple views, none of which made sense to her, other than the few cameras still sending live video streams.

"This is a spectrograph," he said from over her shoulder. His dark, armored hand pointed at a window that was streaked with red and yellow over a purple background. "This gives us clues as to what chemicals have been released into the air. We have a few key things that would indicate greater harm than others."

"I'm familiar with them in lab settings. But here? Apocalyptic chemicals? Radiation?" she asked quietly.

"Yes," he said and patted the shoulder gently. "This one shows detectable radiation."

Persephone let out a deep sigh of relief. The screen showed only a few small peaks in the lines running across the screen. "They didn't use the apocalyptic weapons."

"So far, it seems they were restrained. Well, if you can call their destruction restrained."

"They didn't want to end the world."

"They wanted to end their adversary and take over the remains," he agreed.

"It's not over yet, though, is it?"

"No, but from what we can tell, the locations with those weapons were taken out early. No one wanted to leave that option on the table."

Persephone nodded. "The cameras?"

"Those are the remaining cameras in urban areas. A few are scattered throughout rural areas that support lines of transportation. Those areas seem to have held up. The urban areas have been nearly destroyed."

"Is there anyone left alive?" she whispered.

"Yes," his hand squeezed her shoulder. "We've seen people sporadically and other sensors indicate wireless communication coming from a few areas. There are still people out there and if they don't release some last burst of effort with the ... you know, *apocalyptics*," he said while making an explosive gesture with his hands. "Those people may survive the next few months. If they're resourceful."

"There's hope still," Persephone said with a smile.

Chapter 18
Day 5

Persephone relinquished his chair and Hades signaled for one of his guards to bring one for her. The man returned with a massive padded, wheeled chair, likely from a nearby conference room. Hades gave him a look and the man set it directly next to his digital throne.

The tension in the room returned, but Persephone refused to look at Thanatos or Amalthia. She mustered every bit of poise she had in over-large, borrowed clothes and settled herself with regal dignity. Hades said nothing, but the corners of his mouth twitched into a smile.

They stayed several hours after he pointed out what was on his screens. Being unable to see the screens on the floor or hear the conversations between technicians left Persephone bored. She fidgeted in her seat. Finally, she set her hands on the chair's arms to rise. Hades' hand came down gently but held her firmly in place.

"Not much longer, my Blessed, I'm almost done."

Persephone's mouth set in a frown at his subtle reminder of her place.

Hades turned to her. "I am Lord Commander and King of this and must see it through. I'm almost done. And as the Lord of this realm, it would be best if my Blessed remained by my side." His voice was even, but she could hear the command in it. If she defied him in this moment, they could both pay for it.

She caught the look Thanatos shot her from a nearby desk. Over his shoulder, she could see Amalthia's face turned to them, probably hoping she would step out of line.

"Very well, Hades," she said and settled deep into the chair's padding again.

True to his word, Hades rose from his digital throne a few moments later and offered his hand. Swallowing down her annoyance at being commanded, she rose with a tight smile on her face and placed her hand in his.

"Thanatos, call in Hermes. He can cover the next shift while I sleep. Tell him to wake me if—"

"If anything big happens. I know," he said with a tired smile.

"You need sleep too, my friend. Don't stay after you hand off." He clapped Thanatos' armored shoulder. "You too, Amalthia."

"Yes, my Lord," she said. One eyebrow flicked up before she controlled her face. "Have a good night, my Lord."

Something in her tone made Persephone grind her teeth, her grip tightening on Hades' hand. Amalthia's words were bland, but the tone said she knew Persephone would be unable to fulfill his desires that evening and Amalthia was more than willing. Persephone tucked her arm in Hades' and allowed him to lead her away while she shot Amalthia an icy smile.

Hades led her out without a word or even a twitch to indicate he'd caught their silent duel. They strolled arm in arm through corridors lined with variations on rough stone, dry wall, and wood paneling. Persephone trailed a finger along each wall, taking in the feel of each material.

"How do you decide what is finished and what is raw?" she asked as her fingers skimmed the rough-hewn wall 500 steps from the communications suite.

Hades' stride faltered a moment as if that was the last question he expected from her. "It goes in stages and by utility," he told her. "The only people coming to the command suite or communications center are technicians. They don't need it beautified, they need it functional."

"Who gets the clean walls and nicer look?"

"Common areas, where everyone congregates. The personal quarters for Asphodel and Elysium."

"Tartarus really is a prison, isn't it?" she asked without a falter in her step.

"Not exactly. But you are here to work and survive. You don't need the niceties."

"Or you've fallen from grace and that is a punishment," she said quietly.

Hades nodded. "Yes, that's true."

"Would you put me in Tartarus if I disobeyed you?" she

whispered.

Hades stopped in his tracks. The sudden stop pulled her back and he spun her into his arms. Persephone gasped as he wrapped his arms around her. From here, she could see every emotion on his face. Pain. Anger. Disappointment. Hope. Lust.

He closed his eyes. "I don't want a Blessed subservient to me. I want a partner. I want a Blessed who stands by my side. Like you did tonight. But yes, for now, I can't have you being openly defiant while things are unsettled."

Something in his tone made her wonder if the "unsettled" referred to the war being waged above them or their relationship, whatever it was right now.

"Blessed? You mean wife. Your little woman simpering at your side?" she said with no small amount of venom. Being told to sit quietly beside him while he managed the end of the world still rankled her.

His hands squeezed on her arms. "I told you I want a partner. Wife. Blessed. Whatever you call it, you'd be by my side. Not behind me. Not below me. Beside me."

Persephone's chin came up and she studied him. "That's why Amalthia hates me. She wanted the power." Persephone gave a little laugh. "She doesn't care about you; she just wants to rule."

"Yes."

"It's why you rejected her?"

"Yes. Minthe, too."

"Oh, Minthe too? Who in the world is Minthe?"

Hades' eyebrows rose as he looked at her. "Do you want all the details? Or is it sufficient to say that relationship has ended?"

"Just how many of your lovers are down here waiting to remove me for their chance by your side?" Persephone gave a disgusted sigh. "Every time I think I understand things, something else comes up."

Hades' eyes darted down the hallway. "Not here. Not now," he hissed and started walking again.

Persephone stayed still. "Not now? I obeyed you in there. I kept your image intact. I think you owe me answers."

"I will give you answers, but not here," he said, tugging on her arm. When Persephone wouldn't move, he swept her into his arms and then rolled her onto his shoulder.

She shrieked and howled the whole way back to his apartment, fists pounding ineffectually on his back.

He gave a little hitch to his shoulders. "Any louder and you'd really sell it."

She howled in impotent fury as he pushed his dark wooden door open.

Hades dumped her on the couch.

She popped up spitting mad. "Was that necessary?"

"Yes." He bowed his head. "To anyone watching, that was me putting my Blessed in her place quite effectively."

Persephone gave a huffing sigh. "This is why I can't trust you. Nothing makes sense. You trickle out the truth and withhold anything you can. Hell," she sneered, "I don't even have clothes, shoes, or glasses to be able to move freely without you or Thanatos following my every step personally."

Hades gave her a baleful stare but turned toward his kitchen.

"Do you know," she shouted, "how many times my own mother kept me captive? Contained? Imprisoned?"

Persephone rose from his couch and stalked after him until she stood on her tiptoes to be nearly chest to chest with him in his kitchen, finger pointing at his nose.

"*Years*. Every time I graduated from a new program and thought I might loosen her grip, she only tightened. Every new location, she was there first, manipulating the staff into 'keeping me safe,'" she spat.

"You aren't safe here, if that's what you want to hear," Hades told her calmly. He walked from the kitchen to his bedroom.

Persephone took a step back, unwilling to follow him into his bedroom. "I'm still under lock and key. Under surveillance," she said loud enough for her voice to follow him. "And worse? I don't know why! I'm a threat. I'm a savior. I'm the 'Blessed of Hades' as if that means anything to me."

"I've already tried to explain—" he said as he walked back out of his bedroom.

"Oh sure," she said, cutting him off, "we're in some way 'married' and your, your aura," she faltered, "protects me …"

"It does somewhat, if it's not complete." Hades said and

handed her a flat package. "Clothes. Toiletries. Makeup. Sleepwear. Glasses."

Persephone inhaled to launch into another tirade and stopped. Her eyes went wide and she tore open the package. Ripping through the package, her hands honed in on the leather wrapped glasses case. She tore it open and stuffed the frames to her face.

"Change as you wish, then please join me in the kitchen." Hades closed his eyes and bowed his head.

Persephone gave a confused and frustrated sigh. She stepped into the bedroom, refusing to look at him.

He simply bowed his head again and backed away, closing his bedroom door behind him.

Persephone glared around the room now that she was able to see it clearly. The only word that could describe it was sumptuous. The walls were painted a dark blue, but now that she could see it clearly, Persephone noticed that some insane interior decorator had had the nerve to mix flecks of gold into the paint. She ran her fingers over the wall and sure enough, the tiny flecks of gold gave the impression of staring at a starry night sky. His massive bed was unmade and showed blue sheets only a shade lighter than his walls with white pillowcases. The whole thing had a built-in bookshelf that spanned up the wall and over the bed with discreet, recessed lighting that spoke of late nights reading to himself.

Persephone turned away from the bed, cheeks burning with the memory of that morning. Now that she could see what was in Hades' little care package, she went through it more slowly. The flat box held less than a week's worth of clothing, but what it did hold was beautiful. Three dresses, each in a different color but the same cut, were smooth under her fingers. Each had wide straps holding up an unboned bodice. The bodice was adjustable with ties in the back, a smart call if he didn't know her dress size. Each had layered, flowing skirts with a slit to the mid-thigh. She snorted. They were long enough to be modest, but the low neckline and slit would certainly turn heads.

"Ah ha!" Persephone seized the toiletries, which were exactly what she used. "Wait," she muttered and turned over the bottle of shampoo. A familiar dent from where she'd dropped the bottle told her they were her toiletries. "They managed to grab my soaps but not my glasses?"

The antiseptic smell of the hospital still clung to her beneath the scent of soil. She could see dirt beneath her nails as well. Maybe Amalthia had more than one reason to glare at her. Persephone snatched her bag of toiletries, one of the three dresses, and an opaque bag blandly labeled "underwear," then marched to his bathroom. She locked the door behind her this time.

Persephone stalked through his bathroom, ignoring the white marble countertops flecked with gold. The man certainly had a strong sense of style. She showered slowly, taking her time to not only scrub the dirt and antiseptic smell from her skin but to luxuriate in the shower. Her thoughts intruded on the peace of warm water pounding down her back. She felt caged. With the blast doors closed, she was trapped. Worse, she was tied to a man she knew almost nothing about, in a role that no one had been able to clearly define. Her mother's control, as maddening as it was, could at least be counted on to be predictable. Now? She was thrown into the chaos of a world turned upside down.

She sighed. At least he had good food and wine. And Hades certainly wasn't hard on the eyes. She laughed, his hard parts might be his best parts. She scrubbed her face with soapy hands in an attempt to wipe the memory from her mind, but it was seared to her brain. The feel of him behind her, his hands on her hip as he pushed into her. Persephone inhaled deeply. She had no idea how she could survive the next few years living in this man's home. He clearly felt something for her, but she couldn't name the emotions he brought up in her other than lust.

Groaning, she turned the handle to full cold and stood in the icy water. Letting water only a degree above sleet flow over her body left her gasping but chased the memories from the front of her mind. She stepped from the shower and was relieved to see nothing had moved this time. It was easy to fall into her normal post-shower routine and push out thoughts of the man on the other side of the door. She finally smoothed the dress over her hips, secure in her ability to calm her unexpected ardor and push him from her mind. Persephone even smiled as she opened his bedroom door.

Every thought she had fought to drive away burned back into her mind the second she stepped through the door. Persephone had assumed Hades would be in the kitchen cooking, as that's where he said he would be; instead, the man was sprawled languidly in his armchair facing the bedroom door. He had doffed his armor. Now he wore his dark trousers with the tailored black shirt unbuttoned to the middle of his well-muscled chest, sleeves rolled back to show forearms like chiseled marble. One arm draped casually across his thigh while the other held a blood red wine to his lips, his sip paused as she opened the door.

Persephone stopped. Stopped moving. Stopped breathing. She stared at him. Somehow, sitting and relaxing in his chair, he still threw off an aura of command. Of power. Of pure sexuality. A thought of herself, face buried between those thighs as he gripped her hair, flashed through her mind and she gasped. Persephone bit her lip and turned to flee through the door.

"Stop," Hades commanded.

She paused, her hand still on the doorknob. If she walked through the door, she knew he could avoid all this. If she turned around, she didn't know what would happen next. Or what she wanted to happen next.

"Come here." His voice was low, deep, and it stirred something in her.

Persephone turned around.

Hades regarded her over his wine glass. His eyes were dark, half-lidded, but she noted the feral intensity behind them.

With her new glasses, Persephone could see the most minute flickers of emotion on his face: desire, fear, and curiosity. Her feet started moving before her conscious mind made a choice.

Hades stood as she approached. He set his wine glass on the dark wood table beside him and held out a hand. She placed hers in his, but stopped an arm's length away.

She was able to see him clearly for the first time. He was Henry, but somehow not. His jaw was stronger and sharper than it had been above. His shoulders were broader and his hair was longer. Henry had been good looking, but Hades was gorgeous.

"Do I look different here, too?" she blurted out.

Hades gave a light laugh. "You didn't look in the mirror?"

Persephone shrugged. "A steamy mirror doesn't show much."

"Fishing for compliments then? Yes, there are subtle differences," he told her. His free hand reached out and he curled a lock of still damp hair around his finger. "Your hair is longer and has a more golden tone with the chocolate."

Persephone reached up to touch her hair. She pulled a lock in front of her face. "I guess."

"Come to the table," he said and gestured to the food she hadn't seen when her sole focus was on his gorgeous face.

He settled her in a chair with courtly manners. The table was laid with two meals, neatly plated, and another bottle of wine. He raised his glass in a slight toast, then began to eat.

"Your skin is more luminous, too," he told her a few bites later.

She looked down at her hands, finally free of the dirt. "I can't tell."

"You may not be able to see it yet."

"Why?"

Hades seemed to consider his answer, head tilting slightly as he thought. He took her hand again and ran it lightly up her arm. "I told you that there are those of us who can see auras?"

Persephone nodded. The feel of his hand brushing her arm was electric, the same static she had felt when she agreed to be his Blessed tingled in the wake of his fingers.

"We're different," he told her, "special. And the same thing that allows us to see auras allows us to both see the differences as well as make them above."

"Then how am I able to look different? I can't see the auras."

"You've never practiced. But you already know you're like us, special."

"The plants?" she asked quietly.

Hades nodded.

"It's why you took me. Me, specifically." She looked down at her plate.

"Yes."

His voice was so steady, factual, and blunt. She looked up at him. There was no hint of wavering or prevarication. The level of solid belief in her was heady. No one in her life had ever shown her that level of trust in what she could accomplish. Something in her softened.

Until she remembered that they were by no means the only ones with gifts.

"I need wine," she told him.

If he was surprised, he didn't show it. He gave her a quick nod and went to fetch her a glass of wine from his amply stocked kitchen. It appeared to be the same varietal he was drinking: bold, deep red, exactly how she liked it. At least if she was bound to this man and his home for the next few years, they were compatible in this way.

Persephone accepted it absently. "You throw me over your shoulder like some Neanderthal and I'm just supposed to accept it?"

"I've told you what the stakes are," he said.

"Is that any way to treat your wife?" she countered.

His head rocked back as he considered her question. "No, my Blessed, it is not. I will be more considerate in the future."

She gave him a nod and sipped her wine. "Who else was before me?"

"What?" his fork stopped halfway to his mouth.

"Amalthia. Minthe. Some magical *little death* power. Who else?"

He frowned and let the fork come to rest on his plate. "First of all, Minthe has been out of the picture for years."

"Out of the picture but not out of the Underground," she countered.

"Indeed, she remains."

"Which means she is a direct threat to me."

He didn't comment. "Amalthia?" He gave a chuckle. "She doesn't want me, she wants what I can give her."

"Clearly," Persephone said with a voice as dry as the wine she sipped.

"And," he continued, "I couldn't be with someone who only wants me for what I can give them. It's transactional, not love. I want a love match."

His words hung in the air for a long moment. Persephone decided she had no energy or mental capacity to dive into that now.

"And since Minthe?"

"No one," he said firmly.

"What about this little reward? Your *little death* reward. How many of your faithful followers will I be defending myself against over that?"

Hades looked abashed and sipped his wine. "Yes, I did use that at one time as a reward, but not in the last few years."

"Why?"

"I found you." Once again, his simple statement held such solid truth, Persephone was unable to counter him.

They finished the last of the meal in silence. Persephone was digesting what he had told her and Hades was seemingly waiting for a reaction. When she finished the last forkful, she thanked him for the meal and conversation but claimed sleepiness.

"I'm sorry to kick you from your own living room, but I need sleep," she told him.

He nodded with a slight pause, perhaps having hoped she would join him again. "Feel free to change in my room again, I'll finish the dishes."

She gave him a polite nod and fled back to his room. Her thoughts churned over his answers and her reaction to seeing him clearly for the first time since arriving in the Underground. She returned a little while later in a simple, wholesome nightgown that covered her from neck to wrist to knee.

"Thank you again for the glasses," she told him as she settled onto his couch.

"Of course, I can't have my Blessed running around blind," he said as he draped a blanket over her.

"Ha. I'm blind whether I have glasses or not. They just make it bearable."

He had no answer to that and slipped quietly back to his room.

Chapter 19
Day 10

A few days later, Persephone was in her dedicated lab studying the Underground's cultivars and reasoning out how they fit together. A combination of hydroponics, hot houses, and pure soil horticulture drove the entire Underground. And yet, no one had introduced air-purifying plants to the common areas. Simple ferns would go a long way to cleansing the air that so many thousands breathed every day and she was flabbergasted by the oversight.

Hades' insistence that she was picked for some mystical purpose aside, his primary farmers and scientists were clearly idiots. She typed another note in her ever-growing notepad with a decisive jab of her ring finger.

Hades had installed her in this small lab after she was designated Blessed and let her have unfettered access to the Underground's soil samples, watering patterns, planting cycles, nutrient infusions, and more. She had spent nearly every hour of the last few days playing catch up by herself in her lonely lab, deeply aware how crucial her work was with the Underground sealed. On more than one occasion, she had passed out at her microscope or terminal and awoken on Hades' couch. She respected that he had not taken her back into his bed since the first night when nightmares had plagued her.

A part of her was infinitely relieved and another part wished to wake up pressed against him again, basking in his warmth and feeling his hard chest and ... other things ... against her. A thought that made feelings rush to her belly, equal parts heat and anxiety.

Each day, Hades escorted her to the lab. Each day, nearly every person they passed gave a look of deep resentment, regardless of which badge was on their clothing. They all knew who and what she was, what she represented. He left one of his personal guard, marked by the gold stitched bident emblem on their chest, at her door to keep her safe, only returning at lunchtime to work with her to control her power. They would take a picnic lunch to the fields to work on her control of the local plants and break when her hunger and exhaustion peaked. After lunch, he would escort her to the lab, leaving her to resume her study of the Underground's plants.

It had become routine, predictable if a little nerve wracking, and it was horribly like working in a lab her mother, Demeter, controlled.

Persephone wasn't a slave, per se, but neither was she a free woman. She was well fed, well groomed, well housed. For all the world, she seemed like a well-loved and very smart house pet.

She hated it.

"I need my own space," she said abruptly during one of their lunch-and-learns. She had been struggling to control how much of her power she pumped into the plants, enabling them to grow to just the right level of ripeness.

"The only open rooms are on the Tartarus level," Hades told her calmly. "That would be unsafe for you." He took her hand and kissed the back of her knuckles.

Persephone let him. It stirred something in her. Something wild that longed for freedom, though.

"And just who made the circumstances by which I am so in danger in the Underground?" Her perfectly enunciated sentence was practically spat on the ground under them.

"I did," Hades said simply.

Persephone snatched her hand back. "You. You who tell me I can't break the rules, I have to fall in line, at least in public, and I have to be deemed worthy of the resources put into me. It seems like a lot of expectations are heaped on me without much in return."

"Food, shelter, safety, clothes, and purpose. That's not nothing."

"It's the bare minimum. Even my mother gave me that. But freedom? What I want is freedom. Choice. The ability to choose my own path for once. And yes, working to gain the trust of people here in the Underground. But on my terms. My way." She turned her back and thought. "I didn't ask for this, but I appreciate not being dead. I appreciate that you seem to be working in my best interest, if I'm willing to blindly trust you. But then, what choice do I have?"

"You are right," Hades finally admitted. "I am the Lord Commander and King of this realm. I should be above reproach. I should be the most lawful of all my people if I want them to trust me, but I willingly broke rules to get you here. I did it for my own gain. I did it because I couldn't imagine a world without you in it. And you don't even know me enough to trust me." He hung his head.

"Henry—" Persephone started before she snapped her jaw shut.

Silence stretched between them.

"Maybe I do know you. A little bit. Or at least the part of you that you could show me," Persephone said carefully. "I liked Henry. Maybe more than liked him. I felt safe around him and trusted him. Maybe you aren't the Henry I know, but parts of him are you. Parts of you are him. It's," she paused to think, "a starting point."

Hades nodded. "How do we move forward?"

"First, I need to figure out what is 'Hades' and what is 'Henry,' so I can keep it all straight in my mind."

"How do we do that?" Hades asked. He reached out slowly, telegraphing his movements to give her time to accept or reject them.

She let him take her hand again. He brought it up once more, allowing his lips to brush along her knuckles. A little flutter hit her belly and something clenched deep inside.

"We get to know each other. The real us. Or the real us in this realm, since apparently, we're both different down here," she said quietly. "Okay, first question: Since I look different down here, do you still find me attractive?"

Hades gave her the feral smile she'd seen in his apartment the first day she was there. He leaned across their picnic blanket and caught her chin in his hands. He pulled her close until she had no choice but to look into those beautiful ice-blue eyes. A deep, almost growling noise came from his throat as he pulled her in closer. His lips crashed against hers and the hand on her chin snaked around to the back of her head, gently cupping her neck.

"I would tear the clothes from your body just to worship the beauty of it. I would build monuments to the light in your eyes. You are the most attractive woman I've ever had the honor to behold," he said.

Persephone's kiss-roughened lips fell open and she could

feel a blush heating her cheeks. She closed her eyes to shut him out while she recovered some semblance of balance. His passion infected her and she bit her lip to keep from kissing him back.

She didn't know why she hesitated to return the kiss. He was so damn hot. He was kind and attentive, even if more than a little high-handed. She stared across the fields, lush under the artificial sun, as if they would whisper the answer back to her, but nothing came. Persephone shook her head. She needed to steer things back into calmer waters.

"What are you most passionate about? Uhm, excited. Damn it," she blushed. Clearly, she wasn't steering the conversation at all. "What things here do you enjoy when you aren't working? And don't say the Underground," she clarified, "tell me a hobby you love."

He chuckled at her obvious dodge. "Cooking and wine, clearly."

"Fine. What's your favorite book?"

"Hmm. It's always hard to pick just one. I'd have to narrow it down to *The Quiet Crown* by Vroman, *Station Eleven* by Mandel, or *Orpheus Did Not Look Back* by Walpole."

"Oh, wow. I've heard of *Station Eleven* but never read it. I haven't read much but peer-reviewed papers and journals," she admitted.

"Don't worry, I have paperback copies of all three."

"Really?" There was a hopeful glint in her eyes.

"Yes. And the Underground has an extensive paperback library as well, should you wish to expand from your peer-reviewed reading into something less academic and more entertaining."

Persephone smiled. "That would be lovely."

"Ask me another question," Hades encouraged.

She thought a moment, searching for questions that were still surface-level. "What's the weirdest food combination you've ever tried and liked?"

"Sushi and tacos," he said quickly.

"Wait, that's a thing?"

"Yes. It's more like an unsliced sushi roll. But we have fresh salmon in the farm tanks, then avocado, cucumber, and cilantro, which I believe you've already seen growing. Put it all on a rice paper and a thin layer of rice, a line of spicy sauce and roll."

"I could really have that?"

"Yes?" Hades' answer was more of a question.

"I mean, everything is so limited here and that sounds extravagant. Amazing, but extravagant."

"It's all ingredients we grow here; it doesn't even dip into the stored supplies. So, yes, extravagant sounding but readily available."

"What would you need to pull from storage?" she asked, curious.

"Well, for starters, salt. I can store it almost indefinitely, but it would take more supplies than we have to create sodium. We allow it in cooking because it's so essential to life, but it is still rationed and closely monitored."

"Oh yeah, I guess unless you had a salt mine down here, that makes sense."

"Saffron would be another."

"Oh, yes. Definitely. It takes nearly 150 plants for just a gram of saffron and it has to be harvested in the early morning by hand when the bloom is the most open. I'm sure you could manipulate the lighting for that, but I can't imagine you have that much space to spare."

"Indeed. The space in the fields or the manpower required. We have it in storage and I can authorize its use medicinally or for food during special occasions, but the amount is finite. I will run out eventually."

Persephone leaned back and considered the answer. "I'll need to have a very open mind here and spend a lot of time challenging my assumptions."

"I appreciate you're willing to do that for me. For *us*," he corrected.

Persephone nodded quietly, wanting to steer it back to learning about him. She scrunched her face as she tried to think of more questions.

"If you could have any superpower, what would it be?"

"I would have control over Death."

"Oh yeah, dumb question," she said and blushed.

Hades gave a quiet chuckle. "Where did you come up with these questions?"

"I did speed dating once, it was on the question card."

Hades gave her an appraising look. "How many dates have you been on?"

Persephone blushed and looked away. "Well, Mother kept me practically under lock and key, so not many."

"When did you manage to get out?"

"In college," she said.

"College? So you were, what, sixteen?"

Persephone looked back at him, her blush an even deeper red now. "It was toward the end, so, yes."

"And how did that go?" He took her hand, holding it gently.

"Uh," she looked down and his hand on hers, "well, it was okay. Sometimes less okay. I, uh, managed a third date once before Mother caught on and locked me away."

"Third date, huh?" he asked, something knowing in his voice.

She nodded but didn't meet his eyes.

"And then what?"

"When my mother found out, that's when I was recruited to my first position at the IBCC compound. I went from the IBCC headquarters where she lived to the small compound where you found me. Nearly a three-hour flight away."

"That's," he paused, choosing his words carefully, "brutal."

"Well, what about you? Minthe. Amalthia. Who else?" she shot back.

"Amalthia and I were never together," he said firmly.

"But she wants that."

"She does, but certainly not on terms I'm willing to accept."

"So, who else?"

"A few ladies here and there," he said.

"How many?" Persephone pushed.

"A gentleman never kisses and tells."

Persephone gave a little grunt of annoyance.

"Is it really so important to know? I'm not a blushing virgin, but I'm not some cad either, if that's what you really want to know. I choose my partners based on common interests and my feelings toward them. I am deliberate, if nothing else."

"It is. But I also want to know how many women I need to be

wary around. How many might be happy to see me six feet under?"

"You are already more than six feet underground, Persephone," he said mildly but with a wicked glint in his eyes.

Persephone swatted him playfully. "You know what I mean."

"I do and you will be safe with me."

"I know. Well, I think I know. Time will tell."

"Indeed, time will tell."

They sat in quiet contemplation for a few peaceful moments.

"You really do need more air-purifying plants, Hades," Persephone finally blurted out.

Hades gave a surprised chuckle. "And you really do keep your mind on work, don't you?"

"You've tasked me with improving the Underground's botanicals, which includes more than food crops," she shot back. "But yes, I do tend to hyperfocus."

"Well then, Dr. Kore, how do you propose creating a crop of air-purifying plants and where would you put them?"

"Follow me," she rose and stalked toward the far end of the field. "Various studies promoted that certain plants could 'purify' the air. It's a slight misnomer that led to other studies that debunked the claim in open environments. But," she said, looking over her shoulder to make sure Hades was following her, "the original studies were conducted in a closed system."

"Like the Underground," Hades murmured.

"Exactly like the Underground, just smaller. Additionally, studies have shown that the presence of plants helps lower blood pressure and improve cognitive function." She stopped as the crops turned into row upon row of *nephrolepis exaltata* and *monstera deliciosa*.

"It's impressive to see the switch from Persephone to Dr. Kore," Hades mused.

"Oh?"

"You speak differently when you're describing the plants."

"Oh."

Hades chuckled and took her hand, caressing his thumb along the backs of her knuckles. "Tell me more, doctor."

Persephone's mouth twitched into a little smile. "How many large pots or tubs do you have that could be made available?"

"On hand? Relatively few, but they can be manufactured with ease."

Persephone nodded. "And would you have the manpower to care for the plants? Watering weekly and adding nutrients when needed?"

"I could make accommodations."

"Then I just need space to begin growing more of these," she pointed at the low ferns. "They can be potted and moved to public areas once they mature."

Hades tugged her hand lightly, drawing her gaze. "You know you don't have to wait. You could start now," he said quietly.

"Hades, I don't have that kind of control yet. What if I hurt myself again?"

"You've been working with me for days and your control is already much more refined."

"I know, but," she squeezed his hand nervously, "what if?"

Hades pulled her to him, pressing her body against his. "Concentrate," he said, voice low.

Persephone closed her eyes, savoring the solid warmth of his body against her. She took a deep breath and let it out, noticing that curious static tickle on the back of her neck.

"Feel the life in the plants, encourage it, feel it grow," he commanded, one hand stroking her back.

"How do you know how it feels?" she asked.

"Because that is the opposite of what I experience," he said simply.

Persephone's eyes flew open as understanding struck: This was what it was for him to take a life.

"Concentrate, Persephone."

She closed her eyes once more, focusing on the plants, trying to ignore the warmth his touch ignited in her. Understanding flooded through her, their life humming in her mind, nature's heart beating against hers. Somewhere in the soil at her feet, roots stretched in a lively network of growth. Stems and leaves reached like living fingers toward the grow lights above them. She leaned into Hades and the heartbeat of life grew louder. The sensation expanded and threatened to slip from her control. She held Hades by the hips to steady herself as she exerted control over her own power.

Finally, Persephone released the living power in her grasp and opened her eyes. Hades was looking down at her with an excited smile on his face.

"Look," he encouraged.

Persephone stepped back from him and turned to the plants. She gasped.

Row upon row of plants were now doubled in size. Lush, thick leaves and robust stems marked every plant in a fifty-foot radius. The closer they were to her, the more mature the plant.

"I did this?"

"Yes."

Persephone turned back to Hades excitedly. "I did it! I kept control!" She leapt into his arms. Without a thought, she stood on her tiptoes and kissed him.

Hades pulled her in close, deepening the kiss. His arms wrapped around her waist, pressing himself against her in a way that made her belly clench. Persephone moaned against him.

Hades kept one hand steady on her back as the other trailed down her thigh. Persephone gasped, breaking the kiss when his hand found the hem of her skirt. Her pulse hammered in her ears, a soft *whoosh whoosh whoosh* echoing the heartbeat of her plants and covering all other sounds. She shook her head to clear it.

"No?" he asked softly, face inches from hers, but his hands froze.

Persephone opened her mouth to answer but was robbed of words. She leaned against him, head on his chest. "Not now. Not here. Not yet."

"As you wish, my Blessed," he said, but held her in his arms.

Internally, Persephone kicked herself. She wanted him desperately but couldn't understand why she hesitated.

She stepped back. "I'm sorry."

"There's nothing to be sorry about," he said calmly.

"I don't want to lead you on. I want to," she hesitated, "you know." She made a vague hand gesture. "But I just ..."

Hades regarded her for a long moment before gently asking, "Persephone, what happened on that third date?"

She bit her lip. A deep red blush spread across her cheeks all the way down to blotchy red spots on her neck and chest. Persephone dropped his gaze and stared at the soil underneath their feet. "Nothing," she mumbled.

"Ah," he said simply and exhaled. "I understand."

"Can you take me back to my lab now?" she asked, still not meeting his eyes.

Hades gently raised her chin until she looked at him. "It's nothing to be ashamed of. And yes, I would be delighted to escort you back to your lab."

It was his calm, gentle answer that reassured her the most. Even the arm he held out to walk her back was no match for the steadiness she felt in his respectful response. She didn't even notice the dark stares of the people they passed.

Chapter 20
Day 45

Several weeks later, Persephone was startled by a piercing siren that screeched through her lab. She covered her ears and walked to the hallways where the rising and falling tone echoed down the drywall covered walls. Leuce, one of Hades' personal guards who had escorted her back from the hospital wing, stood beside her door with her face pinched as she clearly fought to keep from putting her hands over her ears as well.

"What is that?" Persephone asked.

"The all-clear siren, ma'am," Leuce shouted between wails.

"All clear of what, Leuce?"

"I'd guess the war above is over."

The sound died as fast as it started and immediately Leuce's radio crackled to life. Persephone listened for only a moment before her mouth twisted into a frown.

"Let me shut down my equipment," she said with a quiet sigh. "I can already hear him calling for me."

Persephone looked down at her dress as she strode back into the lab. For some reason, Hades couldn't seem to find her normal pants and shirts. Either he had some kind of "thing" for women in dresses, or he simply hadn't thought to request pants for her. She would admit that the dress was pretty, a spring green made of soft stretchy cotton that wasn't much more than a fitted t-shirt attached to a knee-length skirt. It was easy to work in as long as she didn't have to kneel in the experimental fields to examine root structures and sprouting plants. Currently, the front hem and her knees were lightly dusted in soil and she had no doubts that if Amalthia was in the control room, she'd endure the woman's haughty looks again.

Persephone shut down the equipment that wasn't actively running diagnostics before trudging to her utility sink to scrub her hands, knees, and hem.

"Ma'am? He's asking where you are," Leuce called from the

doorway.

Persephone frowned. "Leuce, he can have me there fast, or he can have me there presentable. Which does he want?" she snapped.

The woman leaned into her radio, blonde bob shielding her face, but clearly relaying the question.

"I'm sorry, Leuce, that was harsh and I didn't really mean for you to ask," Persephone called. She was still adjusting to people who rushed to fulfill anything that even hinted at a request.

"He says he would prefer you to finish cleaning up, but leaves the decision to you, ma'am," Leuce said with quiet dignity.

Persephone sighed but continued scrubbing a brush under her nails. Over the weeks since their conversation in the fields, Hades had taken to heart her comments about being trapped and having her choices taken away. At every reasonable opportunity, he had allowed her to make her own choices: meals, when she worked, or even how she spent her time in the evenings. The last one had been easy; she had requested a tablet and access to the Underground's vast digital library. She had spent nearly every night curled up on Hades' couch reading until she fell asleep, tablet on her chest.

For as much as she had the illusion of choice, it was still an illusion. As with right now, she could stop to clean up or hurry to the command suite, but either way, she was expected to be by Hades' side, probably as nothing more than some prop he called his "Blessed." Frustration drove her hands to her knees, scrubbing furiously. She knew she needed to confront him, but even now, she knew that a confrontation in the command suite, in front of his retinue, was exactly what he would want to avoid. Besides, if she was going to build her own reputation down here, it was beneath her dignity to fight with him in public.

Persephone swallowed down her frustration and wiped her hands. At least the decades of bowing to her mother's will gave her some useful skills here beyond plants.

"Let's go, I'm ready," she told Leuce.

Five steps into the command suite and Persephone realized she was not, in fact, ready. The bank of screens that had been predominantly static during her first visit now contained a steady stream of photos and what was possibly a live video stream.

Death.
Destruction.
Loss.

Each screen echoed the devastation the war had wrought on the world above. In less than a week, the Sons of Zeus and Forces of Poseidon had brought utter ruin. Bombed-out buildings surrounded by rubble. Open fields, their crops flattened, bisected by a road filled with destroyed vehicles, and ringed with demolished tents. Persephone recognized it was a refugee camp, now empty of people. A street in what must once have been a thriving city, dotted with charred corpses, some so small that Persephone had to turn away, wishing Hades had never been able to secure her glasses.

Anguish lanced her heart. A small sob escaped her and she covered her face, unwilling to let anyone see her break down.

"Welcome, my Blessed," Hades' deep voice cut in.

Persephone took a deep breath and lowered her hands. "Hades," she responded and bowed her head slightly. She caught Thanatos' quick grimace, but she wasn't calling him "my Lord." He'd have to take a nod as the best he would get right now.

"The damage is severe," he said, eyes fixed on the screens over her shoulder, "but it has been a full day since we last saw movement from either aggressor."

Persephone closed her eyes for a moment, then looked up at him. His face was calm, neutral, but something in his eyes said he was roiling under the surface. She gave him another nod and turned around.

"Good girl," he whispered so quietly she almost missed it.

The words made something go through her. Something hot and sensual she didn't want to examine right now. She steeled herself and looked at the screens again.

"It's terrible," he said, loud enough that his assembled leaders could hear, "but there is hope. We've been tracking transmissions and emissions since hostilities ceased."

He pointed to a bank of monitors displaying an array of squiggles across a green and black screen. Beside them, another displayed colorful linear spikes across a dark band.

"Those, the green, are comm signals," he said. He put one hand on her shoulder and pointed with the other. "We've been able to intercept and interpret them. They're civilians. Normal people. Not the Sons of Zeus or Forces of Poseidon."

Persephone gasped. "There's life in all of that?" she asked, gesturing to the live cameras.

"Yes."

She exhaled. Where there was life, there was hope.

"The technicians are still working to pinpoint where the survivors are grouping together, if they are, but people survived. And it would appear that our two aggressors have obliterated one another."

"Good." She spat the word out and felt Hades' hand tighten on her shoulder. She turned her head to see his face and was rewarded with a half-smile. One corner of his lips curled up as if amused, but the look in his eyes was feral.

He was glad she rooted for their demise.

"My Blessed, you surprise me."

"When the plant is rotten at the stem and root, you tear it out," she said quietly. "You don't let blight spread."

The hand on her shoulder turned her gently. He held her gaze as he then ran that hand gently down her arm, eyes still blazing and feral. Hades lifted her hand to his lips and placed a gentle kiss on her knuckles. "I believe we are one mind. Later, we can discuss this further."

He turned away and for the first time, Persephone realized how crowded the space was. Her shock at the destruction and then intense focus on Hades made her miss a crowd that was clearly assembled to hear word on the end of the war. She blushed when she realized that she had delayed them not only to clean up, but also when she stole Hades' attention now.

"Preliminary reports are in," Hades started without preamble. "The war is over and there is no evidence of apocalyptic residues."

A pleased murmur echoed through the crowd and Persephone got a chance to see who was among those with enough rank or precedence to be invited. She had already seen Thanatos when he grimaced at her refusal to call Hades "my Lord." Behind him, a small handful of men and women, dressed in the dark uniform of the Underground's security, stood quietly. Persephone even thought she might have spotted one of the golden bident badges that indicated

Hades' personal guard, perhaps the head of the guard.

To Thanatos' left, Persephone saw Eris, still dressed in dark robes, but she had her hood down now, revealing a beautiful but sharp featured face and glossy black hair that nearly faded into her robes. Behind her were three robed men. Given their proximity to Eris, Persephone assumed they were the Judges she encountered on her first day: Minos, Rhadamanthus, and Aeacus. They wore expressions ranging from pinched annoyance to open curiosity.

On Thanatos' right was Amalthia; the dark blue of her skirted suit sculpting her into a portrait of effortless grace. From every line of her lithe frame to her neatly tied chignon, her look spoke of refinement and restraint, beauty honed to precision. Even the tilt of her matching blue kitten heels suggested composure born not of warmth, but of control. Behind her was a small knot of people in various styles of clothing. Persephone spotted two baggy jumpsuits bearing an unadorned embroidered black disk who looked like they belonged to a mechanic or maintenance personnel. Another stood in a white coat bearing the embroidered gray flower Persephone had seen in the IBCC cafeteria. One man was dressed in a suit with a sheaf of wheat embroidered in golden thread. Persephone realized each symbol denoted where they lived in the Underground hierarchy. Amalthia in her dark blue suit, had no symbol, and was currently smirking as she looked at Persephone's dirt-stained hem.

Hades continued speaking and Persephone stepped up to stand beside him as Amalthia's smirk vanished. She enjoyed annoying Amalthia more than she wanted to admit, but she was comforted by Hades' presence. Like the Henry she knew, he was strong, solid, and stalwart in the face of an apocalypse.

"While our remaining sensors show no apocalyptic residue, other sensors have been destroyed. We don't yet know if they would yield different results in other areas of the world."

A quiet murmur rippled through the crowd as they absorbed that information. Persephone spread her fingers wide, letting her pinky touch Hades' hand for reassurance. Without changing his posture, he intertwined his pinky with hers. Persephone held in a sigh and smile, keeping her face resolute; the only emotion she thought Hades would want at a time like this.

"I know it will take time for any residue, if it exists, to

spread from where our sensors are destroyed to the places we can still receive communications. I propose we remain locked down for the next three months, awaiting a change in sensor data. After that, I believe it will be safe enough to send a team above to repair the sensors, if possible, and report their observations."

The assembled crowd was silent and still.

"We know we have enough materials and supplies to last over five years in the Underground," Hades continued. "Review your logistics. Check on your personnel," he said, looking at Amalthia. "Ready any weapons you feel would be useful above," he said to Thanatos. "And keep the population in line," he told his Judges.

"We will receive updates weekly. Until then, this is our mission. This is why we prepared."

Chapter 21
Day 80

The mood of the Underground shifted after Hades' pronouncement. The anxious waiting was gone, replaced with a sense of resolve. The worst had happened. The war that had been the focus of their entire existence had come and gone, rolling over them with little direct impact on the Underground. Now her denizens were ready to settle down and wait.

Every resident but one.

Persephone grew more agitated by the day. It was subtle at first, barely a whisper across her mind. She found herself glancing up at the false sky more often as she checked on her crops. Hades had granted her an unused section of the farmlands to propagate her ferns and after only a few days, the young bulbils, encouraged by Persephone's touch, were lush and ready for repotting. Persephone felt a sense of accomplishment for creating something of value to the Underground, but it was diminished by the whisper of discomfort in her mind.

Each day, she rose when Hades emerged from his room, broke her fast with him, then allowed him to escort her to her lab. She worked in the lab or walked the fields, always watched by one or two of Hades' personal guards. While the guards' presence gave her a strange sense of home, they also added one more grain of sand to irritate her. Each day as she walked among her plants, she found herself looking up at the fake sky searching for the sun, a cloud, a sunset, a bird, anything that would break up the homogenous overhead glow.

At the end of each day, Hades, ever a gentleman, would collect her and walk her back to his rooms. His physical presence felt like peace. Something, maybe the bond she had unwittingly made when she accepted being his "Blessed," made him a balm to her growing irritation and discomfort. It gave her a break in the whispering irritation that followed her, but even that wasn't enough to stop her from seeing the faces of people they passed. Some were friendly now, mostly from people bearing the embroidered golden wheat of Elysium. She supposed they had the best accommodations and the least reason to hate her, which was welcome relief. Many were a blank neutrality of someone in a hurry to get from point A to point B, usually showing the gray flower of Asphodel but a few with the embroidered black disk of Tartarus. The rest were outright hostile and usually bearing Tartarus' symbol. The last were those who clearly resented her last-minute addition to the Underground while they languished in the depths of the Underground. Even being Hades' "Blessed" wasn't enough to quell their anger.

Almost every night, they enjoyed a quiet dinner, often punctuated by wine and conversation, before Hades retired to his room to allow Persephone peace and solitude in his living room. And yet, in that peace, she found a different kind of discomfort. She couldn't forget the moment in the field, when she'd controlled the surge of power flowing through her and Hades had kissed her. She had enjoyed it. It awoke something in her she didn't know she was starving to feel. She wanted something from him that she couldn't put her fingers on. A sensation, not unlike the static tingle she experienced when they were together; it was a feeling of being on the cusp of something that never came. When and if it did, she knew some level of tension in her would snap, allowing her to sink into something deep and sensual.

Every night he gave her one lingering look as he closed his door. It wasn't an invitation, per se, but it was a gentle reminder. He was there. He was her husband by the rules of the Underground. Their bond was incomplete and if what created the incomplete bond was an indication, completing the bond would be a pleasure unlike she'd ever experienced before.

And yet, she couldn't take the next step. She was trapped. She was bound. Something in her said she hadn't found the strength that let her feel like an equal. Anything short of that was … tainted.

Whatever thought, feeling, or effort it took to move from Hades' last lingering look to walking through that door eluded her.

With each day, her agitation grew, and the looks of her detractors grew darker.

"What would you be doing each evening if I weren't here?"

she asked him the night after she started transferring her ferns to pots that would be placed throughout common spaces.

Hades blinked in surprise. "Meeting with Thanatos or Amalthia, I suppose. Working, certainly."

"Am I keeping you from things you need to be doing?"

"Yes, but in a good way," he said with a smile. "I need the break. I'd work myself to the bone if I didn't have another purpose."

"Oh." She took a small sip of wine to give her a moment to consider his answer.

"It's more than that," he continued, "I feel more relaxed around you. I go to sleep calmer, less keyed up. When I wake, my mind and plan for the day are clear. It's like the bond—"

"Makes us complement one another," she finished for him. "It makes us better together."

Hades set his fork down and rose, stalking to her seat. He drew it back and offered his hand, gently pulling her to her feet. His hands skimmed down her shoulders and settled on her hips, possessive and sure, guiding her body until it fit perfectly against his.

"It's like the bond emphasizes what's already there," he whispered in her ear. His breath tickled the soft skin of her neck.

Persephone gasped. "Henry." She jerked back. "I'm sorry, I—"

"I think that only proves my point. There was something there before and it's still here now. Maybe it feeds the bond, or maybe it's the foundation of the bond. But what lies between us predates your arrival here."

Persephone stepped back but held his gaze. "I'm not ready, Hades."

"I know and I won't push." His grin turned feral. "But when you're ready," he said and closed the gap between them, "know that I will be too." He leaned in to kiss her but shifted at the last moment to place a gentle kiss on her forehead.

The rest of their dinner was finished in a silent tension.

The look he gave her as he closed his door that night was lingering and meaningful. Persephone took a long time to fall asleep.

Chapter 22
Day 81

Persephone woke from a restless sleep, her heart already pounding. The dream that had been so clear moments before evaporated in the dark of Hades' living room. But she knew. It was the same dream, even if she couldn't remember all the details. She caught her lip in her teeth, biting lightly as she searched her memory. She had dreamt of a meadow above, soaked in sunlight with butterflies dancing among the grass and wildflowers. She had walked along a thin trail, letting her hand brush the plants as she passed. When she turned to look back, she could see they'd grown and Hades followed her trail, the people of the Underground in his wake as they plucked fruit and flowers grown from her touch. Hades had caught up to her and kissed her passionately. The world above faded each time she dreamt of him until it was just them entwined in a passionate embrace.

What she remembered fully was how he made her feel. The tension that drew across her, taut and pulling at her until it snapped in glorious ecstasy every night. And every morning, she woke with her body remembering what her mind would not. Today was no different and she could feel the dampness pooling between her legs. She rubbed her thighs together under the sheets, squeezing them as she remembered the phantom touches that ghosted up them in the night.

She didn't remember how the dream started; there was no applying logic to a dream, but she remembered shaking as the last tremor left her body. She reached for him, this dark-haired, pale god of a man. His touch was as familiar as breathing, but it eluded her. In her dream, she pulled him in, kissing the taste of her orgasm off his lips. The feel of him controlling her was exquisite, sending shivers down her spine even now. It was give and take. They had shared their ecstasy. Neither greedy, only demanding in a way that brought both greater pleasure.

Persephone sighed in frustration.

"Persephone?"

She bolted upright and turned to see him in his doorway. Concern was etched into his face. She could see his furrowed brow and slight frown even in the dim light of the living room. She realized that once again, he wore only a pair of loose pajama pants that threatened to slip down his hips at any moment. Her eyes took in his trim waist with muscle pressing against his pale skin. His chest was a broad expanse of marble, only lightly sprinkled with hair. Her eyes reached his face and she saw that same lingering, meaningful look he'd given her as he closed his door. He didn't seem upset at her own lingering look. He seemed to invite it.

Persephone gave up on critical, clinical thought. She didn't want to catalog the series of physical features that drew her to him.

She wanted to act. She wanted to give in to her emotional side. The side that had seen his more human and personable side. The part that enjoyed him as Henry and was attracted to the man before her.

She walked to him slowly, watching him as he watched her. Her fingers gently traced the line of his collarbone and down to his ribs. Her hand continued its trail until she stopped at his hip bone, a feather-light touch on the soft skin, making a line toward his belly. His skin was as soft as silk over iron. She stood with her face inches from his chest, his sandalwood, charged ozone, and burnt cinnamon scent invading her nostrils.

"Hades?" Her question was more of an invitation.

He exploded into motion. His arms wrapped around her, pulling her to his chest and his lips crashed into hers. The kiss was rough with need, commanding, and unrestrained, the sound of pleasure rumbling low in his throat.

Persephone gasped and pulled back. She searched his face, looking for the traces of Henry she knew lurked in there. His face split into a grin and something in his eyes softened, almost boyish.

"Yes, I'm him. He's me. The Henry you befriended is here," he took her head and placed it on his chest, over his heart.

A sense of relief washed over her and she kissed him again, lightly. The touch of their lips was electric, the strange static that accompanied their semi-formed bond spanned at the edges, as if encouraging her to continue. She deepened the kiss, leaning into him. His hands ran down her back and gripped her ass. He pulled her closer and she could feel him pressing hard into her stomach. She let impulse drive her and trailed her hands over his thick shoulders and down his sides. She reveled in the feel of his smooth skin before letting her hands dip into his pajama pants. She grasped him, the same silk over iron sensation as his chest.

"Persephone!"

His cry woke her from the dream and she sat up, panting.

"Fuck," she sighed and flopped back against the couch, wondering if she would ever sleep peacefully here.

After a long night of tossing, turning, and digging a little rut into Hades' couch, Persephone woke tired. The itch of agitation drug fingernails across her brain. When she sat up, her nightgown had ridden up her thighs and the blankets had tangled between them.

"That might explain my dreams," Persephone muttered as she untangled herself.

"What dreams?" Hades' deep voice was thick with sleep, as if he had missed precious slumber as well.

"Nothing," Persephone said hurriedly, in no way prepared to tell him he was the focus of a dream that had her tossing on his couch and untangling damp sheets from her thighs.

"Curious. I had the most vivid dreams last night," he said slowly as he crossed to his kitchen.

"Vivid?" Persephone asked, almost scared to hear the answer and already blushing.

"Yes. Prescient, I think," he mused.

"Have you dreamed in prophecy before, Hades?" Persephone rose and crossed to the kitchen when she smelled his coffee starting to brew.

"Yes, two before this. If this is a prophecy, then it makes the third."

He slid a cup of coffee to her, already prepared with cream and sugar. She gave him a half nod of appreciation as she brought it to her lips. When she set the cup down again, she stared into the curling steam as she considered asking about the prophetic dreams. She knew that some claimed to be able to see the future, but most were hacks and the few that might be telling the truth refused to say what they experienced in their dreams.

"Your face is so expressive," Hades told her. "I can almost read your thoughts as I watch your face. The internal debate. The consideration." He tilted his head slightly as he regarded her. "I appreciate you not outright demanding to know."

"It seems like a personal question," she told him. Knowing what her dreams had devolved into last night, it was a *very* personal question.

"I can't be sure if either of my previous prescience was real or imagined because none have come to life in any way I could pinpoint." He set his mug down. "Would you like to know what I dreamed?"

"If you're willing to share, I'm very interested in listening." Persephone settled onto a stool behind the counter that divided the kitchen and dining area.

"The first was years ago," he said and leaned his elbows onto the countertop, black coffee steaming beside him. "A great storm broke over the shore, lightning striking rocks and trees on the shoreline as the surf pounded both. A hurricane, I suppose." He sipped his coffee and met her eyes. "But when it died, the world was silent. Lightning flashed in the distance and the waves lapped at the shoreline, but the world was quiet and somehow calmer. I could see myself walking the line between land and sea, dressed in shadow, and with every step I could hear the tolling of a bell. A woman walked in the grass beside me. Not behind me, like a concubine or consort, but beside me like a queen in her own right. Where I walked the line between the sea and land, she appeared to walk a line between grass and the char left by the lightning, crowned in blossoms and ash."

"That's ... deep," Persephone finally said. "What do you think it means?"

Hades stood upright again and gave a little shrug. "When I first considered the dream, I thought it meant I would triumph over the Forces of Poseidon and Sons of Zeus but how was never clear. Now, considering the queen who walks beside me, I don't think it was the walk of a conqueror; I think it was the walk of inevitability. We will be what holds the world together after the war subsides, as it's doing now."

"Why did you change your interpretation? I mean, other than

the war has ended. That part must be clear now."

"I had another dream after that. I had already started preparing for the coming war when I had the dream. This facility was going to be a bunker, bristling with weapons and ready to conquer, until I had the second dream."

"You and Thanatos against the world?"

"Perhaps," he said. He took a longer sip and grimaced.

"May I ask about the second dream?"

"Are you sure you want to know?"

"Oh, you can't leave me hanging now!" She set her cup down.

"Even if it's about you?"

"Well, I, I mean …" she stuttered to a halt. "Yes?"

"I dreamt the personifications of the Fates stood before me. Weaving. I inquired about their work, but they stayed silent. The tapestry was a beautiful scene depicting a forest in all four seasons. Trees, birds, a brook bisecting summer and winter, and the flowers done in vibrant silk. Clotho plucked a thread woven into a beam of sunlight, then bound it with black silk. Lachesis pulled the thread tight between her hands and I feared she would cut the threads, but instead she seemed to measure it. The more she pulled, the longer the threads became before she turned to Atropos, holding her blade. Again, I feared the threads would be cut, but she set aside the knife, not severing the thread but knotting it. Golden and obsidian silk, tied gently and clearly stronger together. She then wound the threads into a loop and placed them gently in my hand."

"Threads? You think that was about me?" Persephone's brow furrowed with skepticism.

"The Fates spin threads into the tapestry of life," he told her.

"Yes, I know that," she said with a huff and sipped her coffee.

"They weave them together or they sever them when a life comes to its end. They only pull a thread from the weave of life if that person is destined for something. I knew from my first dream that I would have a queen beside me, but not who or how I would find her. The second dream seemed to clarify that she was picked by Fate and bound to me. From the tapestry's scene, I knew she would be from above, tied to land and growth, a ray of sunlight at dawn that could span seasons."

Persephone arched one eyebrow as she stared over her coffee cup at him. "And that's me?"

"Now that we are half-bound? Yes, I believe so."

"I'm only here because you brought me here. That's not fate, that's manipulation."

"I had the first dream over 200 years ago."

Persephone, who had been mid-sip, spat her coffee out in surprise. "Two *hundred*?"

"Yes." He wiped the coffee with a damp cloth as she wiped her mouth with the back of her hand. "You may ask Thanatos when you see him next. He has been my second for nearly 100 years, although I have known him longer. We are special, Persephone."

"But you're two *hundred* years old?" she asked in shock.

"More than 200. I was in my sixth or seventh decade when I had that dream."

Persephone shook her head. "Thanatos? Amalthia?" She grimaced at the name.

"Thanatos is nearly my age and Amalthia is in her eleventh decade if I recall correctly. There are a few others. Here and above. I've know the Commander of the Forces of Poseidon for as long as I have known Thanatos, he is touched by the Fates as well. I've heard rumors that there are a few in the Sons of Zeus, but nothing confirmed."

Persephone shook her head. "Immortal?"

Hades' coffee paused at his lips. "We can be killed, Persephone. But it takes a lot." His look darkened. "It would take a full-scale war in some cases."

Persephone nodded and sipped her coffee. "What about the second dream? With the Fates? Was that over 100 years ago as well?"

"No. Twenty-five years ago, on the spring equinox."

Persephone stared at him as the implication of his words rolled over her. She was twenty-five. She was born on the spring equinox twenty-five years ago. The exact date the Fates told him he would be bound to a woman of sunlight and growth.

"The day I was born, the Fates told you we would be bound for life? And my thread, stretching like that?"

"You will live a long life. As will I."

"If I weren't sitting down, I'd need to."

"It's a lot to absorb."

Persephone blew out a long, coffee-scented breath. "Wait, what did you dream of last night? I know my dreams weren't prophecy!"

Hades gave her a searching look before he spoke. "I saw bare feet, walking along dark soil and stone, trailing blood. Plants bloomed from the blood as the feet stopped at three skulls. Thorny vines exploded up through the skulls and in a moment, our bond flared to life, full and complete."

"What does that even mean?"

"Well, I believe the bond part was, uh, rather simple to interpret," he said without meeting her eyes.

Persephone blushed deeply. He may have dreamt that the bond was completed, but she dreamt of how they completed it. Or started to before her brain cut her off. Something hot and dark shot through her, making her lower belly clench.

"The rest I'm afraid I don't understand. I assume from how the dream ended that the feet are yours, but I don't understand the skulls." He shook his head. "I won't burden you with the rest of the dream."

"There's more?"

"Hmm. Yes, but it was more," he paused, "personal."

Persephone closed her eyes and held the cup in front of her face. Her dreams were about as personal as it got.

She blew out one more breath. "So, I'm fated to be bound to you, I'll live a long life, and I'm going to be leaving a trail of blood as I walk to a pile of skulls. What a cheerful way to start my day, Hades."

"In my defense, you did ask to hear my prophesies."

Persephone gave an unqueenly grunt. "Fine. But this is still a hell of a way to start my day."

Chapter 23
Day 81

Persephone watched the faces of those they passed as Hades escorted her to her lab. His personal guards trailed behind them, but that didn't stop a few harsh looks thrown their way. She hoped to start turning those around today. Her ferns had matured enough to repot. Today she would transfer as many as possible and start placing them around the Underground's common spaces.

"Are you sure you don't wish for assistance?" Hades asked for the second time on their walk.

"Yes," she told him and her hand tightened on his arm as a particularly nasty look was thrown her way. She pressed on. "It's more personal if I do it. Since the problem I seem to be facing is my place and value in the Underground, I should do it myself."

"My guards won't be burdened. They must have their hands and minds ready at all times."

"I know. I'm doing it myself. They're welcome to keep following me around, but I won't ask for their help."

"I'm glad they're welcome since I insisted they keep an eye out for you," he said, voice sour.

"You're extra grumpy today."

"I'm contemplating my dreams."

"Maybe it's just a dream," she said. Even as the words left her mouth, she knew she didn't believe them. "You waited 200 years for one to come to fruition and twenty-five for another. What are the chances that last night's dream comes true today?"

He looked down at her and the words hung between them like an icicle waiting to fall, sharp and cold.

"I will not be taking chances with my Blessed," he said simply.

Persephone gave him a small nod of acknowledgement. The itch of growing irritation and the curious static around the two of them pulsed across her mind.

"My Lord?" Leuce, her favorite of his guards, interrupted quietly.

"Yes?"

"Thanatos needs you urgently. Something has come up," Leuce's words were quick and clipped and the look in her eyes said it was something big.

"I leave you here, my Blessed. Be safe today," Hades said formally and kissed the back of her knuckles.

"I'll see you this evening," she said by way of goodbye. Her mind had already jumped to the tasks ahead and she was mentally cataloging the supplies she would need to accomplish the day's work.

Hours later, she had soil up to her elbows and dusting across the potting apron she had thought to throw over her dress. Like all the dresses Hades had acquired for her, this was another knee-length dress that was soft, comfortable, and its structure gave an aura of elegance. The green potting apron, all that stood between the frock and stains, complemented the golden yellow dress, a fact that struck Persephone's sense of the absurd.

She was a scientist, but in her heart, she was a farmer. She lived her life in the soil of her beloved plants and carried a bit of them wherever she went, like a mother carries her newborn. To continue that professional tradition in decidedly untraditional garments made her want to laugh.

Seventeen black plastic pots sat in a neat row on her workbench. It was a slightly mismatched gaggle, but they worked for her purposes. Hades had been correct that they had few on hand but had requested more from Amalthia's logistics team. Amalthia, knowing exactly who they were intended for, provided the pots as directed, but they were varying sizes and mismatched designs. The man who delivered them, baring the black embroidered disk of Tartarus on his sleeve, merely shrugged when Persephone asked if he was sure they were for her.

She supposed if he lived in Tartarus, he didn't have much motivation to care about spats and fights among the leadership.

Despite the odd collection of pots, each had a lush fern nestled neatly inside it. Dark potting soil was scattered across the metal table, occasionally combined with splatters of water. Her lab was a mess, but each pot was neatly wiped clean and ready to be placed in common spaces.

Persephone wheeled a long, flat utility cart beside the bench and began transferring the pots to it. A line of dirt smudged her forehead where she had wiped a soil-dusty arm across her sweaty brow.

"I should be ready to start placing these in about ten minutes," she told Leuce. The tall woman was thick with muscle and almost no fat. Exactly the kind of guard Hades would entrust with Persephone's life.

"Yes, my Lady."

Before Persephone could react to being addressed as "my Lady," Leuce turned to speak into her radio. Thanatos had mockingly called her "my Queen" and Persephone had heard people address Hades as "my Lord," but this was the first time anyone had addressed her by a title that mirrored his.

"Any updates from Hades? He sure departed in a hurry."

Leuce gave her a quick look and appeared to weigh something in her mind.

"Yes, my Lady. Earlier, we had a report that one of the hydroponics systems was malfunctioning."

"Oh no, that's really bad, Leuce."

"It's worse, my Lady. They've updated me and it appears to be sabotage."

Persephone gasped and Leuce nodded slowly.

"How many tanks?" she whispered.

"The first estimate is roughly seven percent of our available tanks, but the saboteurs appear to have demolished one of the nutrient vats as well. Overall, they're estimating a thirteen percent loss of hydroponic capacity."

Persephone let her mind calculate through the Underground's various methods of growing food. The hydroponics were a small but not insignificant portion. The attack could be devastating if anything else failed or there was another attack.

"How much attrition did they plan for when they built the Underground?"

"I'm not sure, my Lady. A lot, I assume, but I couldn't tell you numbers. Amalthia would know." Leuce reached for her radio.

"No. No, it's fine. I'll ask Hades later."

Leuce's mouth twitched into a brief smile before she mastered her expression.

"I saw that, Leuce," Persephone said with a laugh.

"You don't like her, do you?"

"Not one bit. She goes out of her way to make me feel small and unworthy." Persephone gestured to the pots.

"She's an idiot."

Persephone gave a harsh bark of laughter and turned to Leuce with her eyebrows raised. "If she thinks she can sink her claws into Hades now that I'm his Blessed, she really is, isn't she?"

They both fell into a fit of giggles that took a moment to overcome.

"Ready?" Persephone asked when she finally calmed down.

"Yes, my Lady. I've alerted the other guards to expect us."

Persephone pushed the cart, awkwardly maneuvering it around her lab tables and equipment to the exterior door. Leuce held the door as she passed through. "Thank you."

"No, my Lady, thank you." For the first time, the woman grinned.

"Ready for some cleaner air?"

Leuce sighed. "You have no idea."

"Tell me about it? What do you hope to get from my plants?"

"You said these would help the air quality?"

"Yes, in an enclosed system, a sufficient number of them should help draw pollutants and irritants from the air. Like natural air scrubbers."

"That would be wonderful," Leuce sighed. "Ever since we locked down, the air feels—I don't know—stale?"

"Recycled," Persephone offered.

"Yes. It's clean, but there's something that lingers. It's especially bad in the living spaces where the recycled air wars with the smell of humanity."

Persephone gave a light laugh as she maneuvered the unwieldy cart around a corner. "Yes, humans certainly have a strong smell when we're grouped together."

She finally stopped the cart and surveyed the open area before her. It was clearly intended as a common space with concrete tables and benches arranged in groupings to encourage community.

But it was currently empty. The area carried the hint of acrid tang, a smell that seemed to cling to everything.

"I'll start here and monitor it daily. If we smell an improvement, then it's working. If we see people using it, then we know it's a success."

"Yes, my Lady," Leuce said as her eyes scanned the area for threats.

Persephone hauled pots off the cart, arranging them on every available flat space. She made mental notes of where the closest water sources were and tried to group them close to each other. She would need to speak with an engineer about adding hoses. That made her realize she would have to go through Amalthia to reach the engineers and she frowned.

"My Lady, are you well?"

"Yes, Leuce, sorry. I'm just tired. This was a lot of work." She gestured to the seventeen new ferns dotting the common space. "And I have one last thing to do."

Persephone sat down on the nearest bench and closed her eyes. She inhaled the stale air and let her senses seek out each plant. They throbbed with life among the inanimate tables and benches. She focused, letting their throb of life match her own pulse. When the two synced, she pushed, gently, sending more life into them.

Leuce's gasp told her she'd been successful. She opened her eyes, and she was greeted with the sight of each fern now cascading out of its pot. The air smelled cleaner, too, the ferns having used both her life force and the pollutants to grow.

Leuce smiled down at her and held out a hand. Persephone grasped it and rose slowly, more tired than she wanted to admit.

"Well done, my Lady." She inhaled deeply. "It smells like ... home," she said with a smile.

Persephone inhaled, letting the smell invade her senses. Soil, compost, and greenery overlaid the flat smell of recycled air. Persephone smiled at Leuce. "It's a start."

Persephone brushed her hands on her apron and a light dusting of soil drifted to the cold stone floor. She felt a pang of guilt that she was leaving her plants in such a sterile, sunless space. When she looked up, she could see people starting to drift in. Drawn by the scent of living plants or just cleaner air, they arrived slowly in singles and pairs.

A soft murmur rose as more people gathered to see what had changed their common spaces. Persephone stood straight and strong with Leuce a pace behind her, watching as people's expressions changed from hostile to neutral and neutral to happy. She gave a small wave to the few folks who smiled at her.

The ferns were doing their job. It might just be a start to setting her place in the Underground.

"Now," she told Leuce, "let me get this cart back and go rest. I'll move the next round tomorrow."

Persephone pushed the flat cart back to her lab with Leuce trailing behind her. Perhaps it was a hopeful imagination at work, but she saw fewer people frowning at her as she trundled through the hallways. Her heart rose until she turned the last corner and was confronted by a man whose frown deepened at the sight of her. She gave him a quick nod and turned into her lab, accepting that not everyone might know what she was doing right away.

Leuce's startled shout was the only warning she got before she was thrown forward onto a lab bench. Her face smashed into the steel table. She took the impact at the bottom of her ribcage and her breath was knocked out of her in a rush. Persephone gasped, her lungs struggling to pull air back in.

Hands grasped her shoulders and roughly spun her around, throwing her back into the table again. As the hard steel lab bench dug into her back, she could see the face of her attacker: the angry man she had passed as she turned into the lab. Over his shoulder, Leuce was struggling against two large men who had her pinned to the wall, a knife at her neck.

Persephone could feel blood starting to drip down her face from the impact as she gave a choking gasp, trying to fill her empty lungs so she could shout for help. A wash of static came over her as the man shoved the flat of his forearm against her throat. She kicked at him wildly but only succeeded in flinging off her slip-on gardening shoes.

Hades' incomplete bond had saved her from a concussion, but it wasn't enough to push the man off her. Her vision began to blur and her fingers clawed at his forearm. The lab around her grayed at the edges as her body struggled for air.

Her lungs burned.

Graying vision grew dimmer as the man's breath, hot with fury, blew across her face, an affront to her starved lungs.

Behind him, Leuce had overcome the two men, but Persephone could see blood soaking the right side of her neck, making her black uniform glisten. Leuce staggered toward her and Persephone realized it would be too late. Her vision went black and her limbs began to grow slack.

Static flashed through her again and this time the stone beneath her answered.

A deep, almost guttural groan rumbled through her lab as the stone floor of her lab ripped apart. From a long crack that started at the door to the farms and terminated under Leuce's feet, thorny vines shot upward. Vines that were thick, brown and sharp shot upward with vicious intent. Thorns like daggers pierced the air, puncturing their attackers. Arms, thighs, calves, and shoulders impaled. The angry man screamed and pulled back slightly.

Persephone pulled in one glorious, lifesaving breath, and her vision returned. She looked down to see a green static scintillating between her fingers.

Persephone locked eyes with the man, dropped her chin with a slight smile, and *pulled*.

The vines obeyed.

The man was ripped back from her, living tendrils wrapped around his limbs. Barbed and unrelenting, they ensnared him and blood bloomed like petals on his skin.

"You take space, time, resources, and attention that don't belong to you," he shouted as the barbed vines crept up him. "You poison Lord Hades' mind."

Persephone flicked her hand and the vines slammed him into the stone floor. Behind where he stood, Persephone could see Leuce speaking into her radio, one hand holding back the flow of blood from her neck. To her shock, Persephone could see a faint white glow, sparkling with blue, emanating from Leuce.

"You're a whore," he spat as if he didn't feel the vines. "Whore of Hades."

Persephone's focus snapped back to him. The restraint she'd held in check ever since she nearly killed herself on the pomegranates broke. Eyes blazing with fury and power, she raised her scintillating hands. The vines holding the man writhed before impaling him with more thorns. Behind Leuce, the men she had fought screamed as vines impaled them, too.

"Why do small men always resort to calling women whores?"

"My Lady?" Leuce choked out.

"They reduce us down to what's between our legs as if my mind and power are trifling things."

Persephone stalked forward. The weariness that had washed over her as they walked back evaporated in her fury. She strode into the hallway, one hand curled as if holding an invisible rope and the vines responded, dragging the impaled men behind her.

"My Lady," Leuce gasped out, "no. Please. Lord Hades is on his way. We can't let people see you like this."

Persephone whirled to her guard and pinned her with a stare as hard as winter frost. "No. They should see. They have to see. They have to know. I am worthy. I am not a burden. And I will not tolerate this." She jabbed a glowing finger at the men and they howled in pain as the thorns pulsed inside them.

Leuce nodded her understanding but pointed to the glass beside them.

Persephone could see herself in the reflection. Or some version of herself. She was streaked with blood and glowed with a sparkling green aura. Her hair danced on an invisible wind behind her and her eyes blazed with green fire.

"Good. Let them see who I really am."

Persephone walked, her powers dragging the vine encased attackers behind her. They left a trail of blood as she stalked to the common area.

Chapter 24
Day 81

Persephone's fury cooled only slightly as she dragged the men toward the common area. They had wailed and spat curses with impotent rage until she wrapped vines across their mouths. They didn't deserve to assault her ears with their bullshit.

"She's moving to common area 12," Leuce whispered into her radio.

"Hades?" Persephone asked. The tiled hallway was cold against her bare feet and a counterpoint to the boiling rage inside her.

"Thanatos, my Lady. But he's with Hades."

Persephone nodded and continued dragging the bloodied men toward her objective.

The common area they had just left was nearly flooded with people. Word of the ferns had spread fast and people had come in droves to see a little bit of lush green life in their stone fortress. They had not anticipated seeing their Lord's woman dragging three bound and bloodied men into the space. People got one look at Persephone, face streaked with blood and still blazing with green light, and they stepped back to let her pass.

She stopped in the center of the room and released the delicate line of shimmering green that tethered her to the vines. She surveyed the crowd and her ferns. The denizens of the Underground had clearly been both enraptured with and respectful of the lush life growing in their midst. Not one fern had been touched, only admired. She smiled.

Persephone stood tall and straight, the bloodied lump that embodied every accusation levied against her writhing behind her.

"There are those among you who believe I am a waste. That I rob you of resources. That I have no claim to what I am given. You believed me weak because I am nothing more than Blessed of Hades." Her voice was steady, fierce, and rose over the crowd like a cold spring after a brutal winter.

Across the crowd, she saw Thanatos and Hades rush in. Somewhere the back of her mind was cataloging their appearance: Thanatos pulsed with a dark aura while Hades radiated a furious red. She caught Hades' eye, his gaze filled with cold fury, and nodded. The fierce smile he gave her in return made her heart skip a beat and another type of heat blaze through her.

"Look around you. I am no thief or waste awaiting a handout. I build, grow, and sow the soil to feed this community."

Hades reached her, but with one look at her, stayed quiet, becoming a silent and towering presence before her.

"Let it be known: I sow, but I also reap," she gestured to the bloody mass behind her. "I am no one's possession," she didn't dare to look at Hades. "If you see me among soil, roots, and delicate flowers, do not think I am gentle. Because like your Lord, I am power. I am life. And life fights to grow. Vines can tear open stone and a seed can split a mountain given time. I am the bloom and the thorn. I am Persephone."

The room held its breath as she finally turned to Hades. They locked eyes for a single moment and in that moment, she saw fear, pride, and a blazing, feral anger that she had been attacked.

"I felt your shield flare." His hand came up slowly to cup her cheek.

She leaned into his touch as he rubbed his thumb across the blood that was smeared across her lips.

"Who hurt you?" His question was quiet, but it carried across the silent, entranced crowd.

Persephone stepped aside to reveal the men, now still and staring at their Lord, eyes round with horror.

"You did well, Dr. Persephone Kore."

Persephone smiled. He had heard her.

"But this cannot stand. I will not allow people to think they can attack our preeminent bioengineer without consequences. Well," he looked at them, "without more consequences."

Hades stepped closer to the tangled men. "Did you touch her? Did you fucking touch my Blessed?"

The only answer they could give were whimpers of fear. They knew what was coming for them. The entire room knew.

Persephone met his gaze again. She recalled how gently he had released Thomas from his pain and how he described executing a traitor.

"Do your worst," she said, still holding his gaze, "my Lord." She moved to stand beside him but caught his dark smile.

The three men died screaming.

When it was done, Hades gave Thanatos a quick nod as he put an arm around her.

"We need to get you cleaned up," he said quietly.

"What about …"

"Leuce? The men? Thanatos will take care of both. I will personally thank Leuce once I've taken care of you."

"Good." She was too tired to help now.

The arm around her gently drew her along. She allowed him to guide her back to his rooms, her bare feet on autopilot and the energy that had filled her slowly ebbing out.

"You did well, Persephone."

"Thank you, my Lord."

He gave a small laugh. "I appreciate that you called me by my title among the crowd, especially in that moment, but when we're alone, let's be Persephone and Hades, okay?"

She gave a sleepy, "Mmm hmm," and leaned her head against his chest.

Hades opened the door to his rooms, nodding to the two guards at the door. "No one in or out without my expressed permission. And no disruptions until I come out. Thanatos is in charge until I am done."

"Yes, my Lord."

He ushered her through the door and gently steered her past his living space and bedroom to his massive bathroom.

"You're covered in blood, Persephone. I need to get you cleaned up before you can sleep." He sat her on the edge of his massive tub and she slumped against the wall. "I don't think you're able to get yourself cleaned up right now. May I assist you?"

"You're always so formal," she told him, head still leaning against the wall. "Just take my clothes off already."

Hades chuckled. "Oh, how I long to hear you say that. But in my dreams, it's under very different circumstances." He started running hot water into the tub.

"Mine too," she said quietly.

Hades' hand paused where they were untying her gardening apron. "You dream of me?" His voice was thick and hushed, like a whispered prayer to an untamed goddess.

"Almost every night," she said with a sigh. "You dream of prophecies and I dream of us." She wobbled to her feet and turned. "Can you unzip the back? I feel like the blood is making it stick to my legs."

Hades pulled the apron gently over her head before his hands went to the zipper. Persephone shivered as the zipper opened, exposing her back to the cool air of his rooms. She felt her skin tighten into goosebumps.

Hades ran a warm hand down her naked back. "Hold on, the tub is almost filled."

Persephone could feel his body heat as he stepped closer. His warm hands slipped the dress off her shoulders and let it drop from her waist. His fingers traced her back, stopping just above her waist.

"You're bruised here," he said quietly.

"Probably on my ribs too," she said and turned around to face him, uncaring that she stood before him in just a thin pair of panties. She looked down to see purple splotches forming over her ribs. "Does it look bad?"

Hades swallowed. After a beat, he dragged his eyes up to meet hers. "The bruising is minor, I'm sure you'll be better after some sleep."

"Good," she said. Without a word or hesitation, she took off her panties too. "Can you help me in?"

Hades took the hand she held up and settled her gently in the warm water.

Persephone sank up to her ears. Still silent, Hades wet a washcloth and started dabbing at the blood on her face. She winced as he reached the place where the force of the impact on the table split her forehead.

"Shh, it's okay. It looks like you're healing already, but I need to clean the area." His hands were gentle as they completed their task and she shivered from their touch despite the warmth of the water. "Do you think you can wash yourself?"

Persephone shook her head vaguely. The warm water and Hades' presence were calming and she felt the last of the adrenaline that had pushed her forward slowly draining from her. She looked up at him. His face, normally neutral or stern, was etched with concern. The diffuse light overhead didn't hide deep furrows that appeared between his eyes and somehow, the fears of a man more than 200 years old blazed in his eyes. She realized that if he truly was more than 200 years old, he had seen more than his fair share of friends, lovers, and enemies die of old age as he remained in perpetual robustness.

"I'll live, Hades," she murmured.

"I know," he assured her. His hands caught hers and gently washed the blood and dirt from them.

"You're worried I won't." It was a statement, not a question.

The concern on his face deepened and he caught her eyes, his hands pausing. "Yes," he whispered.

Persephone let him work in the comfortable silence between them. His hands were gentle, soothing the dirt and blood from her with practiced ease. As they caressed over her breasts, she looked up at him, curious. His face was still concerned. She arched into his hands, letting the washcloth pass over her breasts again. The rough cloth sent sensation through her nipples and Hades pulled back slightly.

"Stay still, please," he said quietly.

Persephone settled back against the rim of the tub and let him continue, reveling in the feeling of his hands over her body, something in her aching for more. He worked over her chest and shoulders, tipping her forward slightly to wash her back. Persephone had a feeling of anticipation as he moved lower. He laid one hand gently on her knee to steady her and gently washed one leg, then the other. When he finished, she met his eyes.

"Do you want to wash yourself?" he asked quietly.

"No."

Their curious static connection crackled with tension.

Hades' hands moved between her legs, but they moved with efficiency, not lust. She arched into him again.

"No, Persephone. I'm not doing this." His words were quiet but firm.

She looked up at him from where her head rested on the rim of the tub, hurt. He spoke so passionately about taking her, making her howl in pleasure, and now ... rejected her?

"But, why?" Even in her own ears, she sounded small and quiet.

Hades set down the washcloth and took her wet hands in his, engulfing them. He looked deep into her eyes. "You're mentally compromised. You've had an extreme shock and you're exhausted. When I take you," his warm, wet hands squeezed gently, "and I want to desperately, I want you to be an enthusiastic and willing participant. I want to know that you are awake and in full possession of your faculties so that I can create a first time that stays with you forever."

Persephone's mouth dropped open and something hot and feral roared to life inside her.

"Does that sound good?"

"Yes," she said thickly, almost too overcome to speak.

"Good." His smile was the dark, feral smile she'd seen when he'd pinned her to his door. "Now, let's get you out of here before you prune."

He released one hand to allow her to rise and helped her from the tub. His strong hands were gentle once again as he toweled her dry. Persephone gave him a shy smile as the towel passed over her breasts and he rewarded her with a quick kiss.

"Later," he promised.

Persephone blushed as her mind ran wild with possibilities.

Hades led her to his bed. "You're almost falling down, you're so tired. Stay here, it'll be a better night's sleep than the couch."

She nodded once before crawling into his bed.

"Do you want a nightgown?" She heard him ask, but she was already drifting into sleep.

Chapter 25
Day 82

Consciousness washed over Persephone slowly, like dawn slowly creeping over the horizon. Somewhere in the twilight between wakefulness and sleep, Persephone dreamt of the sun rising over dew-soaked meadows. Golden light caressed every wildflower, the blossoms turning their heads toward Persephone and the sun, as if to greet her. Half a sob caught in her throat from the raw pain and longing at missing the sun, the real sun, not the Underground's manufactured perfection. Beyond the meadow, she could see the destruction that had been displayed on the command suite's screens stretching out to the verdant growth of a reborn world.

Riding that twilight, Persephone walked slowly toward the horizon, her fingers trailing over the field of flowers. As she grew closer, she realized it was not all death and destruction. In the gaps between the rubble, life stubbornly bloomed despite the war. Flowers, saplings, grasses, and incongruously corn, wheat, and fruit trees all bloomed under her touch. The breeze was warm, humid, and sweet. It stirred her hair and whispered her name like fate given life.

She sighed in her semi-sleep, only barely aware that her fingers were twitching against Hades' skin, as if she reached toward that distant warmth. He didn't wake, but his arms tightened as if afraid the dawn might steal her away. Shadow and light coiled together as they held each other in her semi-sleep—death's finality and life's soft yearning. In the hush of that silent moment, Persephone dreamt of spring, even as the King of the Underground held her close, anchoring her to the dark.

The swirl of light and darkness brought her mind fully awake. She reached out, her hand seeking the reassurance of Hades' warmth. Persephone's fingers brushed across his chest and the delicious feeling of silk over iron. Heat and desire settled in her core. The slow, simmering tension that made her ache was pulled taut and she wondered if her control would finally break.

She checked to be sure Hades was still asleep before she let her hand drift over the fine dusting of hair on his chest, taking one stolen moment in hopes of settling that ache.

"Good morning," Hades' voice rumbled across the pillow. His voice was deep, unhurried, and sounded like distant thunder over her sun-kissed meadow.

Persephone gasped, yanking her hand back only for him to catch it and pull it to his mouth, kissing the back of her knuckles.

"You can touch me, Persephone. I welcome it," he murmured. He placed her hand back on his chest. "How do you feel? You slept soundly."

Persephone wanted to shrink back in embarrassment. "I feel okay," she said quietly, betraying the heat she felt.

"Only okay?" Hades ran a feather-light thumb just under the cut on her forehead. "This seems to be healing well."

"Yes. I mean, it doesn't hurt."

He let his hand drift down her face to cup her cheek. The look in his eyes was deeper than the Underground and far warmer.

Persephone felt her pulse stutter at his touch. The ache in her core swelled and she didn't know how he couldn't feel the heat radiating from her.

"I was terrified when I heard Leuce's call. She was barely able to get out that you were being attacked and she was fighting off two men. Then I heard her scream and she cut out." The muscles in his jaw rippled and he closed his eyes as he shook his head. When he opened them again, they were rimmed with tears. "I can't lose you, Persephone. You are so much more than we all think, more than I ever dreamed, and more than I deserve."

Persephone frowned. *He was now the most powerful man on the planet and he didn't think he deserved her?*

"You were right last night. You are powerful in your own right. You are more than my Blessed." His voice was rough and raw. "Your power extends beyond what you can manifest, Persephone. You hold my heart in your hands."

Persephone's breath caught in her throat and her hands flexed on his chest involuntarily as though pulled by some invisible thread.

"It's the real reason I couldn't leave you above. I knew I needed Dr. Persephone Kore, but once I met you, I knew I needed you, Persephone, in my life. One week in your presence and I knew I never wanted to leave your side. I knew you were the golden cord of life the Fates intertwined with mine."

Persephone met his eyes and saw a mixture of hope, fear, joy, and love. Unmistakably, love. Her chest ached with a fierce delight. When she met those eyes—vulnerable and filled with love—it undid her.

The tension that had held her suspended in the Underground snapped.

Thoughts fled her mind and she surged forward, closing the distance between them, her lips crashing into his. His surprised grunt turned into a deep growl and he leaned into the kiss. His hands began to trace her body, memorizing every curve, and her skin tingled under his touch.

Fire.

Electricity.

The sensation flooded her core and she leaned into him.

His hands reached her hip and brushed to the apex of her legs. Persephone froze—not in fear, but in sudden awareness. She was completely naked, having never put clothes back on after the bath. She should feel embarrassed, shy, or nervous, but his touch was warm, reverent, and utterly natural. When his hands brushed against her she could tell how wet she was, and his touch was as natural as breathing.

"Is this alright?" His voice was low, rough with restraint.

"Yes," she breathed. "Please, Hades." Her hands closed on his shoulders and she kissed him.

The sensation of his finger sinking into her was delicious and filling. His finger curled against her as his palm rubbed against her clit. The ache in her belly blazed with sensation.

"Please, Hades," she begged and he slid another finger into her. Persephone gasped and arched into him.

"Do you want more?" he asked, brushing kisses along her jaw and down her neck.

Goosebumps rose on her arms as he kissed the sensitive skin. "Yes!"

He eased her gently to her back and trailed a molten line of kisses down her chest and belly until he was nipping at her hip. Hades looked up at her, a wicked grin on his face, before he replaced his palm with his mouth.

Persephone cried out in surprise and pleasure. She wound her fingers in his hair and his tongue worked against her. It danced across her slit in tandem with the fingers inside her. Her orgasm built quickly, the feelings she had suppressed for too long bursting to the surface until she was gasping in ecstasy. She let her head fall back and her moans echoed across Hades' dim bedroom.

Hades raised his head and kissed a line of fire up her trembling thigh. When he caught her eyes, his wicked grin promised more. "Good?"

"Oh, yes," she panted.

"Do you want more?"

"Yes."

"Are you sure?"

"I am more sure about this than anything in my life, Hades."

He crawled up her body, every inch of his skin gliding across hers until he was poised between her thighs. Persephone's breath caught when she saw him, hard and ready. Desire flared again, sharp and hot, and she pushed herself up to kiss him.

Persephone gasped, pulling back from the kiss as he pushed into her slowly, and she was awash with intense but thrilling stretching. She looked up at him, seeing concern softening his face. Foregoing words, she pushed her hips up into him, feeling him sink deeper. Hades gave one swift thrust until he was fully inside her.

"Is this okay? Does it hurt?" he whispered like a reverent prayer.

"No," she said slowly, but her voice trembled. "It ... It's different. I feel full. But it's good. So good."

He drew his hips back and sank into her once again. Persephone reveled in the feeling of him filling her. She bit her lip, ready for the next thrust.

Looking deep into her eyes, Hades thrust in again, and again with careful, patient strokes. His movements were steady but unyielding and Persephone could feel the pressure building inside her again. Under his careful onslaught, she found herself rocking her hips to meet him as she gasped his name. The orgasm struck hard and she shattered beneath him.

Hades wasn't done wringing pleasure from her body, though. He withdrew and his mouth claimed her center once again, devouring her like a man starved of love.

"You taste better than ambrosia," he growled against her, "but after your orgasm? Fucking divine. I want to do this every day and taste your ecstasy."

Persephone threw her head back and moaned as his mouth brought her to another quick release.

Hades crawled up her body once more and positioned himself against her again. He eased into her with long, slow, languid strokes.

"Faster, please, Hades. Faster," she begged.

"No," he murmured. "Slow. Trust me, Seph."

Persephone tilted her hips, trying to push him onward. In response, he caught her behind one knee, hitching it up and holding her hips still.

"Slow, Persephone. Trust me."

He kept up his slow strokes until Persephone could feel the ache in her core building to an unbearable level. Hades' pace pushed her to the absolute brink until she cried out, clutching him like a lifeline. With one last deep thrust, Hades followed her into pleasure, calling out her name with a deep groan, shuddering against her.

Persephone came down from her release slowly and as she did, a new awareness opened in her mind. She felt her heartbeat slowing against a counter beat—Hades', she assumed. He lay on his back, panting, and she shuffled closer to put her head on his chest. Under the firm muscle, she could hear his heartbeat, the same that pulsed faintly in her own mind. She sucked in a breath and let it out slowly.

"Do you feel that too?" she asked quietly. She kept her head on his chest, reveling in the feel of him under her cheek.

"Yes. I feel everything. Your heartbeat, the air that fills your lungs, and the pulse of magic that fills you."

Persephone propped herself up to look at him. What she saw made her smile.

"Hades, look at me," she said gently.

His eyes opened and met hers. Sudden realization hit him and he sat upright. Hades caught her cheek, cupping it in his hand

and he ran his thumb over her lip again. His smile radiated from him, literally. The red aura that was now faintly glowing around him pulsed green slightly as Persephone looked at him.

"The aura," he said, "it's—"

"It's changed," she said quickly. "Your red is flecked with green."

"And yours is green, dark like pine, but speckled with red, like mine." His smile deepened as he ran his hand down her arm. "How do you feel?"

"Sore. A little bit sore but also so alive. Like life itself is running through my veins."

"It's the bond," Hades said quietly. He put an arm around her and flopped back onto his bed, pulling her with him.

Persephone snuggled into his chest and pressed her body against him. The static she once felt near him had eased into the gentle pulse of his heartbeat.

"You are semi-immortal now. Like me. Like Thanatos. Like Amalthia." He paused when she tensed. "Don't worry, Seph, this bond is unbreakable. No matter what Amalthia might try, she'll only end up looking like a fool."

Persephone thought about his statement for a moment, considering its implications.

"We may be semi-immortal, but your people are not." Persephone put her hand flat on his chest, feeling his heartbeat in her soul as well as under her hand. "They need to go above again."

"They will. Once it's safe."

"You can't afford to wait that long, Hades." She rolled to her side and pushed up to look him in the eyes. "I know about the hydroponics."

Hades looked away from her. "We have reserves."

"Some reserves. Even," she ground out the name, "Amalthia would agree that this sets you back and you are on a very, very narrow margin of error. One more attack—"

"There won't be another! I have it under control. Besides," he said slowly, like he was pulling himself back together, "it's not safe up there."

"I think it is," she told him.

"We don't have enough evidence of that yet. The sensors—"

"Don't reach everywhere. And the ones that are active show the area is habitable. And," she paused, hoping he would believe what she said, "I dreamt that it was safe."

Silence filled his bedchamber.

"I dreamt I was walking above, the plants grew at my touch. You and your people followed me as I grew the plants above. And then," she propped herself up on one elbow to look down at him, "we made love."

Hades' face was unreadable. "You think your dream was prophecy?"

"I think we can go up sooner than you planned. I think we can start sending parties up now to check. The sooner we can return above, the higher the chances are that we survive."

"I will admit it could be a possibility," he said slowly.

"If you pair it to your dream, the queen who walked beside you, it makes sense." She said and gave a little shrug.

Hades nodded and a rumbling growl echoed across the room. "That's what this is about."

"What?"

"You want to go above."

"Yes? I mean, who would be better?"

"Almost anyone in the Underground!" He exploded. Hades bolted upright and Persephone wiggled back, clutching the sheet to her bare chest.

"Do you happen to have another world-renowned biochemist that I haven't met?"

"No."

"Trained scientists who can take soil and plant samples to analyze in the field?"

"No," he growled.

Persephone looked at him coldly. "Then why wouldn't you send me?"

The muscles in Hades' cheek rippled as he clenched his jaw. "I shouldn't have to say it."

"And I shouldn't have to argue with you over this. Hades, I have no real place here. My existence is only as an accessory to you. No matter what I have done for the Underground, I am 'Blessed of Hades,' not Dr. Persephone Kore. I don't even have my own rooms,

Hades. I sleep on your couch in your open living room."

"You could sleep in my bed, you're here now."

She pinned him with a stare. "You know what I mean, Hades."

Hades' anger broke, his face crumbling into sadness and he looked lost. "I know you don't love it here, but I had hoped you would find fulfillment here. That there would be things to anchor you here."

Persephone put her hand on his chest, seeing the faint glow of green around her hand where it pressed against his chest.

"I do. But I miss sunrises, sunsets. I miss the sound and smell of rain on wet fields. I even miss the sound of birds chirping too loudly before I want to wake up. And you know I need to do this. I need freedom, Hades. Real freedom, not just the illusion. We may be lovers now, but if we remain like this, I will always question if you're my captor or liberator."

Hades hung his head. "I know. I don't like it. I'm terrified for your safety, but I know."

Persephone let her hand rise to his chin and tilted his head up so he met her eyes. "I'm semi-immortal now, remember?"

He gave her a weak smile and pulled her hand to his cheek. "I know. But I will be scared every day you are gone. You are my other half, Persephone Kore, and I cannot bear the thought of losing you."

Persephone leaned forward to press her forehead against him. "I know."

"And I know how much you value your freedom. I know that tying you here will ultimately destroy you and that I have to let you go."

Persephone's breath hitched in her throat. "Yes. I can't grow in your shadow, Hades. I need a place in my own sunlight. To flourish. To grow."

"Promise me when it's time, you'll come home to me."

"I promise, Hades."

Act 3
Ascension

Chapter 26
Day 103

Persephone scooped cool rainwater onto her face and dipped a cloth to tie around her neck. The pool was shallow, broad, and almost perfectly round. Like many areas they had scouted in the world above, the craters left from the bombings had become small pools where rainwater collected.

In the two months since the Underground's sensors indicated the war had ended, the world had started to heal. New shoots of grass, pale green and barely half a hand tall, unfurled from the dirt and ash at the edges of the crater. Trembling in a slight breeze, the bright green shoots were a contrast to the land around them, a whisper of life defying the still grieving world.

Persephone gently stroked her hand across the shoots, tender as a mother soothing her newborn, and they flourished in response. She smiled and rose.

The small team that Hades had chosen for the expedition was breaking camp for the day and Persephone caught a few people surreptitiously watching her. Her lips twisted into a smirk. She knew they wanted to see her at work, so she obliged.

She approached a charred tree with blackened limbs reaching heavenward. Noting the thin blades of grass poking up around its base, she knew the soil would be able to sustain it after she left. Persephone placed a hand on the trunk and felt for the pulse of life that would indicate the tree was salvageable. Life hummed beneath the black ash of charred bark. Once Persephone found life, it echoed and fairly thrummed in her soul. She reached out with her power and cradled the life in her spirit, willing it to flourish inside the tree as she fed it a tiny drop of the power that welled within her.

Ash fluttered down like black snow and she raised her face to see the effect of her work. The tree's limbs stretched toward the smoke-blurred sun and new leaves unfurled as the limbs shed ash to reveal new, healthy bark. She released the tree's life and let her power recede. With a satisfied sigh, she turned to see the entire team watching her.

"Okay, the show's over folks. We need to press on to the next location," she told them.

The team returned to breaking down their camp and setting their vehicles up to trek to the next unresponsive transmitter. Persephone marveled at their ability to move forward with anything. She supposed it was a lingering effect of being in an enclosed society, one that had to find a way through every problem thrown at it. She also marveled at the fact that they had been able to cobble the expedition together in the first place.

***

Three weeks prior

The Underground's comm suite was unusually quiet as Hades escorted her to their meeting. She observed the suite's screens, now dimmed or off except for a few showing the smallest bit of communication still happening on the surface. It was as if the entire comm suite held its breath to see if what lay above was truly alive. Hades' hand was firm and tense against her lower back as he steered her to the small, enclosed conference room at the top, adjacent to his imposing chair.

The room was filled with a massive dark wood table, which spoke to its purpose as a planning room. Thanatos was already seated to the right of Hades' chair at the head of the table. His black armor was faintly scuffed but she could still see his dark aura on it. Behind him stood Leuce, a neat bandage on her neck, and a man Persephone didn't know.

Thanatos rose and quickly nodded to Hades as they entered. He then gave a start and looked between Hades and Persephone before a sly smile spread across his face. To Persephone's great relief, he didn't comment on the auras.

Hades settled her into the chair to his left before seating himself. Persephone gave Thanatos a small smile of welcome and worked hard to keep from bursting into giggles at his expression. He was clearly pained holding back what would undoubtedly be a rapid fire of intense and personal questions.

Amalthia breezed in last, bathed in a light green aura, and the expression on her face made it clear she was late deliberately, wanting to make a grand entrance for Hades. She was neatly dressed and groomed again in her prim and prissy white suit while trailed by four others. Her heels clicked a staccato rhythm as she stalked the length of the table, eyes and smile focused on Hades.

Her cool smile remained in place until the change in his aura registered. Her focus whipped to Persephone and her high heels stuttered to a stop.

"Amalthia," Hades' voice was sharp as a whip crack and Amalthia plastered a brittle smile on her face again. He looked at her entourage and his frown deepened.

"You seem to be a bit behind, Mal," Thanatos drawled.

"I hate that nickname, Thanatos," she snapped. Her anger and frustration at seeing Persephone's aura complete were clearly being taken out on Thanatos. She returned her focus to Hades. "You're out of your mind."

"Amalthia," Hades growled.

"You want to send the Underground's greatest agricultural catalyst into a war zone," she said smoothly.

"Wow. 'Agricultural catalyst' sure is an interesting way to articulate 'multiple PhD holder and world-renowned bioengineer,' Amalthia," Persephone responded coolly before Hades could speak.

Amalthia's mouth dropped open, giving her the appearance of a surprised trout.

"And in case you missed what happened yesterday," Persephone continued, pushing power into her aura until it sparked and crackled with life, "I am fully capable of defending myself and others."

The ghost of thorny vines coalesced in her aura and Persephone stared Amalthia down as thin tendrils wove toward her. Amalthia shrunk back from the vines and shot a pleading look at Hades.

"My Blessed, I think that's enough demonstration," Hades said, laying a gentle hand on her wrist. "Sit, Amalthia."

Persephone released the power with a wintry smile at Amalthia, who thumped down hard into the chair two spots away from Thanatos.

"As I said, we need an expedition above to confirm the active sensors' findings and seek data on the inactive sensors." He gave a small sigh. "We also need to find additional farmland suitable to cover the capacity we lost when the hydroponics were sabotaged. And as my Blessed points out, she is the most suitable lead for that expedition. We need her to go."

Hades' hand clenched on her wrist slightly. Persephone turned her hand over to take his, running a thumb along the back.

"She needs to stay alive," Amalthia snapped. "You of all people should understand how precarious our situation is. One broken filtration system, one unexplained decline in our yields, or one incident of rotting food, people die and you could lose control. And she wants to go skipping off to the surface like some curious child looking for sensors and dirt? She is the only thing that can cover a gap in our yields. Unacceptable, Hades."

Hades gave her a bland look punctuated only by a slightly raised eyebrow. "I'm sorry, Amalthia. I didn't realize you were leading the Underground now."

Amalthia blanched and started stuttering apologies.

"Stop. Just stop," he commanded. "I am more aware of how precarious our situation is than you will ever be. And do not ever contradict me outside of private meetings again, or you will find yourself above, without a team."

Amalthia gave him one quick, chastened nod.

"The best way to mitigate risk is to minimize the size of the team," Hades went on. He turned to Thanatos. "What's the lightest footprint we can have above?"

"I recommend at least two of my best for security."

"I believe I have that covered," Persephone said bluntly.

"When you're awake, certainly. But you have to sleep eventually." He gave her a knowing smile and Persephone blushed. "I recommend Leuce, as you two already work well together. Eudoros has volunteered," he said, gesturing to the man beside Leuce, who also bore the golden bident of Hades' personal guard.

Persephone nodded. "Will you have enough loyal security here if I take two of Hades' personal guards?"

"Of course," Thanatos told her with a smirk. "He has more than enough volunteers for his guard; we'll be covered."

"Very good, Thanatos. Amalthia? We need vehicles and a signals expert who can analyze or repair damaged sensors."

Amalthia's face was pinched, but her voice was smooth as silk when she responded. "For an expedition of this duration, you need at least one signals expert and one technician. For vehicles," she looked down at her papers, "two experts. They'll be covering navigation, driving, and any repairs you require while traveling."

Hades cleared his throat and gave a hum of annoyance. Persephone looked at the three women and one man standing behind Amalthia's chair. A petite blonde, her pale hair swept into a neat bun, gave Hades a demure smile. Like Amalthia, she had a light green aura around her and Persephone realized Amalthia wasn't done taking shots at her.

"If you intend to include Minthe as part of the team, then I'll provide you an opportunity to rethink your assumptions," Hades told her in a calm voice, untouched by the anger she could feel almost pulsing from him.

Persephone caught the flicker of tension at the corner of Hades' eyes, the only indication of his rising fury. Persephone gave him a quick nod and sat up as straight to assume a more commanding posture.

"Take her off the team," Persephone commanded.

"She's the most skilled communications specialist I have," Amalthia snapped back.

"My Lady," Persephone said with the deadly quiet that precedes a storm. "I am Blessed of Hades after all, in more than name now."

Amalthia made a scoffing noise.

With a flick of her wrist, thorny vines ensnared Amalthia. Thanatos pushed back from the table as Amalthia gave an undignified squawk of surprise.

Persephone turned to the blonde cowering behind Amalthia's chair. "Minthe, I trust you are wise enough to understand why I wouldn't be comfortable with my husband's former flame accompanying me in the unknown wilds?"

"Yes, my Lady," she said quickly.

"Lovely. Who is the next most capable signal technician?"

"Melinoë," she said, gesturing to the woman beside her. "After that, Nephele."

"Good. Tell Nephele to start packing her kit." She looked at Hades. "We have a team, but we need supplies."

Persephone regarded Amalthia coldly. She was squirming against the vines, her lips working to get them off her mouth.

"I suppose the supply list is on your little clipboard?" Persephone wouldn't admit how much she enjoyed watching Amalthia struggle after the stunts she had pulled. "If I unbind your mouth, will you act like a professional and Hades' head of Logistics, or will you continue to behave like a petulant child?"

A flash of anger crossed Amalthia's face before she could suppress it.

"I can leave you like this and have Melinoë read from your sheet instead."

"Persephone, enough," Hades' voice was quiet but held a hint of warning.

Persephone flicked her hand again and the vines disappeared. Small red spots where the vines had punctured her skin dotted Amalthia's white suit.

Amalthia pressed her lips together in a thin line as she brushed at her sleeves.

"My Lady," she said with forced calm, "I have already built the supply list and the kits are ready. Additionally, I have two armored vehicles prepped with air quality sensors, fallout sensors, and brush guards. They are ready to depart within thirty minutes of your notification. They're specifically modified to run on solar power, as I did not anticipate you finding working and serviceable fueling stations above."

"Very well thought out, Amalthia, thank you," Persephone acknowledged. She looked at Hades.

"Good. Persephone, you will be the highest-ranking member of the team. I hereby grant you the authority and autonomy to lead the team and act on my behalf in all things," he said. A flare of sadness pulsed across the bond. "You leave at dawn."

Chapter 27
Day 158

Persephone bumped along in the passenger seat of the lead vehicle as they navigated to the next malfunctioning transmitter. It was a slow and arduous process to get to each location. Maps and charts that would have taken them on a direct route were only minimally useful. At any community larger than a town, the roads were littered with the bones of wrecked vehicles. Fire and bomb blasts had twisted many of them into surreal shapes that couldn't be moved from the roadway. The team had also seen evidence that some inhabitants of each community had survived the initial attacks: doors half off their hinges but barricaded, open and uncharred cans littering spaces that appeared bombed out, and most telling, the occasional message or hand drawn map on walls that remained upright.

After the last town sported a message warning off travelers, written in blood, they had agreed to avoid anywhere that humans might group together.

Each day they rose, tore down their camp, made space for Leuce or Eudoros to sleep in the back of one of their vehicles, and resumed their trek. Their knobby-wheeled crawler was laden not only with the team, but a high-tech suite of sensors and receivers. The onboard equipment took continuous air samples and sought evidence of radiation, vital to entering areas with no working sensors providing them with air quality reports. At each stop, Persephone took soil samples and meticulously cataloged any plants that showed signs of life. If a larger plant looked like it might help jumpstart the local ecosystem, Persephone would spare some of her energy to bolster the plant. Leuce, Eudoros, Melinoë, Charon, and Stygia had all seen her powers the day Hades had authorized their departure. Nephele, Minthe's replacement, had jumped back in surprise the first time she witnessed Persephone reviving a plant.

"It's okay, Neph," she had said with a grin. "I'm trying to use my powers for good. Don't let this lot tell you I've ever bound up anyone with thorny vines."

Charon had given a bark of laughter, his brown eyes glittering with mirth. "She has, but only her enemies."

"She's not my enemy," Persephone had said with a smirk. "Not anymore."

"Can you do anything else?" Nephele had asked in amazement.

"You've seen me encouraging the plants along. I can feel life, I guess?" Persephone's voice held the skepticism she felt. "I can feel life in the plants, but only if I concentrate."

"You couldn't feel living people approaching?" Eudoros asked.

Persephone shook her head. "No, I don't think so."

"Charon, Thanatos. Come in."

The group jumped as the radios of both vehicles blasted out Thanatos's voice. Persephone was aware that Charon was providing reports of their finding every few days, but this was the first time anyone in the Underground had initiated contact.

Persephone felt a pang of sadness. It was like Hades had dismissed her from his heart when she had insisted they leave.

Charon tapped his ear, keying his implanted receiver. "Thanatos, go for Charon."

The group watched Charon's face change.

"How bad?" Charon asked quietly.

Not quietly enough, every head whipped to look at him.

Persephone's eyes narrowed and the corners of her mouth tightened as she observed him. Charon was taking the call in his receiver, possibly trying to keep it discreet, but his pinched face and clenched jaw spoke the words he was intercepting.

"Put it on the speakers, Charon. We might as well all hear it," she ordered.

He tapped his ear twice and nodded. "Say that again, Thanatos. We're on vox."

"We lost an additional four percent of the hydroponics which had been fouled, bringing the total to eleven percent of the available units. We've caught the saboteurs now, but," there was a pause, "not before they did irreparable damage."

"How does that impact the current food stores?" Persephone

asked.

There was a crackle of static before Thanatos answered. "We don't know the full impact yet. But it is safe to assume your expedition is now critical to our survival."

Persephone gave a mirthless laugh. "Ah, yes, so critical that Hades is relaying it to us himself."

"He's too busy for the likes of you," Amalthia voice shot across the radio.

"Oh. Lovely. I see Amalthia is there with you too."

"Lord Hades is ensuring we don't have a riot. I've been deputized to relay communications from here out. He *trusts me*."

Her words felt like a stab in the guts. She didn't want to believe any of Amalthia's digs, but the fact was, Hades had delegated what could only be viewed as critical communication to others. He was avoiding her.

"Update us when you know more. We'll be out here searching." Persephone turned to Charon. "Kill the line."

Charon tapped his ear implant once and the barely audible hum of the line died.

"I hate her so much," Persephone spit out and turned her face away from her team. She inhaled deeply, drawing in a breath and composing herself.

"We're on our own," she said when she turned around. "We knew we would be, but now more than before, we know we are what stands between bloom and ruin."

"No mistakes. No unacceptable risks, my Lady," Charon told her.

Since that conversation, Persephone had practiced with her vines at available opportunities. She learned to create thin walls of vines, barely head height, but when Leuce and Eudoros had tried bashing them down with their shields, the vines had held firm. After that, she finished each day by building a wall around their camp, giving Leuce and Eudoros the opportunity to split their evening guard to allow each of them more sleep.

Persephone had thought she would chafe at the two guards' presence on the team. Her whole life had been under the watchful eyes of her mother, her mother's security teams, and now Hades. But these two were different. They weren't there just for Persephone;

they were there for everyone. And even more importantly, they were friendly. The only other "guards" who had been open and friendly with her were Thanatos and Hades as Tony and Henry.

Leuce and Eudoros had been open books the entire trip, freely discussing every topic that came up. Melinoë, Charon, Nephele, and Stygia had often joined in the evenings. Initially, the conversation had been a little strained and punctuated with *my Lady*'s but after Persephone told them to cut the crap, the conversation had flowed much more smoothly.

Their slow wandering from campsite to campsite each day felt freeing. They had a destination, but each day they were able to choose their own path. They had general ideas of where to seek food or water while avoiding people, but it was an unparalleled level of mobility for Persephone.

She smiled as they drove through the bombed-out wastes. The world above was so quiet now and strangely open. Somehow here, at the end of the world, she had found freedom at last.

Sunlight streamed through the vehicle's open windows and the wind that whispered through carried a scent of growing things and ash. The combination of aromas hit her with a pang of sadness and longing. The late evening talks with her team and days spent freely wandering the world in search of transmitters fulfilled a part of her soul, but she ached for Hades. His silence felt dismissive and it nagged at her heart.

"My Lady, look there," Charon told her as he pointed to their left.

Ruins of what might have once been a factory, stripped to its steel bones, stood in the distance. The sun's warmth heated a stretch of pavement between the team and the building, making the air shimmer. The cool floors of the Underground were never assaulted by the beautiful, brilliant light of the sun, and the shimmer, though entirely normal, held an odd aura of magic to her. Persephone squinted through her glasses at the factory, trying to see what Charon was pointing at.

"Stygia, pause a moment," he radioed to the other vehicle.

"See something?" Stygia asked as their armored crawler rolled to a stop beside them, its massive knobby tires crunching in the dirt.

"Check ten o'clock, at the corner of the factory."

Persephone peered over the vehicle's short hood to the corner of the factory and nearly shouted in surprise when she saw figures moving around it.

"We knew some had lived, but I hadn't expected to see anyone. Not with our route," she told Charon.

"Obviously, the air's good," he nodded at Persephone's open window. "Team huddle," Charon radioed and cut the engine.

They gathered in the shade between the two vehicles, Leuce and Eudoros scanning their surroundings while the rest huddled near the vehicles' big, knobby tires.

"Do you think they see us?" Nephele asked. She squatted low and peered under the vehicle's belly.

"Maybe," Leuce answered without breaking her scan. "I don't see them looking at us now, but we're in the open, so they're bound to notice soon. We should move on, fast."

"Agreed, but if they've spotted us, we can't go directly to our next stop. They might follow. They're on foot, but we aren't exactly fast and these beasts leave tracks," Charon said and gave his vehicle an affectionate slap.

"Circle back?" Persephone asked.

"No, we need to keep moving forward. Unless your tests start showing edible food, our supplies are finite. We can't afford too many detours."

"Can we risk a road this one time?" she asked the group at large.

There was a quiet pause before Leuce answered. "It's a risk, but if we're concerned with being followed, a road wouldn't leave tracks. We could stay on it for a few miles, then try to jog down a firm dirt road. That would lessen the tracks."

"Eudoros, does that work for you?" Persephone asked. When he didn't answer, she turned to look at him.

Eudoros had his weapon up and pointed at a small group near the tails of the vehicles. An elderly man wrapped in a stained coat, a thin woman with hollow eyes, and two small children hiding behind the woman's stained pants. The man looked as though he was seeing ghosts and the woman wore an expression of fear warring with resignation.

"Hello?" Persephone called to them. She came to Eudoros' side. "We aren't here to hurt anyone," she said slowly, hoping they would respond that same way.

The two adults merely stared at her, but one of the children, a small boy, looked up at her. "Are you soldiers?"

Persephone knelt to his level. "No, little one. Are you alright? How long have you been out here?"

"Weeks," the woman whispered. "Maybe longer. We fled when the bombs started. I ran to my father," she gestured to the man beside her, "and we got as far from the cities as we could before we ran out of fuel."

"Smart. The rural areas seem to be largely untouched." Persephone told her.

"We've been trying to keep moving, to find food. There's nothing left …" She licked thin, cracked lips. "Raiders roam quicker than we can move and they pick everything clean before we can get to it. Can you help us? Please, you have to help us."

Persephone looked at the two children, thin with more than the slenderness of a youthful metabolism. Her throat tightened and she looked back at her team. Charon gave an almost imperceptible shake of his head: They had to keep moving forward.

Persephone closed her eyes. Their situation was dire, they were hanging on by the barest thread, but she and her team were all the Underground had.

"I'm sorry." Her heart clenched with her words. "I'm so sorry. We're on a mission and we can't stop" she told them.

"Please, I'm begging you!" the woman cried.

Persephone looked back at Charon again.

"We can't, my Lady," he said. "You know our rations are already stretched too thin. Four more mouths reduce how long we can search. If we fail, we risk everything. This is more than us, my Lady; more than four people. You know what's at stake."

Persephone rose under the weight of her responsibility and looked at the woman with tears in her eyes. "I'm so sorry."

The woman surged forward until Eudoros had his weapon pressed against her chest.

"Please. If you can't help me, take my children. I beg you. They're strong and they could work. Help you. They can gather firewood. Please!" Her arm stretched toward Persephone even as her chest pushed against the barrel of the gun.

Persephone's voice broke. "I ... I can't." She stepped back from Eudoros as the woman's sobs cut into her soul. She gave them one last look; the elderly man looked dazed, the woman sobbed loudly, and the two children were now quietly clinging to their mother.

She dug a battered protein bar from her pants pocket and threw it to the woman. It wasn't much, but the woman clung to it as if it were the greatest treasure in the world.

To a mother trying to save her starving children, perhaps it was.

"Go south," Persephone said and pointed out the direction. "There's a shallow river with a wooden bridge spanning it. We saw signs of others near there. Maybe you can group up with them."

It was a thin hope, but it was the only other thing she could afford to give them.

Charon circled his hand to indicate they would move out. They returned to the vehicles silently as the family watched them in equal silence.

"Just what we discussed," she told Charon. "Direct to the closest road, then turn off on a hard-packed dirt road a few miles down. Fast."

He nodded as he started forward.

Persephone spared the family one last glance as her team moved forward. The woman lunged after them. Persephone threw her hand out and a wall of vines sprang up between them, defending the vehicles' departure.

They were silent as the miles flew by. Tears ran down Persephone's face and she sniffled quietly. The silence between the team was heavier than the silence of the desolation around them.

Charon finally broke the silence as they rolled into their planned campsite for the evening.

"Next time, use thorns."

Chapter 28
Day 164

They found their next transmitter six days later. Six days of lurching across rugged fields with nutrient-depleted soil, monitoring air quality like a hawk, halting for Persephone to take soil samples, and constant re-routing to avoid former communities. They had been traveling for several weeks now and the monotony was setting in.

"How many transmitters are we seeking?" Leuce had asked her the evening after they had encountered the small family.

"We had twenty-three candidate transmitters, but based on the calculations Amalthia's team gave us, we would probably only have the time to inspect sixteen."

"Are we making the pace they planned?" Leuce's blue eyes reflected curiosity in the light of their campfire. They had plenty of solar-powered lights but had tacitly agreed to campfires whenever a stop had enough wood to build one. After months of harsh electric lights the flickering glow of the fire had soothed something in them.

"No," Persephone said. "At this rate, we'll have to start turning around after the thirteenth."

"Oh."

Persephone clapped the woman on the shoulder. "Don't worry Leuce, any progress is better than no progress. With each transmitter we restart, we have more data available to plan for coming back above."

Leuce nodded, making the fresh scar on her neck pucker at the edges, and she went silent. The slow pace started to cast gloom over the team. They had tasted fresh air, sunshine, and freedom again and seemed loath to give it up. The sense of fresh adventure had faded in the harsh reality of a land torn apart by war.

The gloom lifted a few days later when Charon spotted what looked like chicken coops at an abandoned farm around their midday break. They had planned to give it a wide berth until he saw the chickens roaming freely in the yard.

"Lunch?" he asked with a grin.

"And dinner and maybe even eggs for breakfast," Persephone said with a smile.

Charon called a halt and they stopped to watch the farm for signs of life. They watched for nearly an hour and saw nothing move except the chickens and occasional squirrel. That was enough for them to decide that fresh meat and anything that could supplement their rations was worth the risk. Eudoros and Nephele made a mad dash to the yard which only resulted in the chickens scattering around the farm.

"I guess it really is uninhabited," Persephone said with a laugh when no one came to investigate their antics.

The team followed the two and in a matter of minutes had snagged five chickens and had filled a small plastic soil sample bin with eggs. The birds had flapped and squawked in fear until Persephone took them one by one and wrung their necks. Eudoros, Charon, and Stygia had looked on with approval while Leuce, Melinoë, and Nephele looked horrified.

"Why didn't you use a stunner set at high?" Nephele gasped.

"One, it's all the way back in the vehicle. The longer they flop around in fear, the more fear hormones their bodies release. Makes the meat less tasty. Plus, I've lived my entire life on or around farms," Persephone told them, "I promise you that is the fastest and most humane way to end their lives."

Despite their distaste for seeing the chickens' lives ended, none of the three were shy about eating the fruits of Persephone's work. She had then handed the dead chickens to Charon with a nod.

"You know how to pluck them?"

"Yes, my Lady," he said with a small bow.

Persephone acknowledged the bow with a nod of her head. "Let me grab the rapid testing kit and we'll see if the birds are edible."

Following the successful test of the chicken meat, Persephone led the rest of the team back to the farm to gather anything else that might be edible. The farm was remarkably intact. A quick tug on the farmhouse door showed it was locked. When Leuce peered inside, she reported back that many cabinets were bare, perhaps indicating the farmers had left in a hurry, but had fled rather than died. When they circled around to the kitchen, they found a faded note written in neat, unhurried handwriting:

"My darling, Kay. I can only assume your return was delayed by the war. The neighbors got wild, waving the wrong kind of flag, and the war crept too close to us. Got scared. Took the kids to your aunt's farm in Aliveri, you know why. Meet us there when and if you can. You are my love forever, S."

"Explains why they turned their chickens loose. They might come back and at least for now, there's a lot of healthy birds still in their flock. We'll limit what we take," Persephone told them.

Half an hour later the team had more of Persephone's sample bins filled with carrots, onions, potatoes, and garlic. She had found the patches that would have borne vegetables growing above the soil, but they had been chewed to nubs by local wildlife. The berry bushes that rimmed the fields had been stripped clean as well, but one touch and a moment of concentration from Persephone yielded overflowing bins of strawberries and blackberries.

She had meticulously tested samples from each type of plant and much to the delight of six folks who'd spent months living on prepackaged rations, they were all deemed safe. Half a box of strawberries disappeared to grabbing hands and hungry mouths before Persephone could even suggest washing them. She'd stifled a laugh and dove in before they ate everything.

The fresh food lightened their mood considerably, finally breaking the gloom that had haunted them since being surprised by the family six days ago.

"Do you suppose they're okay, my Lady? The family we met?" Nephele asked quietly before biting into a chicken leg.

"No," Persephone said, pain lancing through her soul. "They were weak when we met them, I'm not sure they would have made it to the river."

"Do ... are ..." Nephele flushed red.

"Do I regret it?" Persephone asked for her. "Yes and no. I know there was very little we could have done for them without risking our lives, let alone our mission. But they were human and they were alive, unlike so many others. They needed help and I left them behind."

"We've left a lot of people behind, my Lady," Charon said,

joining them around the fire. "Over the course of a decade, we had the time to understand, internalize, make it a part of our culture in the Underground. I'm sorry you have to make it right in your brain now without time to process it, my Lady."

"Stop," she told him.

Charon gave her a steady look over his chicken leg. "We know you're Blessed of Hades, but today you showed you're more than that."

"She's always been more than that," Leuce told him.

"To you? Sure. But to us?" He pointed to the others. "It's the first time some of us are really seeing you. Not just the plants, but checking them, ensuring they're safe. You ensured we were fed today, my Lady, able to stretch our mission longer. And you're going to ensure we're all fed, the whole Underground, with the work you're doing. So, yes, *my Lady*," he said with a nod.

Chapter 29
Day 167

Persephone woke from a vivid dream of Hades. He had been pleasuring her in the most intense ways, his face between her thighs as his hands gripped her hips and she writhed under him. She blushed thinking about it. Splashing cool water on her face from the nearby stream was the best thing she could think of to quench the fire inside her.

"Good morning, my Lady," Leuce said, her quiet voice thick with sleep.

"It's barely morning," Persephone told her, looking at the faint smudge of light on the horizon. "I'm going to wash my face, go back to sleep."

Leuce rose from her cot and made to follow Persephone. "I'm sorry, my Lady. I don't want you out of our sight."

"I'll be fine, Leuce, I'm just washing my face."

"I'm sorry, my Lady. I keep thinking about what the woman said. About raiders?" She peered at Persephone in the slowly growing dawn. "I think we've been incredibly fortunate so far, but I don't think it's luck."

Persephone's stride faltered for a moment. "You think there's someone following us?"

"Yes. Our sensors haven't caught it, but if they aren't actively tracking us, I think we've been observed and deliberately left alone."

"Why? There are only six of us and we aren't heavily armed."

"Mostly true, but we are heavily armored. While they may not think we could fight back based on the few weapons Eudoros and I have, we'd be a tough nut to crack with all our armor. They'd starve before they got one of our vehicles open."

Ever the analytical mind, Persephone shot back, "There are a lot of assumptions in that statement to make a solid conclusion."

"You know your business and I know mine, my Lady."

Leuce laughed quietly. "If they had a one-ton hoist or grav lift and the power to operate it and acetylene torches, then maybe, *maybe*," she stressed, "they could haul us up and carve through the thinner plates on the undercarriage after a week. If they could find a working laser cutter and power it, they might be able to cut it down a few days, but they'd have to haul us there first."

"Oh," Persephone said quietly. "I see your point."

They stopped at the edge of the steam. Persephone scooped water in her hands and onto her face. The water was cool and refreshing after the heat of her dreams.

"Cooling down any?" Leuce asked her. She had her wrist computer off and was scrubbing her arms all the way to her elbows.

When Persephone looked at the woman, she had a sly grin on her face. "Yes?"

"You talk in your sleep, my Lady." Leuce gave a throaty chuckle. "Moan too."

Persephone flushed red from her hairline to her rib cage. "Sorry," she mumbled.

Leuce laughed again and the blue flecks of her aura pulsed faintly. "I'm glad to hear that your relationship with Hades is more than a formality."

It was Persephone's turn to laugh. "Well, we certainly have passion, but it seems like a lot of it is a formality." She shook her head. "I exist in the Underground as an accessory to him, not as my own person. Even after demonstrating my utility to the whole damn group, I was attacked. *We* were attacked."

"By the ignorant. The angry. The people who feel stuck in Tartarus with no chance at upward mobility, short of someone dying." A touch of heat and anger tinged her voice but it didn't seemed aimed at the people who had attacked them.

Persephone realized Leuce was stuck, too.

"You're in Asphodel, though. Aren't you?"

"Yes," Leuce acknowledged. "But unless two of my direct superiors die, I will remain in Asphodel until we can move above again. I'm not far down on the list but just enough that I know it's not likely to happen in my lifetime. Asphodel is nice enough, but it's not homey. And there's no freedom to move anywhere but down. I like you, my Lady, but protecting you was only half my reason for volunteering. I wanted to taste freedom and fresh air again. I wanted to have more than stone walls and a small room each night."

Persephone laid a damp hand on Leuce's shoulder. "Me too."

"After seeing you stop those men, I knew I'd go to the ends of the world to protect you. But now I'm here, at the end of the world, and I realize how much I missed it."

The two women sat quietly on the bank of the stream, watching the sun slowly make its way above the horizon. The gray light turned orange, then golden, before the sun appeared, brilliant and beautiful. Persephone sighed as its glow began illuminating her face.

Before them, on the other side of the stream, the sun's rays touched meadows drenched in morning dew. Golden light caressed every wildflower and glinted off the twisted remains of a vehicle on the far side of the meadow.

"Ready for another day of transmitter hunting?" Persephone asked once the sun's full disk cleared the horizon.

"Absolutely," Leuce said, golden warmth catching in her blue eyes as she looked up from putting her computer back on. In the early morning light, Persephone could see threads of silver lacing her pale blonde hair.

"Thank you, Leuce," Persephone told her as they walked back, bumping the woman's shoulder lightly with hers, "for being my friend."

Leuce smiled and punched her shoulder lightly. Persephone had never had an older sister or young aunt but thought Leuce might be close.

The eggs from the farm had run out the day prior, so the team was off quickly with only a ration pack to break their fast.

"Ten transmitters down," Persephone said to Charon while he drove and she munched on her pressed oat bar. The oats had been grown and pressed into the ration bar well before Persephone had been dragged to the Underground. "The extra food should stretch us to number sixteen on Amalthia's list."

As if summoned by her own name, the radio crackled to life.

"Charon, it's Amalthia, come in."

Persephone rolled her eyes and glanced to Leuce in the back seat.

"This is Charon, go."

"We've finished the audit of our remaining stores and run it against a moderate attrition rate, given the recent loss."

There was a long pause as they waited for her to continue. This time Charon rolled his eyes. "You enjoy bad news too much, Amalthia. Spit it out, woman. How bad?"

"Even with a very conservative attrition rate of five percent, we can't stay down here more than eleven months."

The only sound in the vehicle was the grinding of rocks and soil beneath its tires.

Persephone flipped the vox to mute. "Wasn't it supposed to last for years?"

"Five, my Lady," Leuce whispered.

Persephone toggled the microphone open again. "Are you sure your numbers are correct? You only lost, what, eleven percent of the hydroponics? Surely that's recoverable."

"I am certain of my math," Amalthia said with a scoff. "I've been working *very* closely with Hades on this and he trusts my work."

Persephone's jaw clenched. "Well, thank you for that delightful update, Mal," she said, drawing out the hated nickname. "We'll continue to be out here working to find what will save the Underground."

"Good. As far as we're concerned, your only value is getting food in our kitchens."

Persephone stabbed the line closed, fuming inside. Before she could vent her frustration, Leuce erupted from the backseat.

"That twice damned harpy needs to learn her fucking place! She has no right to speak to you that way, my Lady."

Leuce's forceful commentary made Persephone snort with laughter and the tension on the crawler's cab broke.

"Thank you, Leuce." Persephone let out a frustrated sigh. "I appreciate the moral support. She's just the worst!"

They bumped along in silence for a few minutes. Amalthia might be a thorn in Persephone's side, but her jab made Persephone question how much of it was her words versus Hades' opinion.

She put her half-eaten oat bar, forgotten from the heated conversation, on the dashboard and fumbled with the paper map on the center console. The vehicle gave a lurch and she had to snatch quickly to save her meager lunch.

"At the pace you're setting, we'll get to the eleventh today," she told him with a smile. "You in a hurry or something?"

"Yes, my Lady. This has been a nice break, but I'm ready to get back to my home. And, you know." He shrugged.

"You'd rather stay in the Underground?"

"Indeed, my Lady. I've been there since the beginning, most of my adult life. It's my home. This," he gestured to the pastoral landscape, "is nice and all. But I'm partial to stone walls and steady meals."

"Okay, I think I can see that."

"I miss my wife too. Her touch, her smell, and how she holds me when we sleep," he said wistfully.

A pang of longing hit Persephone. Logically, Hades had taken her from her home, brought her into an uncertain and dangerous realm, and ripped away any of the status and prestige she had earned in the last decade. But at the same time, he had saved her, given her a chance to save thousands, and with every passing day, her status grew, with this team at least. Her heart told her to ignore the negative, look at the good and most importantly, give in to her growing feelings for Hades. He had been nothing but polite to her, clearly respected her as a scientist and a person, and she knew she turned him on.

Persephone gave a small smile. He turned her on as well. Every night they were apart he haunted her dreams. Every night she relived their moment of harmony, aching for more.

"I understand that feeling," she said quietly. They rode on in a comfortable silence.

As the sun met its zenith, Persephone noted the air quality monitor showed the cleanest and clearest air they'd encountered so far.

"This is better than at the farm," she radioed to the other vehicle. "Combined with very little visible damage, I'd guess this area wasn't hit."

"Then why isn't the transmitter working?" Melinoë asked.

"I guess we'll find out when we get there. I'm eager to test the soil too. This air gives me hope it's usable."

The answer to Melinoë's question was apparent as soon as

they got to the transmitter's location: The transmitter was gone. Its concrete pad was cleared of everything down to the bolts.

"I don't like this," Eudoros said. Tension made his voice strained.

Persephone gave a quick nod from where she squatted several feet away, digging up a soil sample. The grass covering had been lush and green with a strong root system she had to cut through to reach the soil below. Underneath the grass, the soil was dark and rich. She pressed her fingers into the spongy mix and could feel it teeming with life. Insects, plants, fungi, and birds singing in the nearby tree line told her this land was untouched by war. The vibrant plant life was responsible for the incredibly clean air.

She popped the sample into her portable scanner and made a mental note to list this as a primary location for starting again above.

Then she heard it.

A crunch.

Not the soft cracking of a stick beneath the feet of a rodent or bird. Boots. Several sets of boots.

Persephone shot up. "Leuce!" she called.

Just then, the brush to her left parted and six figures in mismatched, makeshift armor appeared. Each was dirty and wiry with eyes too bright over sunken cheeks. The one in the front wore a gas mask around his neck like a trophy.

Raiders.

"Well, well," he said, "What do we have here?"

"Farmers?" asked a woman with half her head shaved and blood crusted along her knuckles. "Bunker bastards finally crawling out of their holes? Or looters?"

At the word looters, each of the six hefted a weapon. As mismatched as their armor, they carried a range of knives, spears, a machete, and their leader held a gun. Persephone was no expert in firearms, so she assumed it was loaded.

"I'm not here to fight," she told them. "I'm a researcher. I'm taking soil samples." She gave the portable scanner a small wave.

"Researchers, eh?" The woman spat. "Is that what we call looters now?"

"We're not scavenging," Leuce replied coldly, having reached Persephone's side. "We're taking readings. We aren't looking for trouble. If you don't interfere, we'll be on our way."

The raiders fanned out, their body language fluid and feral, creating the unmistakable tension that preceded a fight. They weren't intimidated by Leuce's armor or the weapons she and Eudoros, now on her left, leveled at them.

"See, I don't think you're just looking," said the leader. He gestured to the concrete pad. "I think you're finding. I think you're taking. Equipment. Food. Places that still grow. Places you want for yourselves."

Persephone's voice rose. "This place could feed hundreds—"

The leader snapped his fingers, and two raiders hefted spears.

"You really believe that, don't you?" he said, amused. "That this is for everyone. That you could save everyone?"

Persephone could hear one of the guards click their safety off behind her. Persephone didn't even flinch.

"Back off and walk away," Persephone told him.

The man grinned, his cracked teeth, pockmarked face, and too bright eyes giving him a manic look. "No. I don't think I will. In fact, I think we'll take what you've got. Suits. Gear. Seeds, maybe? That little scanner of yours?" He gestured at Persephone's hand. "Looks valuable."

"You took the transmitter, didn't you?"

"Sure did. Hawked it. Bought food. You wouldn't believe what folks are charging up here."

"We aren't giving you anything," Persephone told him with more calm than she felt. Adrenaline was coursing through her and she could feel its metallic tang on her tongue.

The man eyed Leuce's and Eudoros's weapons. He seemed to do the math that their two firearms would literally outgun their blades and his one rifle.

"Take us with you then," he said and gestured to their vehicles with his chin.

"Where?"

"Wherever the fuck you came from. You're clean, well-dressed, well-fed, and well-armed. Take us there and we can help you. We can be guards or something." His sly smile told her he'd slit their throats at the first opportunity.

"No. Our home is full and we only take people who are useful. People who can follow rules," Persephone said with all the disdain she could muster.

The tension between them snapped. The raider lunged forward, hand going for Persephone's scanner.

A wall of thorny vines whipped up between them as the sound of gunfire deafened her. Through the vines, Persephone could see bright red blood blossoming from his chest as he dropped to his knees, then slumped to the ground, unmoving. She ensnared the remaining five raiders with thorny vines, letting the thorns dig into unsuspecting shins and ankles.

"Who's next?" she snarled.

"My Lady," Leuce whispered. "We need to leave."

"We do, but we need to ensure we aren't followed," she agreed.

Persephone flicked her wrist and the five remaining raiders were yanked upside down and hoisted aloft by the vines, howling in pain as the thorns dug deeper. She dropped her wall and walked to the leader. There was no life pulsing in his body and the red stain stayed the same size with no heartbeat to pump more blood out. Persephone kicked his gun toward Leuce, who picked it up to inspect it.

"No ammo. No magazine, even. It was all show," Leuce told her, flashing her the bottom of the weapon to show the empty magazine receiver.

"I figured," Persephone said, "when he lunged for the scanner rather than shooting me." She looked up at the dangling raiders.

Five sets of eyes followed her with looks ranging from anger to terror. The smell of urine wafted from them.

"I am Dr. Persephone Kore," she told them, her voice ringing across the open field, harsh with anger. "Bioengineer, Blessed of Hades, and Queen of the Underground." *In for a penny, in for a pound*, she thought. "You were given a chance to let us leave in peace, but you chose violence and for that, I took a life. I don't know if you were always criminals or if war pushed you beyond your normal lives, but I will not stand for it."

Persephone bunched the vines together, bound them with another layer of vines, and directed the whole entanglement to the nearest tree. She left them dangling from a branch, heads bare inches from the ground.

"While I have proven that I will take life, I will not take yours. I will let the Fates decide your end. If you manage to escape, so be it; we will be long gone. And if you don't?" Persephone eyed the lush landscape. "I'd say this area is teeming with small animals, which means it also supports larger predators, and that Fate may have a far more gruesome end for you than I could give."

The woman, hanging at the end of the group spat. Or tried too. It ended up dribbling down her nose and entangling in the dirty hair that brushed the ground.

Persephone looked at her with glacial cool. "May the Fates grant you the life you deserve."

Persephone shivered. The shiver was accompanied by a burst of static, as if she stood beneath a clouded sky just before the first crack of thunder. It sent a jolt of recognition through her.

She gave a harsh bark of laughter and a smile that could start an ice age. "It would seem the Fates have accepted my challenge."

Persephone stalked back to the vehicles, flanked by Leuce and Eudoros.

"My Queen," Charon said and knelt.

"My Queen," Leuce said, kneeling in unison with Charon.

"My Queen," murmured each member of her team, kneeling.

This time, Persephone didn't stop them. She didn't correct them.

This time, she gave them a short bow as she accepted her place and her fate.

Chapter 30
Day 172

Ever since Persephone declared herself Queen of the Underground, the team's energy had shifted. They had reverted to being formal, almost stiff, around her. For the first few days, she had cursed the change from their easygoing banter to their quiet formality, but after two days of quiet contemplation while they sought the next transmitter, she realized it was a necessary step to establishing her place.

Their radio crackled to life once again as they pulled up to a small glade that opened in front of them.

"Charon, state status." Amalthia's voice was cool.

"Pulling into the next search location."

"What percentage of your supplies remain?"

Charon glanced back to the nearly empty shelves then to Persephone. "We've got about a week at most before we need to turn back."

"You're being directed to stretch your rations."

"Is she kidding?" Persephone blurted out.

"No," Amalthia's voice was smooth as silk now. "That won't allow you to reach all the required transmitters. Extend."

"And just who didn't give us enough rations, *Mal*?" Persephone said with venom in her voice.

"You can make the pretty flowers bloom, Persephone. I'm sure making a few more vegetables grow won't be a problem."

"That's not how this works and you know it, Mal."

"Then perhaps you aren't applying yourself enough, Persephone. Try harder. We don't need you here unless you can make your little vacation worthwhile."

Persephone drove her palm into the radio panel, cracking the screen and ending the call.

"She wants us to die out here, doesn't she?" She seethed. "And somehow, I think she's referring to herself as 'we' because no one else would sign off on this."

Unless Hades did. Unless Amalthia wasn't lying and her fleeing to the surface had broken the tenuous thing they had.

Persephone exited the vehicle to survey the land and take soil readings. Charon stepped back, allowing her to pass with a slight bow of his head. On the other side of the second vehicle, Persephone could hear Leuce and Nephele laughing over something, but they fell into a respectful silence as she came into view.

Her jaw clenched and she swallowed down a sigh. Necessity. But once they got back to the Underground, she'd have to seek out anyone else with powers so she might be able to build friendships with peers. She certainly wasn't ever going to become buddies with Amalthia; however, there were more like Hades and Thanatos.

Surely Amalthia would keep unsubtly pursuing Hades in her absence. Doubts slithered across her mind. Her relationship with Hades was new, fragile, and as tenuous as a new blade of grass. She hadn't had the time to grow and nurture it beyond accepting him and completing their bond. She had left and Hades had let her go. She closed her eyes and shook her head, unwilling to contemplate a future where she was trapped in a loveless political marriage to Hades.

The anxiety and doubt warred with facts in her mind. *Hades had let her go because the need to examine the surface couldn't be denied. He let her go reluctantly and had assured her that the bond was unbreakable; no matter what Amalthia did, she would only be making a fool of herself.*

Persephone could feel the breath she had been holding in, the way it pressed against her throat and the pressure that built across her forehead. It was similar to the intense pressure she had felt to fit into something she wasn't in the Underground.

She released her breath and started walking again. She missed Hades. He was occasionally high-handed, often failed to tell her what she needed to know, and was fiercely protective of her. But unlike her mother, he was shockingly devoted to her and listened to her concerns. He made her feel like her thoughts and opinions were worthy of consideration and had released her and the team despite his fears for her safety.

He never said the words aloud, but without question, he was in love with her. From the way he treated her to the way he held her to the look in his eyes.

He loved her.

But Persephone was unsure how she felt.

She had nursed a crush on Henry. An innocent crush that she had no intentions of ever pursuing. Every time Persephone had shown even the slightest interest in a man, Demeter had swooped in and found a way to intervene. Even after moving out to the IBCC compound, far from where her mother held court in the IBCC headquarters, nothing Persephone did escaped her. She never knew who reported to her mother, so she simply assumed everyone did. Armed with that knowledge, she knew she could never have pursued Henry even when he showed occasional hints that he reciprocated her feelings.

Persephone scanned the grass and dirt ahead of her, mind only half on her task. When Henry had been revealed to be Hades, she had felt a sense of betrayal, even if nothing had ever happened between them. She liked him now that she had seen the real Hades. The Hades who treated everyone from his inner circle to his lowliest janitor with dignity and respect. The Hades who had fought against his own leaders to ensure her place and safety. And the Hades who looked at her with eyes that could start a fire.

Persephone had never been in love before, but perhaps this was it. Burning desire coupled with mutual respect. There was just one missing piece: She was afraid they would never be equal partners and she would wither in his shadow.

The sound of Eudoros' weapon snapping up halted her. She realized they had covered the length of the glade and the forest on the other side. They stood only a few feet behind the tree line now. An opening revealed a scene that made Persephone gasp and raise her hand for Eudoros to point his weapon down.

Beyond the tree line was a small but thriving community. It was centered on a small pond and surrounded by life. Everywhere Persephone looked was green, lush, and almost impossibly alive. Wheat and corn stalks waved idly in the wind on opposing plots. Vines climbed low walls surrounding neat rows of tomatoes, squash, and what might have been the leafy tops of carrots.

Between the rows, people moved slowly but purposefully, their sleeves rolled up and hands moving gently between plants and soil. Near a large farmhouse and spindly windmill, the raucous laughter of a gaggle of children drifted to the tree line.

This wasn't some plot taken over recently or hastily. This was real, purposeful agriculture, untouched by the war.

"Eudoros?" she said, her voice tight in her disbelief.

"I see it, my Queen," he said. He flipped up his visor and squinted into the distance. "No weapons. They aren't armed."

"Trap?" she asked softly.

Eudoros gave a shrug.

Persephone scanned the farm again, looking for the inevitable trap. The sound of high-pitched squeals and laughs drew her attention once again. They were a contrast to the small family they had encountered weeks ago. These were well-fed, happy, and thriving children.

Persephone made her choice. She stowed her soil analyzer and walked slowly out of the tree line with her hands raised, palms out.

The farmers closest to her looked up, startled. Hands gripped their spades and hoes tightly, but they didn't raise them. They were clearly as cautious of her as she was of them.

"Stay back," she told Eudoros. Introducing his gun to the mix could make things go sideways fast.

"My Queen?" Anxiety tinged his voice.

"No guns and I can vine them if I have to get out," she told him over her shoulder as she approached the farmers, hands still up.

A small group met her halfway while the rest drew back to the farmhouse. The sounds of laughter faded.

A solid-looking woman broke from the group and approached her. Her hair was graying at the temples, her face only lightly lined with wrinkles made by sun and smiles, and the forearms that extended from her sleeves were thick with muscle.

"You aren't a raider," she stated rather than asked.

"No," Persephone told her. "I'm a researcher." She slowly moved her hand to her hip and patted the scanner.

The woman gave a little bark of laughter. "Researching what? Crop harvest on the edge of war?"

"Exactly."

The woman looked at her with eyes narrowed in suspicion.

"I'm Dr. Persephone Kore, a bioengineer. I used to work in the research division at International Bio-Chemical Corps, IBCC, but now I'm working with a small group of survivors to ensure their harvests flourish."

"I've heard of IBCC," she said. "Might have heard of you, too."

Persephone tilted her head and considered the woman. Her face wasn't familiar, but the dirt under her nails and on her knees said the woman was used to working the land.

"Heather," the woman said and extended a hand. "I own the house and land." She nodded toward the people behind her. "Most of these are kin. A few survivors who proved they could work the soil. A few rugrats who crawled out of the woodwork when we put the kettle on," she said with the smile of a woman used to feeding a crowd.

"I have a team with me. We're looking for sensors that would tell us if areas are habitable again. I'm also taking samples to find usable soil," Persephone told her. Might as well meet Heather with honesty. "I have a bodyguard in the tree line. I asked him to stay back because, well, he's armed, but I didn't want to scare you."

Heather's eyes snapped to the gap in the tree line. "We don't allow weapons here."

"I understand. The rest of my team is beyond the woods, helping me gather soil samples."

Heather sniffed once and Persephone watched her grind her jaw in thought. "You put your weapons back at your camp and I'll let you see what we have."

Chapter 31
Day 172

Hours later, her team sat with Heather's group at several long tables pushed end to end in the farmhouse's backyard. The remains of a large meal lay scattered across the table. Pickled vegetables, roasted squash, and a nearly empty pot of bean stew had been provided by Heather. Empty wrappers left scattered across the table by small hands were all that remained of the sweets Persephone had taken from their stores as a gift.

Persephone was rolling one of the beans between her fingers, studying it as the sun's fading light was replaced by solar-powered flood lights slowly flickering on.

"These aren't wild. These have been cultivated," she told Heather.

Heather was sitting across from her, a slender woman cradled in her arms. "Nope, not wild. I'm no doctor, but I've worked with plenty." She patted the woman's arms. "Lily worked at IBCC, too."

"That's how you heard of it!" Persephone exclaimed.

Lily gave Persephone a shy smile. "I've read your papers, Dr. Kore. Your work was inspired. I never could replicate your yields here after I quit IBCC, but we've done well."

"I'd say!" Persephone told her with a smile. "You hybridized this against surface mold?"

"Yes," Lily said proudly and Heather gave her a hug.

"She's been helping us since before the war."

Persephone gave the nearly mature wheat stalks a glance. "I can tell."

"The soil is good here, I know you saw that with your scanner. We're far enough from everywhere that the bombs gave us a miss and raiders haven't been able to get here."

"Yet," Persephone said.

"Yet," Heather agreed.

Inspiration that had been lurking at the back of her mind all afternoon finally struck Persephone and she smiled at Heather. It was a risk and Hades might hate it, but it was exactly what the Underground needed.

"I think we can help each other." Persephone leaned forward and put her elbows on the table. "I have a few varietals that will work well in moist conditions. We're able to control the moisture of our soil down to the milliliter, so I don't need it. I could also send folks who could help protect your farm."

"And what do you want in return?" Heather asked with a raised eyebrow.

Persephone met her with a level gaze. "Three things: access to a small plot of land, you to allow my personnel to carry weapons in your defense, and," Persephone smiled, "a diplomatic exchange. I want to establish a trade corridor between your community and the Underground."

A soil sample and plot of land today could be a functioning farm tomorrow. They desperately needed plots of good soil and this could be what saved them.

"Land, I can do. We have more than we can work now, even when I can get the little ones to work. But weapons on my land? What's stopping you from taking what you want and leaving us with nothing?"

Charon, who had been nearly silent all afternoon, spoke up. "Because she's asking instead of taking. That's more than most do."

Heather released Lily and let her eyes dart between Persephone and Charon.

"I'm not a dictator. I'm not really a politician, even if I'm negotiating on behalf of the Underground. I don't want control. I'm a scientist," Persephone nodded at Lily. "I want collaboration. I want to share knowledge and exchange resources. You need long-term defense and access to medical care. We need fertile soil and the chance to expand the genetic pool of our plants and animals."

Heather nodded slowly. "We're all Friends here. I'm against violence. It's against my faith. But," she dropped her head, "I know we can't last up here without defenses. I also know the first time someone gets more than a skinned knee or a splinter, we'll be in piss poor shape to heal them. And if raiders attack …"

"They will. It's only a matter of time," Persephone confirmed. "But if we work together, maybe we can both survive."

"Tell me about the Underground. What do you bring to the table, what do you need, and why?"

There was a long silence. Persephone looked at Charon, waiting for him to elaborate, but he remained silent.

"It's a lifeboat. It's a way to survive the darkest of times. But it's enclosed like a terrarium," Persephone finally said.

"A terrarium is only as good as its starting state. If anything is out of balance, it fails."

"Yes."

"So, something failed?"

Another long silence stretched. Persephone looked at Charon again, but his face remained blank.

"Yes," she admitted.

"How?"

Persephone's team seemed to side eye her at once, each of them vehemently opposed to giving more information than absolutely necessary.

Persephone, however, was all for a useful exchange of information.

"They planned for a lockdown with a set time limit. Everything was based on that. All the logistical attrition was based on that length. They never expected there would be saboteurs among them. Or that any one person or group could hate another so much."

There was only a small pause before Heather responded. "They don't like you much, do they, my girl?"

"No. They do not." Persephone sighed. "But they're the best hope I have. They mean well, even if they're hard-nosed and parochial about roles and ranks. They know their stuff too. I've been through every inch of their data and they have a working grasp of how horticulture should function. Couple that with Lily's work and it could improve your farms."

A long silence stretched between them. Then Heather reached across the table and tapped a dirty finger on the map Persephone had unrolled.

"You can have access to one field. This one. Small, on the south ridge. You can send envoys to take soil from there. If it satisfies your need, bring us the seeds you spoke of and we'll exchange. But any hint of exploitation and we cut ties."

Persephone nodded. "Deal."

Heather held her gaze. "And if I find out you lied about the Underground ..."

"You won't," Persephone said. "In fact, I'll personally bring the first batch of seeds and medical supplies myself."

Charon's posture stiffened. "That wasn't in the plan."

"It is now," she said, her eyes still on Heather's. "This is the future."

Heather nodded. "It's the growth, life, death, and regrowth of the world. Let's plant something worth growing."

The next morning, as her team re-packed the vehicles to depart, Charon approached her.

"My Queen, Lord Hades may not have agreed to this. You know, you just made a promise that could shift our entire governing structure," he said quietly so the people loading the other vehicle couldn't hear him.

Persephone smiled faintly. "Good. Maybe it's time the Underground started growing, too. And as I am Lord Hades' Queen, I think that gives me the right to make rulings and diplomacy above in his stead."

Chapter 32
Day 177

The soil sample from the small plot on the south ridge rattled only slightly as Charon led their two-vehicle convoy across rolling terrain. Small and almost insignificant among the trays of meticulously labeled soil samples, it was the most important sample Persephone had.

It was more than dirt. It was life forged through diplomacy, not domination.

Where the Underground was institutionalized, insular, and stifled, this represented the opportunity to accept growth, change, and new life. Persephone hadn't entered the Underground with the intention of changing it. She hadn't even intentionally entered the Underground. But if she was going to be tied there by duty and her bond to Hades, she was going to make it a place she would be proud to call home.

Like Charon, not everyone on the team shared her enthusiasm. Once they rattled to an early halt that day, Leuce approached her while she was alone, checking the samples after a day of rugged terrain.

"My Queen?"

"Hey, Leuce. Just checking the vials. I heard a few unsettling clanks as Charon rolled down those hills. Wild, right?"

"Yes, my Queen. Is this," Leuce paused, seeming to steel herself, "is this worth it?" She gestured to the neatly stacked racks.

"Worth it?"

"My Queen," she said and gave a deep nod, "I don't mean to infer that your judgment is impaired, but that deal was not what Lord Hades would have done." She snapped her mouth shut and rocked back slightly, as if waiting for the inevitable scolding.

Persephone drew in a deep breath and let it out slowly.

"Is this what the entire ride back will be like?"

"My Queen?"

"Each of you maintaining a respectful distance from me until you can get me alone, then questioning my actions?"

"I'm so sorry, my Queen!" Leuce backed up a half-step.

"Stop." Persephone held up a hand. When Leuce met her eyes again, Persephone sighed and ran a hand through her hair, the dirt from her fingers blending in with the dull brown of her tresses. "You're the third person to ask, Leuce. You all were fine and companionable until we met those asshole raiders. Then you all became super formal. Now? Now that I've taken strides to live up to the title I bestowed upon myself, you're all questioning my actions. So, which is it? Am I your Queen in name or in actuality?"

Leuce goggled at her. Her mouth opened and closed rapidly as thoughts must have crossed her mind and she discarded them, unsure of how to answer.

"Leuce, you were the first to call me 'my Lady.' You were the first to truly witness what I could do with my power. And now you're one of the first to see what I can do when I'm unconstrained by the threat of Hades lurking behind my actions."

"Threat?"

"Yes," Persephone said and shook her head. "The entire time I was in the Underground, I was Hades' Blessed, for whatever that's worth."

"A whole lot," Leuce interjected.

"Fine. But I was also his kept woman in their eyes. I'm sure everyone assumed I was his consort. And anyone with two brain cells to rub together could figure out that if they displeased me, it would make it to Hades' ears. Nothing I could request was answered because I asked for it. It was answered because people feared Hades' wrath if it wasn't."

"Many of us were aware the bond had not been completed," Leuce said with a blush. "There are only so many who can see it, but word traveled."

"Amalthia," Persephone growled under her breath.

"Yes, but there are others." Leuce shook her head. "I see your point, my Queen. This journey has shown me you are more than your power and more than whatever title Hades' relationship with you creates."

"Then can you trust that what I did, the deal I struck, is for all of us? That I did it with the betterment of the Underground in mind?"

Leuce was quiet for a long moment. "Despite the brief time you have been there, I believe you understand the intricacies and power dynamics of the Underground. Yes, I believe you."

"I can't guarantee I know exactly how this will impact the way Hades holds power, but," her mind drifted back to Hades' describing a queen, walking beside him, "I think I'm on the right path."

Leuce gave her a deep bow.

"Can you help convince the others? You know me better than anyone else on this trip and you know them better than I do as well."

"Anything, my Queen."

Persephone stood in silence, the pain of missing Hades in her chest. She ached for his touch. Nighttime was the worst. She had dreams filled with his hands, his mouth, the heat of him beside her that left her trembling and damp with memory. She had never known another lover and knew she never would. But now she feared that by stepping fully into the role she envisioned, she would provoke a fury that stripped their bond of everything tender, leaving nothing more than a political alliance. The warmth she felt from him stripped away for duty.

"I know I can make the people accept it. But will he?" she whispered.

Leuce reached out and took Persephone's hand. "My Queen, Hades' heart has awaited its queen for two centuries." A look of hope warring with joy wiped the serious look that had dominated her face. "He will accept it."

Persephone gave her a tremulous smile. "I hope so." She sighed again. "Two centuries? You too?"

"One hundred and forty-nine this year, my Queen."

"You're as invested as him. That's why you guard me so closely." Persephone's face was calm even though she was roiling inside.

"No, my Queen. I *was* guarding you for him. I am loyal to my King. But once I met you. Once I saw what you could do?" Leuce was silent for a moment. "I am here to support you, my Queen. Any benefit Lord Hades gains from it is inconsequential."

Persephone stared at her in shock. "Can you see the auras,

Leuce?" she asked quietly.

"Yes," she smiled at Persephone. "Barely. It's dim to me, not like Thanatos describes it, all blazing, like sparkles."

Persephone giggled at the description.

"It's dimmer here too. Like something above suppresses it and something below enhances it." She shrugged.

"Okay, back to reality. I have to finish my inventory and you have work to do on my behalf."

Leuce took her leave and by the time Persephone finished and joined them at the fire crackling between the noses of the two vehicles, the mood of her team had already shifted. She gave Leuce a discreet, appreciative nod.

"We have two transmitters left, my Queen," Charon told her as she settled to her rump in the dirt with a plate of rations mixed with vegetables from Heather's compound.

Persephone looked down at her plate. "How long can we stretch the rations now?"

Charon frowned. "Even with Heather's gifts? Not long enough."

"Skip Amalthia. Message Thanatos. Tell him we're returning directly and we'll address the remaining transmitters on a second trip."

"Yes, my Queen. I sent a first message giving our state and letting him know we would send our final decision once you had been presented with the information."

Clear, direct, and awaiting her final say. Leuce had done as asked and well.

"How many days until we return?"

"We've been doing a rough circle since we left. Given the terrain? Three days, maybe four."

"Very good. We'll be home soon."

Chapter 33
Day 180

"Five minutes out, my Queen," Charon told her between radio calls. "This is CHARON 02, two vehicles, five minutes out."

"Hermes copies. State authentication passcode."

Silence was broken by the crackling static of the radio.

"Authentication?" Persephone asked as she squeezed her hands together. Every mile they got closer to the Underground increased her anxiety.

"Yeah, I don't know."

"Hermes, it's Charon. Open the damn blast doors." He slapped his hand on the wheel, mic still in his hand.

"State authentication passcode," was the only reply.

"Fucking hell. Months on the move and he's greeting us with this."

Fear built in Persephone's belly. She was well aware that Charon had been relaying status updates every time they found a working transmitter. No doubt Hades knew about everything she had done. Was this retaliation?

"What does the authentication normally entail?" she asked him.

"A specific password or phrase that shows you're someone from the Underground. We used them before we closed the doors, but with them closed for the time before our departure, no one had updated them and three … four … months later, I've forgotten the damn thing."

"Something only someone from inside would know?" she asked.

"Yes, my Queen."

The massive steel blast doors came into view as they rounded the last bend in the road leading to the Underground.

"Give me the mic," she said and snatched it from Charon. She thumbed the transmit switch. "Hades' aura is crimson tinged with pine, Hermes."

There was a squeal of static on the radio then silence. Persephone looked at Charon, her eyes pinched at the corner.

"Welcome home, my Lady."

Persephone let out a breath and let her shoulders relax.

The massive steel doors split and opened outward with a groan that penetrated the cab of their vehicle. Charon edged the vehicle forward slowly, checking the mirrors to ensure their teammates made it. As soon as both vehicles cleared the portal, the doors began their slow swing inward.

Personnel in protective suits appeared beside the vehicles and motioned for them to move forward. Someone plugged a cord into a portal on the side and the radio crackled again.

"You've been outside, we have to take you to decontamination and possibly quarantine. Keep going forward. Once we have you at the opening of the decontamination line, you can exit the vehicles."

A wave of fear rolled over Persephone. She knew what quarantine looked like in the Underground. The memory of a cold, dark room filled her mind. The openness of the world above had healed something in her and seeing the stone walls of the Underground sent a wave of claustrophobic fear through her.

"Charon, I can't do that again," she whispered.

"I'm sure we'll be clean."

"Get Hades," she said into the mic. "We will do decontamination, but we are not doing quarantine."

The person plugged into their radio turned their suit's faceplate to peer inside. His eyes went wide when he saw her face.

"Yes, Queen Persephone," came the clipped reply. He unplugged and jogged forward.

"You told them about that?" she asked Charon. A cold feeling washed over her.

"My reports have been concise, but yes, they covered everything."

"Shit."

"My Queen?"

"I was going to—" she paused. "I wanted to have a chance to explain my choices to him in person. This wasn't the type of thing I wanted relayed concisely without context. Some things require you to have a greater understanding of the foundations first ..." she said, thinking back to how Hades slowly wound out the truth about her position in the Underground.

"I'm so sorry, my Queen. I didn't know."

"I know," she said through a clenched jaw.

She'd lost her ability to control the narrative. Another wave of memories hit her. Any time she had made a decision on her own, Demeter would subject her to a long inquest session, grilling her daughter until she had dug up every aspect of the choice and made Persephone feel like nothing she chose could ever be as good as her mother's choices. Years of defending every decision she'd ever made had anger bubbling under her skin.

Something in her snapped. She wasn't subject to her mother's rule. She had fought for and won her own path, even if it started in confinement. She was her own person and she'd fight everyone in the Underground, even Hades, to make it known.

"Damn it all," she swore. "He will listen to me and he will accept it. If he didn't want me making choices for the Underground, he shouldn't have brought me down here, then let me lead the expedition."

The ghost of a knowing smile crossed Charon's face. He inclined his head, "My Queen."

"Yes. Yes, I am." She looked at Charon, a wicked gleam in her eyes. "You know what I need to do from here already, don't you?"

"Yes, my Queen."

"Good."

Charon parked the vehicle where directed and hopped out. Persephone stayed in the cab and watched him whisper quickly to the other members of the team as Underground personnel scrambled around the vehicles with scanners. Leuce glanced her way and nodded with a grin on her face. Charon came around to her door and opened her door with a bow.

"My Queen," he said, loud enough to be heard by the workers in the area.

Persephone stepped out of the vehicle with all the regal bearing she could muster: spine straight, shoulders back, and chin held up proudly. Her team, now standing near her door, dropped to a knee with murmurs of, "My Queen."

The workers noticed the change almost immediately. A ripple of movement spread across the open bay floor as people dropped to a knee. "My Queen," "Lady Persephone," and "Blessed" rippled throughout the room.

A woman jogged up to her and handed her a note with a bow.

It read: "*Lady Persephone the Blessed, Queen of the Underground, You changed everything. We need to talk. — Hades*"

Persephone clutched it to her chest, her heart pounding. She wasn't sure if it was an invitation or a warning.

"Tell Lord Hades I will meet him in his command suite," she told the runner. The woman turned to deliver the message and Persephone halted her. "Wait. Gather Thanatos, Amalthia, and the Judges, too. And get me a dress. A long one." She glanced down at her hands where dirt was still trapped in her cuticles. No time to get a full shower, but she would at least dress the part.

"Bring it back here, I clean up in the machine bay."

If the woman thought it odd that a queen would scrub up in a machine shop, she didn't dare say it. She merely bowed and jogged off.

Persephone turned to the kneeling crowd. "Thank you," she told them and indicated they could rise.

"Gearing up for a fight?" Charon asked, having clearly heard her instructions. He handed her the soil sample from Heather's farm, already anticipating her needs.

"He called me a queen once before. I don't know if he meant it. But I'm coming back, finally knowing my place and wearing a crown; I don't intend to take it off."

Chapter 34
Day 180

The messenger must have read her intentions because the dress she returned with wasn't from Persephone's small box of clothes in Hades' apartment. The dress didn't seem to come from any mortal plane Persephone knew of, either. She fluffed out her chocolate hair, once again threaded with gold, let it fall over her shoulders, then smoothed the dress over her hips.

Two lengths of gathered white fabric came up the bodice, each covering one breast, and connecting at a single point at her left collar bone, leaving a small gap over her cleavage. A royal blue capelet trailed over her shoulder and down her back from the silver fastening point. The skirt of the dress flowed gently over her hips, trailing lightly behind her and opening with every step from a slit that went to the top of her thigh.

She looked like an ethereal goddess as she strode toward Hades' command suite.

One would never have guessed she had been furiously scrubbing dirt from her skin and fingernails only a few minutes before.

Leuce trailed behind her left shoulder and Eudoros off her right. The rest of her team followed with data pads filled with the data they had gathered. Persephone came armed only with the soil sample negotiated from Heather's farm.

Despite holding her head high and walking like she owned the Underground, anxiety washed through Persephone. Hades' message had been terse and calculated. He wanted to talk.

A *"We need to talk"* message was never a good thing. She ached to speak to him about their relationship but knew his message was about what she had done to the Underground, and it was why she had asked for the heads of his various political branches to be present. After months of threats, both covert and overt, she needed to know where she stood in the Underground. Might as well face them all at once.

But she still longed to see him alone. To know how he felt. If his heart had changed. Her only hope that there might be something salvageable between them was that in his note, he had called her "the Blessed" and not "Blessed of Hades."

Her sense of dread ratcheted up several notches when the first face she saw through the suite's windows was Amalthia's. The weasel of a woman was dressed in an elegant and tightly tailored suit. Two buttons of her blouse were unbuttoned to show off her minimal cleavage. Persephone's teeth ground when she saw Minthe behind her, oblivious to everything except Hades.

Hades, to his credit, was clearly ignoring both women and had his face down, presumably reading something. To his right, Thanatos sat with Hermes behind him and the three Judges along the sides of the table.

Thanatos saw her first and his jaw dropped as he beheld her. The shock was over in an instant and he rose to open the suite's door for her.

"Perfect," he whispered as she reached the threshold. Turning to the room, he spoke louder, "Dr. Persephone Kore the Blessed, Queen of the Underground."

Persephone gave him a little smile as she stalked forward, her team in tow. She settled herself at the end of the table, opposite Hades and gestured for her team to sit along the sides. The long conference table was full and both Minthe and Hermes remained standing.

"You wished to talk, my Lord," she stated rather than asked. Her voice was calm, cool even, as if she wasn't boiling with anxiety inside.

At the other end of the table, Hades' face was impassive. The only sign of his agitation was his aura pulsing red so strongly that she couldn't make out any of the pine green tint that had laced in it since their bond completed. The shock of the missing green lanced through her heart and she was glad she was farther down the table so he couldn't see her blink back tears.

"It would seem that your disruption of the Underground continues," Hades stated. Also not a question.

Beside him, Amalthia had a smug smile and Minthe shuffled uneasily. Anger flared inside Persephone and burned away the anxiety. She hadn't asked for any of this, but she'd be damned if they shamed her for building her place.

"Yes, it does," she agreed. "My Lord," she said belatedly.

Persephone held up her soil sample for everyone to see. She looked at it, giving it a little shake so they could see the rich, dark soil inside.

"I'm bringing you your future," she said simply. "You tasked me with leading an expedition to seek out our broken transmitters, determine the true extent of the destruction, and to analyze and cataloge the soil in the areas we traversed. You sent me because the Underground might fail without additional growing spaces to cover the gap from the broken hydroponics. To that end, you gave me the authority and autonomy to function as an arm of your leadership while above."

Persephone turned her attention to Amalthia. "We were given enough supplies to address only sixteen of the twenty-three transmitters and yet, the team was resourceful enough to forage for food, which extended our trip to eighteen transmitters. We encountered three different groups while we traveled. Each brought a different challenge but the most difficult was not the group that sought to kill us for our equipment," she said with a cold smile, "but the one that offered us a future."

Persephone waved the soil sample. "There is life above. Hope. A chance to leave the Underground or at least open avenues for trade. Trade that would bring new supplies and mean the Underground is no longer a closed, insular system. A single failure or sabotage would no longer be a life-ending fear."

She raised her chin and looked each person at the table in the eye before moving on. "Yes, I'm changing things. Yes, I established a diplomatic relationship beyond the political structure you all represent. And yes, I made a trade deal between the Underground and a farming compound above. I will continue going above to establish more trade routes and diplomatic relationships to keep the Underground from failing."

Her eyes flicked briefly to Amalthia and Minthe before she pinned Hades with a hard stare. His face gave nothing away and Persephone felt her heart breaking even as she steeled herself. "When I was brought here, every single person told me I was a threat, a disruption, or that I was a problem. I didn't ask to come here; I didn't ask to take up space in a world where every role was filled. So, I made my own role. You needed a diplomat, so I became your Queen."

Chapter 35
Day 180

Persephone had stalked out, dress and capelet swirling in her wake. She didn't bother staying to hear protests from the Judges or to hear Amalthia passive aggressively denigrating her work.

She was tired. She was upset. She was filthy from head to toe under the elegant dress. She wanted nothing more than a chance to shower, put on comfortable clothes, and sleep for a week.

"Let me in," she told the guards outside Hades' door.

"My Queen, this isn't—" the guard protested before she cut him off.

"Open the door or I will hang you by your damn toes with vines."

The golden bident on his chest flashed as he whipped around to unlock the door.

Persephone sighed and slumped against the door as soon as it closed behind her. She was glad Hades hadn't followed her out. She wanted a moment alone to collect her thoughts before facing him. She pushed herself off the door and strode to his bathroom, unbuckling and unpinning the dress as she went. She left a trail of underwear and pooled fabric in her wake, pausing only long enough to snag a dress from the one drawer Hades had allotted her.

Every fear and worry she'd held in, too proud to show in front of her team, flowed out of her as the water sluiced over her body. Before she left, she had thought she and Hades had come into balance. She had been able to exert her power, control it, and in doing so, they had found their harmony. She had finally opened her heart to him and completed the bond. For a single shining moment, it looked like she had a chance at happiness with him.

Then she had to go and ruin it by saving the Underground.

Tears flowed down her face and mingled with the shower. His note was so terse. His face had been so completely devoid of emotion. And worst of all, the beautiful pine green that had tinged his aura was gone. Maybe she had been right when she spoke with Leuce about missing him. Maybe Amalthia or Minthe had made their move and won.

She scrubbed weeks of dirt that accumulated despite frequent dips in the creeks and ponds they encountered. If he was mad she had changed things, or if he had decided she wasn't what he thought, she would need a new space. She couldn't be expected to stay in his quarters if that was the case, bond or no. Persephone groaned when she realized that meant she would have to petition Amalthia for space. Well, if the woman had won Hades over, then it would be a small concession to get Persephone out of her hair.

She stepped out of the shower and toweled off vigorously, scrubbing as if pushing Hades from her body and soul. As she donned the dress like armor, she knew the first step would likely be gathering her meager belongings, then seeking a temporary place until they could find her something else. If she wasn't "Blessed of Hades" anymore, perhaps she would find a space in the Elysium dormitories.

She strode out of the bathroom and his bedroom, intent on gathering her things from his living room. She didn't expect to find him lounging on his sofa, knees apart and both arms resting on the backs of the cushions, looking like he was as comfortable as ever. Persephone opened her mouth to speak, but he beat her to it.

"I took the liberty of having your belongings packed and moved," he said quietly.

She thought she was ready for this conversation, but his words crushed her. Sadness and loss washed over her as she looked at him, so relaxed and easy on his sofa. She closed her eyes so she didn't have to see his pure red aura again. She had heard others describe heartbreak but never thought she'd be crushed with such calm words.

Sadness faded to anger and she lit into him.

"You couldn't handle me being gone? Or you couldn't handle me finally finding my place in the Underground?"

"What?" His voice seemed genuinely shocked.

"You're throwing me out because I was successful? That's pretty damn cold, Hades. Are you so insecure about me leaving that you're pushing me all the way out of your life? Or you're mad I'm not dependent on you and have achieved my own renown in your world?"

Hades rose from the couch and stepped toward her, body rigid. Persephone flinched back as he reached for her. A look of hurt crossed his face.

"You think I wanted you to go? That I wanted you to leave? I wanted nothing more than for you to stay, but I let you go because I knew you had been caged your whole life." Hades reached for her again, gently pulling her toward him.

His hands were warm on her skin and in the moment, she hated that her body reacted to his touch.

"I knew you were stronger than you looked and that your power would continue to grow once you saw and accepted it, but I also knew you wouldn't keep growing here." He shook his head as he looked at her. "Do you really think I would cast you aside?"

"You've barely looked at me! You've only addressed me by a title."

"I wanted you to know I was overjoyed that you finally accepted your place by my side, as my Queen. My equal." His hands gently squeezed hers. "My partner."

Persephone blinked up at him, not daring to hope he was being truthful. Something in her melted. "You wanted that?" she whispered.

His hands moved to her shoulders, then pulled her into a crushing hug. "I have waited for this day for twenty-five years. I have dreamed of a queen by my side for two centuries. Yes, my sweet, golden, shining Seph, I wanted that so badly."

"But," she stuttered, "but my things. You moved everything out already." Tears lingered in her eyes, bordering between fear and hope.

"Come with me," he said. He released her from the hug and pulled her to his door by the hand. They stumbled into his hallway, leaving two confused guards in their wake. "I started this the day you left. I knew, well, I hoped, that you would accept who you were."

He stopped by a door she had stalked past earlier, ignoring it in her turmoil.

"Go ahead, open it."

Persephone opened the door and stepped inside. She gasped

at what lay beyond the door.

The room—rooms—were almost a mirror of his spaces. Except where his space was dark and accented with gold, these rooms were light and lively. Rooms were painted in a soothing taupe but accented with shades of green. Ferns, *her ferns*, dotted countertops and end tables. Two boxes sat on a low table and she realized this was where her belongings went.

She walked deeper into the spaces to see a well-appointed kitchen and large dining area.

"A queen and a diplomat will need space to entertain other diplomats and form alliances," he whispered in her ear. The feel of his breath across her ear made her shiver and something hot coiled in her belly.

"Seems awfully formal and, well, businesslike for a living space," she told him.

"Yes, that's true." He tugged her hand and led her to the bedroom beyond the sitting room.

A large bed dominated the room. It was covered in a dark green blanket and pillows that had been shaped to resemble various leaves. A smile tugged at Persephone's mouth.

"It's lovely, Hades."

"I know it's stressful for you living in my spaces. I know you deserve a space of your own. But," he said shyly and put his hand on another door she hadn't noticed, "I had them build a door for us."

He twisted the handle and gave it a tug. Persephone gasped once again when she realized it opened to his bedroom.

"If you would honor me by being my partner, my lover, my wife, and my Queen, then we have an option for traveling between each other's spaces."

Persephone smiled and leapt on him, not bothering to answer with words.

Chapter 36
Day 180

Hades stumbled backwards from the momentum of Persephone throwing herself at him. The stumble carried them onto his bed. Persephone gave a little squeak of surprise and looked down at him from where she now lay on his chest.

His silver-rimmed blue eyes searched her face, seeking the answer to his question. For a long moment neither spoke, and the only sound was the steady rhythm of her breath, matched by his.

"Persephone," he murmured.

"Are you asking me to marry you, Hades? Because I hate to spoil a moment, but we're already married."

He growled and rolled them over, flipping Persephone on her back and pinning her hands over her head.

The sound unraveled her. She leaned up to kiss him before she could stop herself and he kissed her back with startling gentleness for a man forged of iron command and currently holding her down. He broke the kiss to smile down at her. Persephone arched into him, demanding more without words.

He kissed her again. It was consuming, fierce with restraint barely held at bay. He broke away from her again, this time moving to pepper her neck and collarbones with kisses that burned like fire in Persephone's core.

"I've missed you," he said between kisses.

"I can tell," she said with a gasp as he nipped her shoulder.

"Marry me," he said. He released her hands and skimmed his down her sides.

"I *am* married to you," she reminded him. His touch left trails of fire down her sides and she could feel her wetness already.

"I'm asking, Persephone," he said and pushed the slitted hem of her skirt aside, exposing her upper thighs. "You didn't know what you agreed to when you became my Blessed. So, this time, I'm asking you. Would you marry me?"

His fingers slid up her thighs to hook into her panties and pull them down past her knees.

"Yes," she gasped.

Hades kissed his way down her inner thigh then stopped, his panting breath inches from her core.

"Yes, Hades, I would marry you," she answered and bucked her hips toward him.

Hades slipped one finger into her and she moaned. Months. It had been months since she last felt his hands on her and she had ached every day for him. But it wasn't just his hands, his mouth, or his cock she missed. She had missed him. Genuinely.

"I want to marry you properly," he said as his finger curled inside her, tickling her spot.

Persephone could feel her face flushing and her breath was coming fast. If he kept this up, she'd explode.

"I want to marry you in front of everyone. I want to give you vows that say that I choose you. That I choose to be your partner. That I choose to honor you every day of our very long lives."

"Yes," Persephone cried as she exploded under his touch.

He kissed another line of fire up her thigh as she came back down.

When she had caught her breath she looked him in the eyes again. "Yes, I will marry you. And yes, it will be my choice." She smiled at him. "And yes, I want to make a vow to you that says I choose to be your partner, your lover, your Queen. For every day of our very long lives."

The air between them crackled. The static before thunder feeling Persephone had come to associate with the Fates pulsed between them.

"It would seem the Fates accept our vows," Hades chuckled and he stroked the tops of her thigh.

"We should probably do it again in front of our people," she said with a laugh of her own.

"I agree, but the next time you'll be in a gown and not shattering in my hands."

Persephone tried to sit up, but he gently pushed her back down and settled between her legs. She gasped again when his mouth found her core and began to lap up her wetness. He had her exploding again in moments.

This time he let her sit up and before he could initiate, she threw him on his bed and straddled his hips. She met his eyes as she rocked her hips against him, her core making a wet line up his length. Fire burned in his eyes as she looked down at him, echoing the heat coiled in her belly. She leaned over him, one hand bracing herself and one hand caressing his shoulder. She kissed him as she kept rocking her hips, teasing him.

Hades finally broke, growling as his hand moved between them, and he put the head of his cock at her entrance. Persephone deepened their kiss, her tongue stroking his as she let her weight pull her down his length. She gasped when he was fully inside her, enjoying the exquisite stretch.

His hands went to her hips and he thrust up in time with the rock of her hips. "Slow, Seph, slow," he mumbled against her lips.

Persephone ignored him and kept up her tempo , feeling the tension build inside her core. His hands flexed on her hips but he matched her pace. Her pulse raced under his hands, her skin alive to every brush and caress.

For a frozen moment in time the world beyond them ceased to matter. A war. The Underground. Above. It all faded away as they moved together. Only the heat of his breath against her skin, the strength of his arms anchoring her, the quiet promise of a life together existed now. Her driving pace pushed them both until she tipped over the edge into ecstasy with Hades following a moment after.

Later, once they had sated their passions, Hades and Persephone lay in his massive bed together. She curled up at his side, gently running her fingers over the sparse hair on his chest.

"You know I will have to leave again, right?"

He turned on his side to face her and his arms drew her close.

"I know. I don't love it, but I know."

"For all my bluster with Amalthia in the room, the patch of land we gained is very small. It will allow us more growing spaces, but for it to be worth the trip, I'll need to provide my own special touch to increase the yields."

"I know, love. I know you also have to build and maintain more ties to ensure we can trade for what we need." He pressed his forehead against hers. "I'm pleased to have you. I'm overjoyed that you will be my Queen. But I also accept that it means you will only be here part of each year. Not just for the crops, you need your freedom as well."

"You don't begrudge me that freedom?"

Hades rolled her onto her back and showered her with kisses, trailing them down her chin and neck. "Never. If months apart mean months together, I don't begrudge the time away. I waited 200 years for you. What's a few months here and there?"

Acknowledgements

Dear Readers,

I am so thankful to all of you who have taken the time to enjoy my spin on the Hades and Persephone myth. I have loved Greek mythology for as long as I can remember and have always wanted to do modern retellings as novels. So much so, in fact, that this book is now the fastest I've ever completed primary writing for a novel after Pantheon.

Of course, no story comes together without an army of supporters! First, my thanks to my Beta Squad. The Squad grows with every new book and I'm honored to have brave souls willing to read the unedited and only lightly polished version. Your feedback helps me spin a literary pile of straw into gold.

Shout out to my editor Donna who keeps me from sounding like the country bumpkin I am at heart. Your funny quips in the comments make me bust out laughing and push me to improve my writing. Thank you for catching all my n-dash/m-dash shenanigans.

Big thank you to Stephanie. My chaotic book gremlin, margarita bestie, alpha reader, and smutty book subject matter expert. I've asked and you've answered questions that I wouldn't dare put in Google.

Last, to my Hades, my love, my partner, and my King . . . my husband. Thank you for your support, for your insight, and dragging me back into reality when I would otherwise write all night long without intervention! You inspire me to be more, to be better, and I live happily in the emotional, physical, and mental safety you give me.

KR Paul
FL Panhandle
December 2025

About the author

KR Paul was born in California but moved to North Carolina as a child. She grew up rock climbing, horseback riding, and writing fan-fiction like so many other '90s kids. Her love of adventure took her into the US Air Force where her love of writing grew.

She has written non-fiction for business, industry, academia, and leadership education. Through it all, she kept her love of writing and continued to write fiction in her free time.

Today, KR still works her military day job but writes short and novel-length fiction when not being an absolute jock or absolute nerd. When not at work, her hobbies include competitive body-building, video gaming, kayaking, cosplay, skydiving, and playing with light sabers.

Her work serves up a blend of powerful action and the vivid world of urban fantasy. She draws from her own life experiences to fuel the emotionally charged, fast-paced plots found in the Pantheon series.

For more information on this and other exciting new authors, please see KRPPublishing.com

EMAIL **WEBSITE**

This narrative is a work of fiction. Nothing in this work constitutes an official release of U.S. Government information. Any discussions or depictions of methods, tactics, equipment, fact or opinion are solely the product of the author's imagination. Nothing in this work reflects nor should be construed as any official position or view of the U.S. Government, nor any of its departments, policies, or personnel.

Nothing in this work of fiction should be construed as asserting or implying a U.S. Government authentication or confirmation of information presented herein, nor any endorsement whatsoever of the author's views, which are and remain her own.

This material has not been reviewed for classification as it is not required per DAFI 35-101.

www.ingramcontent.com/pod-product-compliance
Lightning Source LLC
LaVergne TN
LVHW030320070526
838199LV00069B/6512